George Jacob Holyoake, Henry Rogers

**Rudiments of Public Speaking and Debate**

Hints on the application of logic

George Jacob Holyoake, Henry Rogers

**Rudiments of Public Speaking and Debate**
*Hints on the application of logic*

ISBN/EAN: 9783337392635

Printed in Europe, USA, Canada, Australia, Japan

Cover: Foto ©Andreas Hilbeck / pixelio.de

More available books at **www.hansebooks.com**

# RUDIMENTS

OF

# PUBLIC SPEAKING AND DEBATE;

OR,

## Hints on the Application of Logic.

By G. J. HOLYOAKE,

AUTHOR OF "MATHEMATICS NO MYSTERY," "LOGIC OF FACTS," ETC.

WITH AN ESSAY ON SACRED ELOQUENCE, BY HENRY ROGERS.

REVISED BY REV. L. D. BARROWS.

Common sense is the genius of humanity.—GUIZOT.

New York:

PUBLISHED BY CARLTON & PORTER,

200 MULBERRY-STREET.

1861.

# INTRODUCTION.

It is a question of the first importance to all public speakers, especially ministers of the Gospel, how their utterances can be rendered the most effectual. Whatever promises aid in this direction will be seized with earnestness and appropriated with care.

It has become obvious to careful observers that the modern pulpit is more distinguished for strong ability, sound learning, and deep piety than for its eloquence. Since it is true of the thousands now annually entering the ministry, so few are remarkable for their power and success as speakers who are distinguished scholars and writers, their study and training for speaking are either greatly *neglected* or fearfully *misdirected*. The numerous text-books on rhetoric, in every liberal course of study, with the corresponding professorships and hebdomadal declamations, do not indicate a neglect of this branch of education. We therefore conclude, that by some means *its cultivation has become sadly defective.*

Public speaking, and even rhetoric, as taught and practiced of late among students and young speakers, have fallen into great abuses. They are exceedingly *superficial.* The very name of rhetoric strikes one now as implying little or nothing more than a painting, or outside adorning of discourse, adding a little

flippancy to please the unthoughtful.  It is supposed
to imply something *showy* and trifling, rather than
substantial and excellent.  In a thorough course of
study, and with good scholars, it does not seem to be
generally regarded as an element of *power* like that
of logic and philosophy, but a kind of educational
plaything.   Hence no moral quality is attached to
its study or practice, nor is it coveted as among "the
best gifts" so much for what it has power to accomplish, as for what it *appears* to be.

Because rhetoric deals so much in forms, it does
not follow that it is destitute of principles, and that
its foundations do not lie deeper than the drapery of
spoken or written discourse.  If novices and sophomores treat the powers of oratory as a toy, upright
and conscientious speakers should regard it as involv-
ing a *moral responsibility,* such as always accom-
panies all great powers.

Sacred eloquence especially should be studied and
practiced from another standpoint, high, pure, and
commanding, like itself, or it will never occupy its
true relative position in a course of education.  If
eloquence in its true character and purposes does not
originate in moral emotions, if it does not deal with
the moral element of humanity, if it does not propose
moral achievements, we cannot affirm what other
branch of science or education does.   By what
authority then has it been brought down, shorn of
its inherent merit, and degraded in scholastic estimation ?  If it has sometimes been used improperly, to
influence men against their judgments and interests,
that does not show its nature and designs are such, any
more than the perversion of any other science shows
it useless or vicious.  But, on the other hand, we claim

that there is not in all the wide range of education any other department that leads us so directly into, and takes such a firm hold upon, the highest elements of our nature, and influences so powerfully the great interests of humanity, as this. Benevolence and religion covet power to do good ; and with men possessed of these qualities, all power will be used exclusively for that purpose, and with this view will be earnestly sought.

We are confirmed in the opinion that the essential qualities of good speaking are not correctly taught generally in modern training for that purpose, from the fact that of those who have studied the most carefully, written the most extensively, and taught the longest, there are found scarcely more really eloquent speakers, in proportion to their number, than of the uneducated. This, however, by no means indicates that this branch of education is not to be elaborately studied, provided it is under the right masters, and in a successful manner. Cudworth says : "Knowledge is not to be poured into the soul like liquor, but rather to be invited and gently drawn *forth from it;* nor the mind so much to be filled therewith from without like a vessel, as to be *kindled* and *awakened.*" The application of this fine thought to our modern instruction in oratory would be of decided advantage.

Let us inquire if there are not in operation several causes, forestalling or undermining to a great extent everything that is now done to improve our public speaking. One formidable obstacle in the way of general success in improving pulpit oratory is the *force of precedent,* and the fear of breaking away from established style. In the ministry of every

Christian Church there is a *way, or manner*, which, if it does not amount to a tone, does to a style, and this must more or less fashion every man's mode of speaking in the ministry. If the individual speaker does not wish it should be so, his associations, with the power of habit, will make it so, unconsciously it may be to himself. Provided he does not feel that his denominational reputation depends on his following the beaten track of style and mannerisms, he will not be above the fear of being thought odd or singular in breaking away from usage. The result is, no matter what a man's *natural* utterance, he will be to some extent squared to these lines, which so far makes him *unnatural*. Who ever was or ever can be eloquent who is not natural? The least constraint is perceptible to an audience and crippling to a speaker. The bar and the stage are comparatively free from this incubus which weighs upon the pulpit. Speakers must be natural or they are *repulsive*. This naturalness comprehends alike tone, or modulation of voice, position of the body, and gesticulation. A practiced observer will detect the least affectation in any one of these particulars. Here lies the danger in all anxious and critical study of eloquence—its continual tendency to interfere with nature, except when taught by masters of the subject. When this occurs, it is mainly to be attributed to the direction of the speaker's attention to wrong points. The young orator resolves to excel, so he speaks and acts as much like an eloquent man as possible, drops everything natural, puts on airs, assumes the gestures and tones of voice which he has observed as pleasing in others, and calls it a success! A burlesque of eloquence. His efforts should be first to ascertain his *own faults as a speaker.* Is he too fast, too slow, too calm, too excited, too loud, too low, too argumentative, too superficial? Having learned by some means what his faults are, he should remove them, no matter what the cost, or despair of success. This was the great effort of Demosthenes, and other great masters of the art, *who succeeded by study.* A short breath, a stammering tongue, or indistinct articulation were impediments to his eloquent nature, such as could be overcome only by the greatest painstaking. This is the point to which all public speakers can direct their attention safely and continually. But, alas! almost any and everything else will be studied before this, which accounts largely for the surprising non-improvement in modern oratory.

When from any cause ministers of the Gospel cease to feel a deep and thrilling interest in their own *utterances,* they are no longer eloquent. Then the most profound logic and finished rhetoric, though applied to the vital truths of Christianity, will fall dead upon an audience, for in *hearing* hearts answer only to hearts in *speaking.* Without a vital interest of the speaker in what he says, his melodious voice will be like a sounding brass or a tinkling cymbal, and the people will sleep on. If a minister of Christ does not " grow in grace," and make continual progress in personal and experimental religion ; if he studies but superficially the great truths of Christianity ; if his discourses are, with himself, old and stale ; if his illustrations are trite and worn ; if his attention is drawn off from the salvation of souls, while he preaches or studies to the securing of popular favor, or to his own livelihood ; if the great truths of God, eternity, and the soul are not deeply impressed on his mind, his own soul will grow less and less susceptible, and his speaking more and more ineffectual. When he becomes conscious of this lack of feeling, his first *expedient* will be to raise his voice, throw about his hands, stamp with his foot, or smite with his fist; and thus, by a superabundance of sound and bluster, strive to atone for lack of thought or *real feeling*. Should this fail, he will probably start a torrent of exclamations, " O my hearers," " O my brethren," etc., repeated so frequently and with so little emotion that it becomes insipid. Such unmeaning phrases, and any sort of clap-trap, used to fill the blanks of thought and real emotion in a discourse, are ridiculous. They discover the nakedness of the land, and show the speaker anxious to be pathetic without the power to be so. The Greeks and Romans made but little use of these empty sounds, or of the exclamation ; neither have such strong and modern writers as Barrow, Sherlock, and Atterbury. Swift says he knew a man who, when he spied an exclamation point at the end of a sentence, skipped the whole sentence. Those speakers might do the same who have to manufacture their feeling to order as they go along with their discourses. Exclamations, personifications, and apostrophes are dangerous in the hands of unskillful workmen, especially such speakers as attempt to warm their lips with words from frozen hearts.

The forbearance and kindness of a pious people, and their reluctance to find fault with their ministers, we fear have contributed to a growing self-complacency among the clergy, and moreover to a false view of their real abilities. This doubtless has had considerable influence in producing the deficiency of the modern pulpit. We do not think it uncharitable to say, that with a large class of clergymen there is a sad deficiency in hard consecutive study; in profound vigorous original thought; in a clear and impressive apprehension of divine truth; in a bold, comprehensive, and earnest diction; in a fearless and manly energy, such as a Christian honesty inspires. But instead of this kind of pulpit attraction we have commonplace thoughts, tame and insiped illustrations, a hesitating and patronizing air of delivery, and apparent indifference to probable or possible results. Such public speaking as this is tolerated nowhere else but in the pulpit, and only *tolerated* there. Under its deadening influence the lawyer would lose his business, the political orator his audience, and the tragedian would be hissed from the stage. These feeble and forceless incumbents seem quite at ease if they have gained the doubtful compliment: "They are good men, though not great preachers." They should know that this is said often, more because nothing else can be said of them, or because this cannot be well disproved, than because they have any special goodness of character.

The speaking of the pulpit, unlike that of the bar and rostrum, does not furnish the speaker with the immediate and ocular proofs of his success or failure. Hence his constant and imminent danger of deceiving himself, alike as to his success and real abilities. This has a tendency to satisfy him with ordinary efforts, and this cannot fail to make him an ordinary man. In ministerial qualifications *goodness* should surely be held as a *sine qua non;* but if the days of miracles are past, *strength*, both human and divine, is its right arm of power, now as of old.

This state of things in the ministerial profession of the present age has had a tendency to invite into it a class of men who are too weak and powerless to get a living in any other way. In all other professions the incumbents must have some talent and vigorous application, or fail; but a young man who has not tact or courage to badger a false witness, or extract a tooth, will do for a minister, for " he is a very *good* young man." By this means the eloquence of the pulpit is greatly marred. For a discourse superficially studied, made up mostly of commonplace and stale thoughts, with dry and antiquated illustrations, no man of sense can deliver with interest or enthusiasm to himself; and then he will fall into a dull, empty, and indifferent way of speaking—the tomb of all eloquence. But when the speaker feels he has elaborated something new, worthy of himself and his hearers, his eye kindles, his spirit rises, his soul is stirred, his voice adjusts itself to his thoughts, and then he has the people with him, and lo, he is pronounced an eloquent man ! Non-progressive, unstudious, and unthinking clergymen are often if not generally monotonous in style. This is a common and ruinous feature in pulpit speaking. So little variations of the voice stupefy the hearers, and obscure the fine thoughts of the speaker, if he utters them. Says one writer: " The monotonous wearisome sound of a single bell might be almost as soon expected to excite moral impressions, as the general tenor of our pulpit discourses, which are, with few exceptions, drowsily composed and drowsily delivered."

The basis of delivery in preaching should be a dignified and earnest conversational tone ; and there

should be no departure from it, except when strong
excitement compels it. Let the clerical reader now
cast his eye over the circle of his ministerial acquaintances, and ask himself how many of these
would, and how many would not be improved by
some change in this respect. There is generally too
much volume of voice used, *too loud and harsh.*
This diverts attention from the thought of discourse
and deadens the feeling. This fault, though common
and very detrimental, is easily remedied with care
and perseverance. It is said of Cicero, that before
he went into Greece he had a rude and coarse voice;
but after remaining there for some time, by industry
and force of habit he brought it to a charming
smoothness and delicacy.

The little attention paid to the voice, its tones and
culture, by public speakers, is really surprising. In
noticing other speakers, nothing sooner attracts our
attention than the voice. We at once determine
whether it is base, tenor, or soprano, as we do also
whether it is agreeable or otherwise. The voice is
not only susceptible of these essential qualities, but
also of various gradations between them. Its flexibility and susceptibility of culture are almost incredible. It can express every emotion of the soul, and
every degree of that emotion. More, it is almost
sure to utter the speaker's soul whether he will or
not! It will not play him false, but may expose his
hypocrisy if he has any. Such is the power of the
human voice; yet how few public speakers ever attempt in earnest to change their harsh and stupefy-
ing tones, *tones* which not unfrequently utterly ruin
their efficiency as speakers; men whose chief business, too, is speaking!

The base voice has great dignity, and is not at first repulsive ; nor is it when occasionally used, but it will soon grow heavy, and become monotonous, and when long continued it is sure to produce drowsiness. To listen for an hour to a sermon in a uniformly deep and heavy base voice, is about as entertaining as to listen as long to a solitary base singer.

The tenor voice is the best adapted to public speaking, and hence should be cultivated by those whose voices are base or soprano, as all these tones can with ease be greatly modified. This tenor voice, occupying a middle position between the other two, plays up and down most readily.

This tone is also more *persuasive* and *sympathetic*, a secret few understand and none can explain, yet an element of great power in a speaker. It has greater variety, and is less inclined to monotony.

The highest voice is sharp and ungraceful. It is more liable to impair the organs of speech, and health, and also to create uneasiness with the hearers. It approaches a scream when long continued. It can be used only occasionally with pleasure to the hearers, or with safety to the speaker, except where it is natural, and even then it is disagreeable to the ear.

Speakers cannot be too cautious in watching against *bad habits* until they are wholly removed. Yet it is possible to become so careful and anxious about the grammar, rhetoric, and pronunciation, and to allow the whole attention to be absorbed, so that the subject *itself*, and the results of its delivery, may be entirely forgotten. Many of our most learned and polished speakers, we judge, fall into this grave mistake. Impression and success are sacrificed to a cold exactness, to a dead orthodoxy. Rather than this, let them speak right on, in the fullness of their souls, trusting to the force of accurate habit of study and speaking; then the mind and feelings will be unembarrassed, and free to enter directly and earnestly into the *subject itself.* The preacher must not be fastidiously solicitous, or elaborately nice in the arrangement of his sentences and in the marshaling of periods; for, as Milton says, " true eloquence I find to be none but the serious and hearty love of truth; and that whose mind soever is fully possessed with a fervent desire to know good things, and with the dearest charity to infuse the knowledge of them into others, when such a man would speak, his words, like so many nimble and airy servitors, trip about him at command, and in well ordered files, and as he would wish, fall aptly into their own places." Such speaking as this, with a tolerable accuracy and clearness of utterance, constitutes, a manly and impressive eloquence, scorning the tricks of the stage, the buffoonery of mountebanks, and the bombast of sophomores.

We have been induced to offer to the reading public a republication of this volume, chiefly because we think it supplies a long-felt desideratum in the literature of public speakers, a kind of connecting link between the *theory* of rhetoric, as taught in our textbooks, and the application or practice of it. In this most important aspect of this noble subject, we think the remarks of this author the most highly suggestive and pertinent of any we have ever read. In his sententious and terse style, he sparkles with thought and abounds with practical hints. He assumes from first to last what we think is true, that public speakers generally are more familiar with the rules of rhetoric than they are skillful in the application of them.  Could our countless corps of public speakers be reached at this point and thoroughly roused, we might hope to see a much needed improvement in public speaking.  It will be noticed that the idioms, or forms of expression, are not all modern, nor exactly American.  Many not such, however, have been changed; but some are left as we found them, where a severe literary taste would seem to require change, fearing we might lessen or mar the author's thought by introducing our own phraseology.

The careful reader will observe that in what we have said in this introduction, and in the notes, together with the valuable essay of Henry Rogers in the appendix, we have aimed at producing a book worthy of the attention of clergymen, and such as we think is adapted to promote the efficiency of the pulpit.  And if our clerical readers can read this little work as many times as we have, with unflagging interest, they will not regret that it has fallen into their hands.                    L. D. BARROWS.

SANBORNTON BRIDGE, N. H.
  FEB. 16, 1860.

# PROEM.

THE highest truths of transcendental metaphysics will one day reach the populace. Not only the standard of intellect, but that of morality, will be raised. The race of the Papinians, the Cromwells, and Marvels, will be multiplied. It was once said all could not learn to read, write, and account. Now they do learn these and other things. They will one day learn all things. Intellect will conquer all obstacles, and teach the human race to realize untold perfection.

But it will be accomplished piecemeal. Progression is a series of stages. Individuals first, then groups, then classes, then nations, are raised. You can no more introduce, at once, the multitude to the highest results of philosophy, than you can take a man to the summit of a monument without ascending the steps, or reach a distant land without traveling the journey. This book is a stage. As the preceding ones in this series, it is designed for the class of young thinkers to whom knowledge has given some intellectual aspiration, and fate denied the means of its scholastic gratification. It is therefore neither elementary nor ultimate, but a medium between the two. It addresses itself to a want. It deals in results. It dictates doing.

Spontaneous life is the life of the people. Their knowledge is confined to phenomena. Their *practical* philosophy is the reality of Hobbism. Disguise it as we may, their sole business is the betterance of their condition. All you can do is to guide their rude interpretation of nature, men, and manners—to give plain method to their classification, coherence to their inferences, justice to their invectives. They want no new philosophy. There are more old ones which are good than they can study. There is more wisdom extant than they can master, more precepts than they can apply. Weapons innumerable surround them, of which they have to be taught the use. Their watchword is *work*. The scaling-ladders of the wise which they, having mounted the citadel of wisdom, have kicked down, are yet of service to those who are below. I have picked a few of these ladders up, and reared them in these pages for the use of those who have yet to rise.

Fastidious punctilios of scholarship would be out of place in such a book as this. He who addresses the artisan class must, like the Spartans, write to be read, and speak to be understood. Mechanics and literary institutions cannot *cultivate* their frequenters, and those greatly mistake the requirements of learning and the state of the people who think they can. They can *stimulate* improvement, and this is their province. Nations never become civilized and learned till subsistence is secure and leisure abundant. So of individuals. The populace are still engaged in the lowest battle of animal wants; and even the middle classes are in the warfare of intellectual wants. In the ancient state of society war was the only trade, force the only teacher, and the battle-ax the only argument. A transition has indeed taken place; the time, and means, and ends are changed; but not the relative position of men. No more do we struggle for the victory of conquest, but we struggle for wages and more intelligence. Knowledge has reached the mass so as to make them sensible of their ignorance without diminishing their privations, and they are now engaged in a double battle against Want and Error. The struggle, therefore, is resolute. The training wanted is practical; the weapons serviceable and ready for use. Provided the literary sword will cut, few will quarrel about the polish. If the blade has good temper, he who needs it will put up with a plain hilt.

When I contemplate the appliances which learning and science present to the scholar, and see how multiplied are its means of knowing the truth upon all subjects, I cannot conceive that he can be struggling like the untaught thinker between right and wrong. To the scholar, truth and falsehood must be apparent; and since the learned do not penetrate to the intellect of the populace, and establish intelligence among them, it must be that the learned want courage or condescension, or that common sense among them is petrified in formulas. We want either a hammer or a fire to break the spell or dissolve the ice.

Those words of Guizot which I have placed on the title-page indicate the broad obviousness of precept aimed at in this work. Hudibras tells us that

> " All the logician's rules
> Teach nothing but to name their tools."

I have attempted to recast this order. In the " Logic of Facts" I have dealt with the *materials* of reasoning. This is such "Application" of them as I should make. In this matter I have striven to speak without affecting superiority or infallibility. Writer and reader stand on the same level, and from a common ground thus established mutual inquiry starts. The information attempted is essentially practical. It is not the heavy inexorable theory of the last age applied to the bustle and elasticity of this; but upon the learning of the schools is endeavored to be engrafted the learning of life, the literature of the streets and of trade, the logic of the newspaper and the platform, and the rhetoric of daily conversation; that the reader may acquire a public as well as a scholastic spirit: the aim being to elicit originality, to realize a *distinct* individual, who shall go forth into the arena of the world with determinate and disciplined powers capable of usefully influencing its affairs.

In the division of the Parts and the succession of the Chapters, there is no pretension to scientific classification. The distinction drawn between the Parts, though not recognized, will, I believe, be found practically suggestive. The order of the Chapters is that which seemed to me to be natural, at least to throw light, one upon the subject of the other. In "Hints" a greater license is allowed, and strict sequence is not so much looked for as suggestiveness.

The FIRST PART treats of the Rudiments of Rhetoric, the elements which the student derives from the instruction of others. After the "Proem" has informed the reader of the design of the book, "Rhetoric" defines and explains the subject; "Delivery" commences with the laws of tone, founded on the study of feeling. "The Theory of Persuasion" accu-

mulates materials from the study of manifestation;
"Method" teaches how to use these materials with
power; "Discipline" teaches how this power is confirmed; "Tact" teaches its special application.

The SECOND PART includes those topics, a knowledge
of which is not so much, or rather, not so well, derived from the instruction of others, as acquired by
the personal observations of the student. Doubtless
the teacher can impart them, but only in a qualified
sense. The student will never excel unless he trust
to himself and to his independent exertions. The
practical relation between the subjects in this Part
seem to be this: "Originality" is a source of independent power; "Heroism" its manifestation; "Proportion" prunes "Heroism" of Exaggeration and
Declaration; "Style" indicates individuality of expression; "Similes" offer themselves as weapons of
expression; "Pleasantry" its relief; "Energy" is a
species of lemma to Eloquence; "Eloquence" mar-
shals the powers to effect conviction on a given
point; "Premeditation" teaches how effect is to be
provided for; "Reality" infuses confidence; "Effectiveness" sums up the condition of complete impression; "Mastery" denotes the signs of rhetorical
perfection.

The THIRD PART, again, relates in its distinction
rather to the student than to the subject intrinsically
considered. This Part treats of topics in which the
student finds the application of previous acquisitions.
"Criticism" applies preceding topics to the development of beauties and correction of faults; "Debate"
is tact applied to conversion; "Questioning," or
Socratic Disputation, is the auxiliary of Debate;
"Personalities" treat of the conduct of Controversy;

"Repetition" is the philosophy of Reformation; "Poetry" is the highest result of Rhetoric.

Whatsoever well expressed thought I have found which illustrated my subject I have taken, and, what is somewhat more unusual, I have acknowledged it; because the author of a useful idea ought to be remembered as one who leaves a legacy. Through this punctiliousness the critics will say that I have not composed, but that I have compiled a book; though I see books published around me in which there is more that belongs to others than in this book, but the obligations being concealed, the ostensible authors get the credit of being original. We are all of us indebted to those who have thought before us, and we say with Montaigne: "I have gathered a nosegay of flowers in which there is nothing of my own but the string which ties them." But in this case the string which ties them is my own. The architect (to pass from nature to art) has the credit of his conception and erection of an edifice. Yet he does not *create* the materials. The materials he finds, but he gives them proportion, place, and design. The *idea* is his; and if good, we credit him with distinct merit. Why, therefore, should not the author of a book, even if made up of other men's materials, be credited also with distinct merit, if his work has an idea which subordinates the materials he employs and shapes them to a new utility? G. J. H.

# CONTENTS.

## PART I.—DERIVATIVE POWERS.

CHAPTER                                                             PAGE

   I. RHETORIC .......................................... 23
  II. DELIVERY .......................................... 27
 III. PERSUASION ........................................ 35
 IV. METHOD............................................ 44
  V. DISCIPLINE ........................................ 59
 VI. TACT .............................................. 65

## PART II.—ACQUIRED POWERS.

   VII. ORIGINALITY....................................... 73
 VIII. HEROISM .......................................... 77
   IX. PROPORTION ....................................... 80
    X. STYLE ............................................ 83
   XI. SIMILES .......................................... 90
  XII. PLEASANTRY........................................ 95
 XIII. ENERGY .......................................... 97
 XIV. ELOQUENCE........................................ 100
  XV. PREMEDITATION .................................... 105
 XVI. REALITY .......................................... 109
XVII. EFFECTIVENESS .................................... 113
XVIII. MASTERY.......................................... 121

## PART III.—APPLIED POWERS.

   XIX. CRITICISM ........................................ 127
  XX. DEBATE .......................................... 130
 XXI. PERSONALITIES ..................................... 139
XXII. QUESTIONING...................................... 153
XXIII. REPETITION........................................ 155
XXIV. POETRY .......................................... 157

NOTES ................................................. 167

SACRED ELOQUENCE: THE BRITISH PULPIT .................. 179

# PUBLIC SPEAKING AND DEBATE.

## PART I.

### DERIVATIVE POWERS.

## CHAPTER I.

### RHETORIC.

RHETORIC is the application of logic to mankind. By reasoning we satisfy ourselves, by rhetoric we satisfy others. The rhetorician is commonly considered most perfect who *carries his point* by whatever means. Men like to see the man who is a match for events, and equal to any exigency. But it is plain we must make some distinction as to the manner in which a point is to be carried. We may as well say that a man may carry the point of life, that is, fill his pockets by any means, as influence men by any means. A low appeal to the passions we call clap-trap. I know no better definition of rhetoric than Dr. Johnson's definition of oratory. "Oratory," said the doctor, "is the power of beating down your adversaries' arguments and putting *better* in their places."

Descending more into detail, the description given by Lord Herbert of Cherbury is the happiest and healthiest delineation of rhetoric that has fallen under my notice.

" It would be fit that some time be spent in learning rhetoric or oratory, to the intent that upon all occasions you may express yourself with eloquence and grace ; for, as it is not enough for a man to have a diamond unless it is polished and cut out into its due angles, so it will not be sufficient for a man to have a great understanding in all matters, unless the said understanding be not only polished and clear, but underset and holpen a little with those figures, tropes, and colors which rhetoric affords, where there is use of persuasion. I can by no means yet commend an affected eloquence, there being nothing so pedantical, or indeed that would give more suspicion that the truth is not intended, than to use overmuch the common forms prescribed in schools. It is well said by them, that there are two parts of eloquence necessary and recommendable ; one is, to speak hard things plainly, so that when a knotty or intricate business, having no method or coherence in its parts, shall be presented, it will be a singular part of oratory to take those parts asunder, set them together aptly, and so exhibit them to the understanding. And this part of rhetoric I much commend to everybody ; there being no true use of speech but to make things clear, perspicuous, and manifest, which otherwise would be perplexed, doubtful, and obscure.

" The other part of oratory is to speak common things ingeniously or wittily ; there being no little vigor and force added to words when they are delivered in a neat and fine way, and somewhat out of the ordinary road, common and dull language relishing more of the clown than the gentleman. But herein also affection must be avoided; it being better for a man by a native and clear eloquence to express himself, than by those words which may smell either of the lamp or inkhorn; so that, in general, one may observe, that men who fortify and uphold their speeches with strong and evident reasons, have ever operated more on the minds of the auditors than those who have made rhetorical excursions. Aristotle hath written a book of rhetoric, a work in my opinion not inferior to his best pieces, whom therefore with Cicero de Oratore, as also Quinctilian, you may read for your instruction how to speak; neither of which two yet I can think so exact in their orations, but that a middle style will be of more efficacy, Cicero in my opinion being too long and tedious, Quinctilian too short and concise."

" Between grammar, logic, and rhetoric there exists a close and happy connection, which reigns through all science, and extends to all the powers of eloquence.

" Grammar traces the operations of thought in known and received characters, and enables polished nations amply to confer on posterity the pleasures of intellect, the improvements of science, and the history of the world.

" Logic converses with ideas, adjusts them with propriety and truth, and gives the whole an elevation in the mind consonant to the order of nature or the flight of fancy.

" Rhetoric, lending a spontaneous aid to the defects of language, applies her warm and glowing tints to the portrait, and exhibits the grandeur of the universe, the productions of genius, and all the works of art, as copies of the fair original."*

He who gives directions for the attainment of oratory is supposed, if a public speaker, to be capable of illustrating his own precepts.

" He may be thought to challenge criticism, and his own performances may be condemned by a reference to his own precepts ; or, on the other hand, his precepts may be undervalued through his own failures in their application. Should this take place in the present instance, I have only to urge, with Horace in his Art of Poetry, that a whetstone, though itself incapable of cutting, is yet useful in sharpening steel. No system of instruction will completely equalize natural powers ; and yet it may be of service toward their improvement. The youthful Achilles acquired skill in hurling the javelin under the instruction of Chiron, though the master could not compete with the pupil in vigor of arm.†

But there is little danger, in these days, of any serious judgment being passed upon the indifferent exemplar of the rhetorical maxims he lays down. Our orators escape as our statues do. Good public monuments are so scarce that the people are no judges of art, and great speakers so seldom arise that the people are no judges of oratory. England has not reached the age of excellence in this respect. Great events can excite it, but only a national refinement, including opulence and a liberal philosophy, can sustain it. The power of oratory requires the union of intellect, leisure, and health, discipline of thought, accuracy of expression, method, a manly spirit, an absolute taste, copiousness of information upon the

* Spectator, No. 421.          † Whately's Rhetoric, preface.

given subject, a vivid imagination and concentration. Oratory—by which term I always mean the highest efforts in the art of public persuasion—might exist in the Church but for its dread of imitating the theater.* It is suppressed among the Dissenters by the influence of evangelism. Did this not exist, their precarious pay would deter them from the pursuit of the art. The bar is too full of business and too anxious for fees, to reach much distinction where leisure and choice are necessary. The politician is generally indolent if not dependent, and if necessitous he has to struggle for himself when he should be struggling for excellence. Besides these drawbacks, there are various popular prejudices which few minds are strong enough to withstand, and which deter the young aspirant after eloquence. Under various heads, as "Premeditation," "Discipline," and others, these points of prejudice will be discussed.

# CHAPTER II.

### DELIVERY.

"Elocution," says Walker, "in the modern sense of the word, seems to signify that pronunciation which is given to words when they are arranged into sentences, and form discourse." The power of distinct and forcible pronunciation is the basis of delivery. Between deliberate, full-toned, and energetic speaking, and feeble, indistinct, and spiritless utterance, there is the difference of live and dead oratory.

* See Note A. page 167.

The rudiments of speaking are few and simple. Vowels should have a bold, round, mellow tone. This is the *basis* of speaking. A slight, short, mincing pronunciation of the accented vowels is the prime fault to be avoided.

Audibility depends chiefly on articulation, and articulation depends much on the distinctness with which we hear the final consonants.

R has two sounds, a rough and a smooth one. The rough *r* is proper at the beginning of words, and the smooth *r* at the end of words, or when succeeded by a consonant. The audibility of the *r* in each case gives strength to the utterance.

In about twenty-two words in our language, beginning with *h*, the *h* is not sounded. These words must be carefully attended to, and all other words beginning with *h* must have that letter distinctly heard. In illustration of this neglect of aspiration where proper, teachers of elocution are accustomed to say, that if the Indian swallows the sword we (h)*eat* the poker.

A strong delivery is to be constantly cultivated— that is, an energy that shall prevent drawling, and a slowness that shall avoid mumbling words or chopping half the sounds away, as hasty speaking does. Take time to articulate fully and intonate. Speak "trippingly" without tripping. If you must be extreme, better be solemn than hasty.

Robert Hall, whose talent for extempore speaking was such that, when eleven years of age, he was set up to preach extempore to a select auditory of full-grown men, says of himself: "To me to speak slow was ruin. You know, sir, that force or momentum is conjointly as the body and the velocity; therefore, as my voice is feeble, what is wanted in body must be made up in velocity." This is a mathematical figure of speech, and is more true of dynamics than rhetoric. This remark has seriously misled many young speakers. There is a distinction to be noted between a small voice arising from peculiarity in the conformation of the larynx, and the feeble voice which arises from the narrow chest or from physical debility. Unless there is a great strength to support any momentum imparted, indistinctness and alternations of screechings and whispers will be the inevitable results.

At a Corn-law meeting held in Glasgow, in 1845, I sat at half distance from the platform. Having offered my services to the Lord Provost, I was uncertain whether I should not be required to take part in the proceedings. I was therefore anxious to hear all that was said. It was at this time that I first felt perfectly the annoyance of indistinct speaking. At the Newhall Hill meetings in Birmingham I had been accustomed to hear the Warwickshire orators *roar*, but in Glasgow I found they only spoke, and spoke as though they were paid for the sound they made, and did not get a good price for it. At length the Rev. Dr. King arose, who spoke with strong deliberateness. His speech was ably conceived and wisely delivered. Every word fell on the ear like the steady tolling of a bell. His voice was the anodyne of the night. Whenever I go to a public meeting I pray that one Dr. King may be present.

It is said of Mr. Macaulay, (I think by Francis in his "Orators of the Age,") that when an opening is made in a discussion in the House of Commons, he rises, or rather darts up from his seat, and plunges at

once into the very heart of his subject, without exordium or apologetic preface.  In fact, you have for a
few seconds a voice pitched in alto, monotonous and
rather shrill, pouring forth words with inconceivable
velocity, ere you have become aware that a new
speaker, and one of no common order, has broken in
upon the debate.  A few seconds more and cheers,
perhaps from all parts of the house, rouse you completely from your apathy, compelling you to follow
that extremely voluble and not very enticing voice,
in its rapid course through the subject on which the
speaker is entering, with a resolute determination, as
it seems, never to pause.  You think of an express
train, which does not stop even at the chief stations.
On, on he speeds, in full reliance on his own momentum, never stopping for words, never stopping for
thoughts, never halting for an instant, even to take
breath; his intellect gathering new vigor as it proceeds, hauling the subject after him, and all its possible attributes and illustrations, with the strength of
a giant, leaving a line of light on the pathway his
mind has trod, till, unexhausted and apparently inexhaustible, he brings his remarkable effort to a close
by a peroration so highly sustained in its declamatory
power, so abounding in illustration, so admirably
framed to crown and clench the whole oration, that
surprise, if it has even begun to wear off, kindles
anew, and the hearer is left utterly prostrate and
powerless by the whirlwind of ideas and emotions
that has swept over him.  This, however, only illustrates the liberty a man may take with elocution if
he has genius to compensate for it.  That member
must beware, who attempts to charm the House of
Commons by a monotonous alto without Macaulay's

wit, his power of enlightenment, and fecundity of illustration.

From Quinctilian to Blair, rhetoricians have insisted on the value of accuracy of expression as promotive of accuracy of thought. Accuracy of delivery tends equally to this result; it does more, it improves the memory as well as the understanding, and imparts the power of concatenation of speech. The naturally voluble may dispense with this aid, but others will find it the only mode of learning public speaking.

A clergyman, who in his early days denied that grammar or emphasis had anything to do with pulpit exercises, one day found his mistake by the laughter created on his reading this text: "And he spake to his sons, saying, Saddle *me*, the *ass*, and they saddled *him*." Of this same divine it is told that a man whom he reprimanded for swearing replied that he did not see any harm in it. "No harm in it," said the minister; "why do you not know the commandment, "Swear not at all?" "I do not swear at *all*," said the man, "I only swear at those who annoy me."

The emphasis which is suggested by the sense is the best guide. Let a person make sure of the sense and his emphasis will be natural and varied. An active and original conception can alone produce personality of enunciation, which is the chief charm of oratory. Conception is the sole governor of intonation. Of the delicious magic of inflection Eben Jones has given us a poet's idea in his lines "To a Personification of Ariel at the Theater:"

"If a new sound should music through the sky,
    How would all hearing drink the challenging tone;

And when thou uttered'st thy denying reply
To this questioning of love, as Ariel alone
Only could utter it, suddenly making known
New voice, new human music; then did burn
Each listener, to divine, ere it was gone,
What feelings toned it; though none might learn,
How many, divine and deep, in that sweet 'No' did yearn."

The offensiveness of affectation was justly satirized
in the confessions of a dandy given in a recent ro-
mance.   Mr. Affection is recounting his rejection
by a young lady, upon whom he had inflicted his at-
tentions.   "'You are mistaken!' said she, replying to
my look, 'it was *not* your dress, it was *not* your manners.   The young gentleman who comes from Bond-
street to tune our piano, is quite as affable and much
more dressy.'   'The people at the Royal Lodge, probably, afford you some little insight into my condition,
as a pretext for your doing me the honor of admitting me into your acquaintance,' said I with considerable bitterness, for I was stung home.   'No,
it was your *voice;* it was the hypocritical modulation
of your voice that satisfied me you had moved in the
best society,' replied Miss Vavasour, with provoking
coolness ; 'I saw that you were a most delicate mons-
ter ; that you had a voice for me and another for
Annie, a third for the pony, a fourth for the lodge-
keepers ; there was nothing *natural* about you!'"

Attracted by the pretensions of a placard, adorned
by a testimonial from the "Times," I went, in Glasgow, to hear some professional recitations.   One of
them was the "Story of a Broken Heart."   The unfortunate girl of whom it was told did not die immediately, but it struck me she would have done so had
she heard Mr. Wilson recite her story.   The subject
was that piece of graceful effeminacy in which Wash-

ington Irving has told, with drawing-room sentimentality, the story of the proud love of the daughter of Curran for the unhappy and heroic Emmet.

No one can recite with propriety what he does not feel, and the key to gesture, as well to modulation, is earnestness. No actor can portray character unless he can realize it, and he can only realize it by making it for a time his own. Roger Kemble's wife had been forbidden to marry an actor, and her father was inexorable at her disobedience; but after he had seen her husband upon the stage he relented, and forgave her with this observation: " Well, well! I see you have not disobeyed me after all; for the man is not an actor, and never will be an actor!"

As the presence of genius will compensate for the neglect of the elocution of utterance, so earnestness and great ideas will produce eloquence of effect without gesture in delivery. It is said of Robert Hall that the text of his discourse was usually announced in the feeblest tone, and in a rapid manner, so as frequently to be inaudible to the majority of his congregation. After the exordium, he would commonly hint at, rather than explicitly announce, the very simple divisions of the subject on which he intended to treat. Then his thoughts would begin to multiply, and the rapidity of his utterance, always considerable, would increase as he proceeded and kindled. He had no oratorical action, scarcely any kind of motion, excepting an occasional lifting or waving of the right hand, and, in his most impassioned moments, an alternate retreat and advance in the pulpit by a short step. Sometimes the pain in his back, to which he was so great a martyr, would induce him to throw his arm behind, as if to give himself ease or support in the long continued, and, to him, afflictive position of standing to address the people. Nothing of the effect which he produced depended on extraneous circumstances. There was no pomp, no rhetorical flourish, and few (though whenever they did occur, very appropriate) images, excepting toward the close of his sermon, when his imagination became excursive, and he winged his way through the loftiest sphere of contemplation. His sublimest discourses were in the beginning didactic and argumentative, then descriptive and pathetic, and finally, in the highest and best sense, imaginative. Truth, to him, was their universal element, and to enforce its claims was his constant aim. Whether he attempted to engage the reason, the affections, or the fancy, all was subsidiary to this great end. He was always *in earnest*, profoundly in earnest. But it is also true that as a chaste, concise, and energetic style is more effective than a florid, turgid, and prolix one, so the judicious employment of moderate gesture is more effective upon the genius of the English people, who love moderation, than any possible amplification of spasmodic attitudes or redundancy of grimace.

The prompting of Lucio to Isabel, when pleading before Angelo for the life of her brother, as rendered by Shakspeare in Measure for Measure, is one of the happiest practical lessons in elocutionary art on record. As a piece of preceptive teaching, neither the rhetoric of ancient or modern times has produced anything so happy, so concise, and yet so comprehensive, as Hamlet's directions to his players. It is a manual of elocution in miniature.*

* See Note B, page 168.

# CHAPTER III.

## THEORY OF PERSUASION.

"Rhetoric," says Plato, "is the art of ruling the minds of men;" but to rule mind you must know it. One touch of nature makes the whole world kin : but we cannot touch nature through the rules of art without knowing nature. "He who in an enlightened and literary society aspires to be a great poet must become a little child. He takes to pieces the whole web of his mind."* This is what the young rhetorician must do. He must tread backward the path of life to the first moment of consciousness, and ask all possible questions of his own experience. Carlyle has said that a *healthy* man never asks himself such personal questions. But a *thoughtful* man does. Could the disembodied experience of men be presented to view, so that the conscious life of each could be palpable in bodily form, how few figures would present the entire lineaments of mankind. We should behold an assemblage of mutilated figures, the limbs of some, the arms of others, the trunk, or the head, would be invisible; so little, as respects consciousness, do men generally possess themselves. As, however, man is himself essentially his own standard of judgment, is himself the measure of other men, it is inevitable that *he* will form a defective estimate of others who is defective himself. The rhetorician, then, who would hope to operate on the natures of others, must primarily make himself acquainted with his own.

* Macaulay, Crit. and Hist. Essays, vol. i.

An appeal to experience is the best test we have
of the force of an inducement. "The argument,"
says Emerson, "which has not the power to reach
my own practice, I may well doubt will fail to reach
yours. I have heard an experienced counselor say,
that he never feared the effect upon a jury of a lawyer who does not believe in his heart that his client
ought to have a verdict." A remarkable instance of
the result of an appeal to personal conviction is afforded in Bailey's Review of Berkeley's Theory of
Vision. "Many years ago," says Mr. Bailey, " I
held what may be styled a derivative opinion in
favor of Berkeley's Theory of Vision ; but having in
the course of a philosophical discussion had occasion
to explain it, I found on attempting to state *in my
own language* the grounds on which it rested, that they
no longer appeared to me to be so clear and conclusive as I had fancied them to be. I determined to
make it the subject of a patient and dispassionate examination. The result has been a clear conviction
in my own mind of its erroneousness, and a desire to
state to the philosophical world the grounds on which
that conviction has been formed." A philosophical
illustration of the truth of Emerson's observation, that
that statement is only fit to be made public which you
have come at in attempting to satisfy your own
curiosity. Men may live, and think, and reason, with
the mere surface knowledge which life presents to
every observer; but no one can master persuasion, as
an art, unless he passes in review the origin of ideas
and analyzes the motives of men.

A sound theory of intelligence is the basis of all
systematic persuasion. Metaphysical philosophy has
been prolific in its dissertations on the facts and attri-

butes of human mentality ; but the classification of intelligence laid down by some of the more judicious followers of Gall is the most scientific, and, consequently, the most intelligible which the student can follow. It is not possible to indicate a particular theory in detail with a chance of its being universally useful. For the general characteristics of humanity are variously combined with the national, local, and individual, in every audience who may be addressed by tongue or pen. The simple elements of humanity, like the letters of the alphabet, are, according to the arrangement of circumstances, spread out into countless volumes of character, each written in a peculiar language, and requiring a copious lexicon to render it intelligible to the reader.* The general principles, say of phrenology, indicate the outlines of human nature, and the study of men and manners fills up the detail. An old writer, I think Ralph Cudworth, says : "It is acknowledged by all, that sense is passion. And there is in all sensation, without dispute, first a passion in the body of the sentient, which bodily passion is nothing else but local motion impressed upon the nerves from the objects without, and thence propagated and communicated to the brain, where all sensation is made. For there is no other action of one body upon another, nor other change or mutation of bodies conceivable or intelligible, besides local motion; which motion in that body which moves another, is called action ; in that which is moved by another, passion. And, therefore, when a compound object very remotely distant is perceived by us, since it is by some passion made upon our body, there must of necessity be a

* Mrs. L. Grimstone.

continual propagation of some local motion of pressure from thence unto the organs of our sense or
nerves, and so unto the brain. As when we see
many fixed stars sparkling in a clear night, though
they be all of them so many semi-diameters of the
earth distant from us, yet it must, of necessity, be
granted that there are local motions or pressure from
them, which we call the light of them, propagated
continually or uninterruptedly through the fluid
heaven unto our optic nerves, or else we could not
see them." This indicates very plainly the philosophy of impressions. We have nothing to do here
with the controversies of metaphysicians concerning
the transcendentalism of intuitive knowledge. It
may be supernatural. It is, however, certain that a
great proportion of human knowledge is the result of
material relations, and to these relations the precepts
of knowledge apply. We may therefore indicate
with sufficient accuracy for practical purposes, that
the consciousness of external things is produced or
generated by the actions of those things on the organs of sense. The brain has no power to create,
only a susceptibility to receive notions. The brain
is the forge of thought,* and the rhetorician is the
smith who hammers out ideas in it.

So far as human conduct is influenced by material
considerations, and these are capable of being combined into a system, confidence can be imparted to
the speaker, and certainty infused into his efforts.

It might be illustrated at considerable length and
by distinguished examples, that appeals to religious
sentiments will always be avoided by a judicious
orator when addressing mixed assemblies.† They

* Carlyle.                    † See Note C, page 170.

are proper enough when spoken to a religious audience, but when employed for the purpose of influencing a mixed meeting they may fail to affect a considerable portion.   The experienced and well-informed speaker has always a wider resource.   He can draw his arguments from moral and political considerations, founded on utility.   These all men can understand and feel.   In those cases in which an orator cannot conscientiously restrict himself to this species of reasoning, he must take the other course, but let him not calculate on complete success or universal impressions.

The great business is to find out the right notion, and adapt it to the understandings of those whom we address.   This world is very matter-of-fact; men are very much the creatures of ideas.   Notions govern everything.   Impulses are the real destiny; men follow them as surely as the stars or the planets, and it is in this sense that what is to be *is*.

> As garment draws the garment's hem,
> Men their fortunes bring with them.*

From lowest to highest all are attached by that which has the attractive relation.   Matter draws matter.   The magnet has no attraction for gold or copper, but how it clings to the iron!   Man has various attractions—gold, honor, love.   To know what ideas are common to men, is to know humanity; to know how they are gained, is to know how to govern men by speech or pen.

*Every* man, said Walpole, has his price.   Whether Walpole had sounded the venality of all patriotism I know not.   Of course he had fixed the market price

* Emerson.

of his own virtue. But with more truth and less offensiveness it may be said that every man has his reason, which, when once presented to him, will sway him; and to find this out is the problem rhetoric has to solve. I am not more favorable than Hood to the plan of dropping truth gently, as if it were china, and likely to break. But if a fair case be so stated as not to mortify others by assumed arrogance, as not to annoy by ceaseless importunity, as not to disgust by seeming vanity, but accompanied by evident indications of disinterested sincerity, it will nearly always prove acceptable. It is not the truth men hate, but the unwise and untutored auxiliaries which so often attend its enunciation. "He who would correct my false view of facts," said one who understood the despotism of a wise method, "he must hold up *the same facts* in the true *order of thought*, and I can *never go back*. A man who thinks in the same direction as myself, but sees further, who has tastes like mine, but greater power, will rule me any day, and make me love my ruler."*

The young orator will do well to notice that morality is better understood, at least in theory, than in former periods of our history, and that the public require sincerity on the part of a speaker; and a life which shall illustrate what the orator seeks to enforce, will add materially to his influence. The reader may ask: May not a recommendation be a good one though the giver of it be bad? This is not the question. Is it not an advantage when both are worthy? The public may accept good advice from men who will not take it themselves. But is it not the object of a wise rhetoric to increase the number of men

* Emerson.

who will take sound advice? If the public should be composed of men who hear only and never practice, who does not see that we may give over all exhortations of amendment. Mankind reason that whatever is good for the public is good for individuals, since individuals make up the public. And when it is seen that a man does not follow his own advice, it is concluded that either he is a simpleton, and consequently is not to be heeded, or that he is secretly conscious of some inapplicability in his own recommendations, and consequently is to be suspected.

The moral existence of men is made up of a few trains of thought, which, from the cradle to the grave, are excited and re-excited, again and again, at the suggestion of sensitive impressions. These leading ideas rule despotically over conduct, and whoever awakens these associations governs those whom he addresses. It is in the appeals to these ancient impressions that we recognize the power and genius of the poet. It is in these leading ideas that we see the source of character. These are the great features in the lives of men which the rhetorician studies. His knowledge of them constitutes the weapons with which he works. When Napoleon in Egypt was threatened by his disaffected generals, he vanquished them by an appeal to the three leading traits in their character—their pride, their honor, and their bravery. Walking coolly among them, he said: "Soldiers, you are Frenchmen! You are too many to assassinate, and too few to intimidate me." The rebellion was blown aside with the breath of these words. The fury of the men was subdued to admiration, and they turned away, exclaiming: "How brave he is." Truly is it said the heart has no avenue so open as that of flattery, which, like some enchantment, lays its guards asleep.

A groundless outcry has been raised against speakers who appeal to the feelings. The only question to be decided is, What are the proper feelings of men? To appeal to these must always be right. The conclusions arrived at through the medium of such feelings are as legitimate as conclusions arrived at by appeals wholly belonging to the understanding. Feelings are the stays of intellect, the first links in the chain of powerful argument. The appeal to reality is the foundation of conviction. The lion was not to be subdued by pictures of Hercules and Theseus; he wanted the fact of his superior strength displayed. It was necessary that Hercules and Theseus should appear.

In nine years' experience in the office of a public tutor in one of the universities, Paley found, in discoursing to young persons upon topics of morality, that unless the subject was so drawn up to a point as to exhibit the full force of an objection, or the exact place of a doubt, before any explanation was entered upon—in other words, unless some curiosity was excited before it was attempted to be satisfied—the labor of the teacher was lost. When information was not desired, it was seldom, he found, retained.

The art of education consists in finding out what the child or adult *wants* to know. Inspired with desire to know, he is inspired with power to learn, and excited aptitude is the happy moment of acquirement. This neglected progress is arrested. This fact explains the failure of half the orations and lectures of these days. An audience is an adult school. It has, in the short space of an hour, to be educated in a new purpose. The undertaking is presumptuous, and is only to be accomplished by the union of rare judgment, disciplined powers, a store of means, and unfaltering energy. Yet how many rush into the arena of oratory without forethought, and go home wondering why they failed, and blaming the apathy of the people. Humanity is an instrument not to be played upon by unskillful performers. Had we men who studied oratory as great artists do music, painting, and sculpture, the majesty of ancient eloquence would yet flourish among us.

We can do without any article of luxury we never had, but when once obtained it is not in human nature to surrender it voluntarily. Of twelve thousand clocks left by Sam Slick, only ten were returned. "We trust to soft sawder," said Sam, "to get them into the house, and to human nature that they never come out of it." Yet how many persons expect to produce effects upon assemblies of men who never bestow half the time upon the study of their natures as was given by our American clock-seller!

The wise persuader will therefore treasure up all striking facts connected with the influencement of character, adapting, with rigid justice, the motive to the condition; to the great occasion, the strong inducement. Then, to borrow the words of Hazlitt: "The orator is only concerned to give a tone of masculine firmness to the will, to brace the sinews and muscles of the mind; not to delight our nervous sensibilities, or soften the mind into voluptuous indolence. The flowery and sentimental style is, of all others, the most intolerable in a speaker. He must be confident, inflexible, uncontrollable, overcoming all opposition by his ardor and impetuosity. We do not command others by sympathy with them, but by power, by passion, by will." On other occasions the orator is not reluctant to remember that the words of sincerity and kindness never fail when addressed to people not stirred by passion or rendered sullen by real or fancied contempt. Then the iron argument and the imperious air give place to the happier philosophy sung by Darwin, which teaches

> " How Love and Sympathy, with potent charm,
> Warm the cold heart, the lifted hand disarm;
> Allure with pleasures, and alarm with pains,
> And bind society in golden chains."

## CHAPTER IV.

### METHOD.

THE art of persuasion is dependent on no one thing so much as method. To have the fact, and to know how to tell it, is to hold rhetorical success in our hands. But it is of no use to have the fact unless we know how to tell it, and it is this which method teaches. There is, said the "Quarterly Review" lately, no power over human affairs like the *right* word spoken at the *right* season.

Method is derived from a Greek word signifying a path, a way, or transit. Where there are many transits, step follows step in pursuit of an object. And as there must be, for a true pursuit, a *definite* object in view, the principle of *unity* is implied in that of *progression*. Hence in a true method there must be a definite pursuit, otherwise circumstances will create sensations; but there will be no thought without method; and there may be restless and incessant activity, but without method there will be no progress. When the mind becomes accustomed to the outward impressions of objects, it turns to their relations, which hence become its prime pursuit, and may be called the materials of method.

The kinds of relations are two, the one arising from that which *must be*, the other that by which we merely perceive that *it is*. The former is called law, in its original acceptation, laying down the rule; the other is called the relation of theory.*

This is the method of science; it applies to the order pursued in the arrangement of encyclopedias. The method of art, if not so rigid, is yet regular, and marks both performances and character.

Coleridge asks: "What is it that first strikes us, and strikes us at once, in a man of education, and which, among educated men, so instantly distinguishes the man of superior mind? Not always the weight or novelty of his remarks, nor always the interest of the facts which he communicates, for the subject of conversation may chance to be trivial, and its duration to be short. Still less can any just admiration arise from any peculiarity in his words and phrases, for every man of practical good sense will follow, as far as the matters under consideration will permit him, that golden rule of Cesar's: *Insolens verbum, tanquam scopulum, evitare*. The true cause of the impression made on us is, that his mind is *methodical*. We perceive this in the unpremeditated and evidently habitual arrangement of his words, flow-

* See Encyclopedia Metropolitana, Art. "Method."

ing spontaneously and necessarily from the clearness of the leading idea, from which distinctness of mental vision, when men are fully accustomed to it, they obtain a habit of foreseeing at the beginning of every sentence how it is to end, and how all its parts may be brought out in the best and most orderly 'succession. However irregular and desultory the conversation may happen to be, there is *method* in the fragments."* The illustration of this is easy.

Two persons of opposite opinions will often meet; the one to convert the other. For instance : A seeks to bring B to the adoption of his opinions. I have witnessed the experiment often. The general course of procedure is this. A commences to unfold, expatiate on, and enforce his views. He expects thus to win B to their entertainment. But the mistake is a grave one. A argues *at* B when he should reason *with* him. A thus stands on the platform of his opinions and preaches to B, who is perched upon a platform of his own. A thus expects B to come to him. B probably expects the same of A. Thus both expect what neither intends.

A, in expecting B to come to him, assumes that on the part of his opponent there exists a predisposition for his views. This should never be assumed. It is the first endeavor of a wise propagandist to *create* it if it does not exist, and strengthen it if it does ; and whether it exists or not he should always condescend as though it did not. The business of A, the converter, is to go down to the platform B stands upon, to inquire his principles, study his views and turn of thought until he finds some common ground of faith, morals, opinion, or practice, with which he

* Encyclopedia Metropolitana.

can identify himself. The propagandist should commence by playing the pathfinder. The business of
A is to find a path from B's platform to his own, down
which B can agreeably walk. When a common
ground is found, A argues on that to B. The narrow
spot of identity soon enlarges if A has truth on his
side, for all truth, like electricity, has a tendency to
pass into all bodies uncharged with it, until an equi-
librium of light is established, and the current is
universal.

A, in finding a common ground in B's intellectual
sphere, establishes an equality with B. This gives
A an advantage. By studying B's views, instead of
making B study his, he condescends to B; he thus
establishes fraternity. This predisposes B to good
will.

Equality and fraternity are the two inlets to the
understanding. Conversion is uniformity. It ends
in intellectual equality. It must begin so. The
pleasure of universal opinion is the harmony it cre-
ates; the propagandists commence in fraternity, that
being the auspicious harbinger of harmony.

It is of no use to say you cannot find a common
ground. He who cannot find it, cannot convert.
How can persons, any more than bodies, cohere who
never touch? So long as each denies to the other a
particle of reason on his side; so long as each main-
tains an infallibility of pretension to complete truth;
they both assume what is contrary to the nature of
things, and exclude the common ground which must
be established between them, where truth and error
can join issue. There is no impassible gulf between
contending men or contending opinions but that dug
by pride and passion. We all have a common start-

ing point. We have a common consciousness of impression; a common nature to investigate; a common sincerity actuates us; truth is our common object, and we have a common interest in discovering it. Nature made us friends: it is false pride that makes us enemies. A common ground exists between all disputants. This is an important fact too little attended to, or indeed too little understood by inexperienced thinkers. The common ground which exists is not one which policy makes, but one that nature provides.

These remarks make conviction to depend upon truth, not upon forms of procedure. Nothing is recommended here which is inconsistent with truth; no cunning questioning, no sophistical entrapment. The sole precepts are those of condescension and contrast. Find a common ground of agreement, and you find a common point of sight, from which all objects are seen in the same light; and a clear plane is obtained on which principles can be drawn, and a perfect contrast of truth and error displayed. He who has the truth will make it plainer by wisdom of procedure. Differences are often made wider by irrelevant, repulsive debate. Differences which did not exist are often created in this way. All men desire the truth, and there is a way in which all can find it. The understandings of men run in a given channel; each thinker looks as it were through a telescope of his own. Let A bring his views within the vision of B, and the chances are in favor of B seeing the truth, if truth there be. If he sees error, A is benefited by the discovery made by a clearer sight than his own. "The faculty of speech," says Quinctilian, "we derive from nature; but the art from observation. For as in physic, men, by seeing that some things promote health and others destroy it, formed the art upon those observations; in like manner, by perceiving that some things in discourse are said to advantage and others not, they accordingly marked those things in order to imitate the one and avoid the other."

It is a maxim of the schoolmen, "*contrariorum eadem est scientia;*" we never really know what a thing is, unless we are also able to give a sufficient account of its opposite. This is the maxim of contrast that enters into all effective persuasion.

Various rules are given to direct the treatment of regular subjects. We are to begin, says Walker, with: 1. Definition, 2. Cause, 3. Antiquity or Novelty, 4. University or Locality, 5. Advantages or Disadvantages.

A theme, which is proving some truth, is said to have these parts: 1. The proposition or meaning of the theme; 2. The reason in favor of it, 3. The Confirmation or display of the unreasonableness of the contrary opinion; 4. The smile or illustration; 5. Example from history; 6. Testimony of others; 7. Conclusion or summary.

Writers are not all agreed in determining the parts of an oration, though the difference is rather in the manner of considering them than in the things themselves. Cicero mentions six, namely: Introduction, Narration, Proposition, Confirmation, Confutation, and Conclusion.

Writers are not agreed upon the division of orations, because nature has not agreed. All subjects will not admit of being treated under so many heads, and some audiences will not admit of the formality.

4

Sometimes an exordium is a bore, and a peroration tedious. Tact retrenches method as circumstances dictate. Paley's custom was to break down a subject into as many distinct parts as it really appeared to contain, and make each of them the subject of a separate and rigorous investigation. This seems a wise rule; we then take such parts as the subject affords, in the order prescribed, abbreviating them as the knowledge or temper of the audience may require.

The facts of necessity and discretion premised, the most practical formula of general procedure seems to me to be: 1. Give the introduction. 2. Explain the terms of the proposition, show what is granted and what disputed on each side, and then state the point of controversy. 3. Examine objections, and establish your own proposition. 4. Refute objections, and expose fallacies. 5. Make observations of enforcement naturally suggested by the subject:

> These rules of old discovered, not devised,
> Are Nature still, but nature methodized.

It is our opinion, says one of our critical journals, that all things should be made known in their proper places. No knowledge can be complete or thoroughly wholesome which is partial.

Dr. Paley has furnished two observations which may be usefully borne in mind in the enforcement of topics:

1. In all cases, where the mind feels itself in danger of being confounded by variety, it is safe to rest upon a few strong points, or perhaps upon a single instance. Among a multitude of proofs, it is *one* that does the business.

2. A just reasoner removes from his consideration not only what he knows, but what he does not know, touching matters not strictly connected with his argument, that is, not forming the *very steps* of his deduction : *beyond these* his knowledge and his ignorance are alike relative.

The simplicity and wisdom of profound method has been illustrated in the works of Morelly. Villegardelle says of Morelly's Essays on the Human Mind, treating on the analysis of the *intellectual* faculties, published in 1743: "The substance of this small educational treatise, which contains the developed germ of the method of instruction to which Mr. Jacotot has given his name, is comprised in the two following propositions :

" 1. The inclinations of the mind are reducible to two, namely, *Desire to know* and *Love of order ;* to these two ends we must refer all, even the amusements of children.

" 2. It is sufficient to present to the soul [understanding ?] objects in the same order as it generally follows, without making it perceive that it must attend to them."

The first essential of any kind of greatness is that it should have a purpose. We do not suspect the presence of genius till we feel this manifest. The Duke of Wellington has few arts which win applause. He is illiterate. All the school-boys in the kingdom laughed at his letters. Instead of the refinement of the classic council-table, his " Dispatches " are as coarse as fish-market bulletins; yet has he achieved greatness of a certain kind because he has decision of character.

One of his biographers—I think it is the Rev. Mr.

Wright—has given us the key to the duke's success in a few thoughtful words: " One characteristic of the Duke of Wellington strikes the reader from the very first, even when but a novice in war or statesmanship: his resolute will and unbounded self-reliance. Confident in his own capacity, he thinks, decides, and acts while other men are hesitating and asking advice. He is evidently conscious that *decision and promptitude, even though sometimes a man may err for want of due deliberation, will, in the long run, more often conduct to success than a slow judgment, that comes too late.*" This is the secret. The capacity to see this truth and the resolution to act upon it, is the capacity to rise above common men. Innumerable people will strike out a course and pursue it while all goes well; but the temper of greatness ever remains unshaken by reverses. It places its life on the hazard of a well-chosen plan, and looks for failures and defeats, but relies on the "*long run*" of persistency for success.

The intellectual character of the Duke of Wellington, so far as it has been displayed in civil affairs, accords with what his military exploits indicate. A simple and brief directness are the qualities of his speeches. " He strips a subject of all extraneous and unnecessary adjuncts, and exposes it in its natural proportions. He scents a fallacy afar off, and hunts it down at once without mercy. *He has certain constitutional principles which are to him real standards.* He measures propositions or opinions by these standards, and as they come up or fall short, so they are accepted or disposed of." The Duke of Wellington early took sides; he learned well the principles of which he would become the partisan. I have *itali-*

*cised* the words in the sentence just quoted from
" Fraser," which indicates his intellectual habit.   It
is hard to tell, generally, what are the " constitutional principles " of British liberty.   But it is not
hard to tell what they are when you know who uses
the phrase.   The principles of the throne and court
may be expressed in three propositions.   The duke
having adopted these, sits at ease, and measures the
plausible speeches of progress by them, and unmasks
the sophism of the quasi-liberal.

But, however directed, men will ever respect
straightforwardness of character.   It is heroic in that
man, whoever he may be, who looks over the
troubled sea of time and manfully elects his course.

> "Stern is the on-look of necessity :
> Not without shudder may a human hand
> Grasp the mysterious urn of destiny."

There is heroism in the very act, which cannot be
too much applauded.   It is this which converts life
from being a phantom or a maneuver into a reality
and a process.   It throws into ignoble shade your
petty men of expedients.   Principle either gives
success or confers dignity ; by chicanery all may be
lost, and nothing noble can ever be gained.   By
maneuver weak men seek to cheat human nature,
cajole fate, and win a glorious destiny by paltry tricks.
But the whole order of things is against it.   Such a
course may triumph, but it is the triumph of luck,
not success.   It is accident, not merit.   Dignity is
alone borne of principle and purpose.

> " He who by principle is swayed
>     In truth and justice still the same,
> Is neither of the crowd afraid,
>     Though civil broils the state inflame,

Nor to a haughty tyrant's frown will stoop,
Nor to a raging storm when all the winds are up."

Horace, Ode 3, Lib. III.

What decision is to character, what principle is to morals, so is method to literature. To have a clear purpose, and vigorously pursue it, is the strong element of rhetorical success. It is this feature which leads to the delineation of individual character. Coleridge has shown that the character of Hamlet is decided by the constant recurrence, in the midst of every pursuit, of philosophic reflections. Mrs. Quickley's talk is marked by that lively incoherence so common with garrulous women, whereby the last idea suggests the successor, each carrying the speaker further from the original subject. After this manner: "Speaking of tails, we always like those that end well—Hogg's, for instance. Speaking of hogs, we saw one of these animals the other day lying in the gutter, and in the opposite one a well dressed man; the first had a ring in his nose, the latter had a ring on his finger. The man was drunk, the hog was sober. A man is known by the company he keeps," etc. As Dr. Caius clips English, some of Bulwer's characters amplify periods. Dominie Sampson exclaims, "Prodigious." Sam Weller talks slang. In other cases an overwhelming passion pervades a character, or an intellectual idiosyncrasy is the peculiar quality, leading the possessor to look at everything in a given light. But whatever may be the feature fixed upon, its methodical working out constitutes individuality of character.

In the courts young barristers are drilled in an iron method. A judge always expects, at the outset, the enunciation of the object of the speech. A judicious speaker will always observe this rule for the sake of his audience. As a system of reasoning proceeds from certain axioms which can never be lost sight of except at the peril of confusion, so a discourse proceeds on something which is taken for granted, and which must be confessed and explained at the beginning, or the speaker will be considered only as indulging in airy speculations, and his hearers will be bewildered instead of enlightened, and be anxious about the danger of a fall instead of intent on the scene placed before them. The advantages of the course here advised have been well enforced in the Encyclopedia Metropolitana. "In purely argumentative statement, or in the argumentative division of mixed statements, and especially in argumentative speeches, it is essential that the issue to be proved should be distinctly announced in the beginning, in order that the tenor and drift that way of everything that is said may be the better apprehended; and it is also useful, when the chain of argument is long, to give a forecast of the principal bearings and junctures whereby the attention will be more easily secured, and pertinently directed throughout the more closely consecutive detail, and each proposition of the series will be clenched in the memory by its foreknown relevancy to what is to follow." These are well-known rules which it were superfluous to cite except for the instruction of the young. But examples may be occasionally observed of juvenile orators, who will conceal the end they aim at until they have led their hearers through the long chain of antecedents, in order that they may produce surprise by forcing a sudden acknowledgment of what had not been foreseen. The disadvantage of this method is that it puzzles and provokes the hearer through the discourse, and confounds him in the conclusion; and gives an overcharged impression of the orator's ingenuity on the part of those who may have attended to him sufficiently to have been convinced. It is a method by which the business of the argument is sacrificed to a puerile ostentation in the conduct of it, and the ease and satisfaction of the auditors sacrificed to the vanity of the arguer.

But though the purport of a speech must be avowed, the drift of an illustration may be concealed. One of Mr. Fox's Covent Garden orations affords a brilliant example. He took the case of certain poachers who had about that time suffered imprisonment in Ashby-de-la-Zouch, and he calculated the days of their incarceration, and the pecuniary loss their families had sustained by their detention from labor. The statistics were dry as summer's dust. What this had to do with the question of the corn laws no one could divine, when, by a masterly turn of thought, he asked: "If poachers are so punished who take the rich man's bird, how ought peers to be punished who take the poor man's bread?" The house rose with surprise. The climax had the effect of a light applied to a funeral pile, in which the arguments of the protectionists were to be consumed before the meeting.

Method is often of moment in trivial things. Some years ago it was the custom in Glasgow, when a fire broke out in the evening, for the police to enter the theater and announce the fire and the locality, that if any person concerned was present he might be apprised of the impending loss. On one occasion, when the watch commenced to announce, " Fire, 45 Candleriggs," the audience took alarm at the word "fire," and concluded that it applied to the theater. A rush ensued which prevented the full notice being heard, and several persons lost their lives. The inversion of the order of the announcement, "45 Candleriggs, Fire," would have prevented the disaster. But afterward the practice of such announcements was forbidden, it being impossible, I suppose, to reform the rhetoric of policemen.

Of the effect of the want of method in neutralizing the most magnificent powers, Burke is a remarkable instance. As an orator, Burke dazzled his hearers, and then distracted them, and finished by fatiguing or offending them. And it was not uncouth elocution and exterior only which impaired the efficacy of his speeches. Burke almost always deserted his subject before he was abandoned by his audience. In the progress of a long discourse he was never satisfied with proving that which was principally in question, or with enforcing the single measure which it was his business and avowed purpose to enforce; he diverged to a thousand collateral topics; he demonstrated as many disputed propositions; he established principles in all directions; he illuminated the whole horizon with his magnificent but scattered lights. There was, nevertheless, no keeping in his spoken compositions, no proportion, no subserviency of inferior groups to greater, no apparent harmony or unity of purpose. He forgot that there was but a single point to prove, and his auditors in their turn forgot that they had undergone the process of *conviction* upon any.

When Fadladeen essays his critical opinion on the poem of Feramorz, he commences thus: "In order to convey with clearness my opinion of the story this young man has related, it is necessary to take a review all the stories that have ever "——-"My good Fadladeen!" exclaimed Lalla Rookh, interrupting him, " we really do not deserve that you should give yourself so much trouble. Your opinion of the poem we have just heard will, no doubt, be abundantly edifying, without further waste of your valuable erudition." "If that be all," replied the critic, evidently mortified at not being allowed to show how much he knew about *everything* but the subject immediately before him, "if that be all that is required, the matter is easily dispatched." He then proceeded to analyze the poem. The wit of Moore was never more happily expended than in satirizing this learned discursiveness. The race of Fadladeen is immortal.

A few years ago a distinguished clergyman of the Universalist denomination was accused, while in Lowell, of "violently dragging his wife from a revival meeting and compelling her to go home with him." He replied: "Firstly, I have never attempted to influence my wife in her views, nor her choice of a meeting. Secondly, my wife has not attended any of the revival meetings in Lowell. Thirdly, I have not attended even one of those meetings for any purpose whatever. Fourthly, neither my wife nor myself has any inclination to attend those meetings. And, fifthly, I never had a wife!" This divine must have had " Order" large.

Next to those who talk as though they would never come to the point, are a class of bores who talk as though they did not know what the point was. Before they have proceeded far in telling a story, they stumble upon some Mr. What's-his-name, whom they have forgotten, and though it does not matter whether he had a name or not, the narrative is made to stand still until they have gone through the tiresome and fruitless task of trying to remember it, in which they *never* succeed.

A gorgeous instance of method occurs in W. J. Fox's Sermon on Human Brotherhood,* in which polished taste has so adjusted each clause that they reach the climax worthy of that Grecian art which the passage celebrates.

" From the dawn of intellect and freedom Greece has been a watchword on the earth. There rose the social spirit to soften and refine her chosen race, and shelter, as in a nest, her gentleness from the rushing storm of barbarism—there liberty first built her mountain throne, first called the waves her own, and shouted across them a proud defiance to despotism's banded myriads; there the arts and graces danced around humanity, and stored man's home with comforts, and strewed his path with roses, and bound his brows with myrtle, and fashioned for him the breathing statue, and summoned him to temples of snowy marble, and charmed his senses with all forms of eloquence, and threw over his final sleep their vail of loveliness; there sprung poetry, like their own fabled goddess, mature at once from the teeming intellect, gilt with the arts and armor that defy the assaults of time and subdue the heart of man; there matchless orators gave the world a model of perfect eloquence, the soul the instrument on which they played, and every passion of our nature but a tone which the master's touch called forth at will; there lived and taught the philosophers of bower and porch, of pride and

* Sermons on Christian Morality.

pleasure, of deep speculation and of useful action, who developed all the acuteness, and refinement, and excursiveness, and energy of mind, and were the glory of their country, when their country was the glory of the earth."

———————

# CHAPTER V.

### DISCIPLINE.

SINCE custom, says the wise Bacon, is the principal magistrate of a man's life, let him by all means endeavor to obtain good customs. Digressiveness is the natural state of the human faculties, till custom or habit comes in to give them a settled direction. Man is as liable to be influenced by the last impression as by any preceding one; and the *liability* of man is the characteristic of children. The teacher knows this, for it is only by infinite diversion that children can be instructed for hours together, or governed without coercion. It is the object of discipline to check the tendency to diversion, and give stability to method. A man may be made to perceive method, but not to follow it, without the power of discipline. A child accustomed to it will go to bed in the dark with peace and pleasure, but all the rhetoric in the world would not accomplish the same end without habit. Nothing but habit will give the power of habit.

Mr. John Foster, in his prospectus of his ruled copy-books, remarks that "the grand secret in teaching writing is to bestow much attention upon a little variety. The necessity of a *continued repetition* of the same exercise till it can be executed with correctness, cannot be too strongly insisted on. But as this reiteration is tedious for an age so fond of novelty as that of childhood, we should keep as close to the maxim as possible, and by a judicious intermixture of a few slightly differing forms, contrive to fix attention, and to insure repetition. 'The method of teaching anything to children,' says Locke, 'is by repeated practice, and the same action done over and over again, until they have got the HABIT of doing it well; a method that has so many advantages, whichever way we come to consider it, that I wonder how it could possibly be so much neglected.' Again: 'Children should never be set to perfect themselves in two parts of an action at the same time.' We have here the highest authority insisting on the very points which we labor to enforce, namely: 1. That it is only by constant reiteration, and persevering, pains-taking efforts, that ease and correctness in penmanship can be attained. 2. That the pupil should not advance too hastily, but proceed by natural gradations, from the simplest to the more difficult combinations." The discipline of penmanship may stand, also, for the discipline of elocution, for *men* are as children on the verge of a new art.

A speaker, like an actor, is subjected to the criticism of a casual hearing. The auditor who hears you but once will form an opinion of you forever. Against this injustice of judgment there is no protection but in acquiring such a mastery over your powers as to be able always to exert them well—to strike, astonish, or impress, in some respect or other, at every appearance. A man, therefore, who has a reputation to acquire or preserve will keep silence whenever he is in any danger of speaking indifferently. He will practice so often in private, and train himself so perseveringly, that perfection will become a second nature, and the power of proficiency never desert him. The uninitiated, who think genius is an impulsive effort that costs nothing, little dream with what patience the professional singer or actor observes regular habits and judicious exercise; how they treasure all their strength and power for the hour of appearance.

From Demosthenes to Curran, the personnel of orators has illustrated the triumphs of application as much as the triumphs of genius. "One day an acquaintance, in speaking of Curran's eloquence, happened to observe that it must have been born with him. 'Indeed, my dear sir,' replied Curran, 'it was not; it was born three and twenty years and some months after me; and if you are satisfied to listen to a dull historian, you shall have the history of its nativity. When I was at the Temple a few of us formed a little debating club. Upon the first night of meeting I attended, my foolish heart throbbing with the anticipated honor of being styled "the learned member that opened the debate," or "the very eloquent gentleman who has just sat down," I stood up; the question was the Catholic claims or the slave-trade, I protest I now forget which, but the difference, you know, was never very obvious; my mind was stored with about a folio volume of matter, but I wanted a preface, and for want of a preface the volume was never published. I stood up trembling through every fiber, but remembering that in this I was but imitating Tully, I took courage and had actually proceeded

almost as far as " Mr. Chairman," when to my astonishment and terror I perceived that every eye was turned
upon me. There were only six or seven present, and
the room could not have contained as many more, yet
was it, to my panic-stricken imagination, as if I were
the central object in nature, and assembled millions
were gazing upon me in breathless expectation. I became dismayed and dumb. My friends cried "Hear
him!" but there was nothing to hear. My lips indeed
went through the pantomime of articulation, but I
was like the unfortunate fiddler at the fair, who, upon
coming to strike up the solo that was to ravish every
ear, discovered that an enemy had maliciously
soaped his bow. So you see, sir, it was not born with
me. However, though my friends despaired of me,
the *cacoethes loquendi* was not to be subdued without
a struggle. I was for the present silenced, but I still
attended our meetings with the most laudable *regu-
larity*, and even ventured to accompany the others
to a more ambitious theater, the club of Temple Bar.
One of them was upon his legs—a fellow whom it
was difficult to decide whether he was most distinguished for the filth of his person or the flippancy of
his tongue—just such another as Harry Flood would
have called " the highly gifted gentleman with the dirty
cravat and greasy pantaloons." I found this learned
personage in the act of calumniating chronology by
the most preposterous anachronisms. He descanted
upon Demosthenes, the glory of the Roman forum ;
spoke of Tully as the famous cotemporary and rival
of Cicero, and in the short space of one half hour,
transported the straits of Marathon three several times
to the plains of Thermopylæ. Thinking that I had
a right to know something of these matters, I looked

at him with surprise. 'When our eyes met there was
something like a wager of battle in mine, upon
which the erudite gentleman instantly changed his
invective against antiquity into an invective against
me, and concluded by a few words of friendly counsel
(*horresco referens*) to "orator mum," who he doubted
not possessed wonderful talents for eloquence, although he would recommend him to show it in future
by some more popular method than his silence. I
followed his advice, and I believe not entirely without effect. So, sir, you see that to try the bird the
spur must touch his blood.'

"The discovery on this occasion of his talents for
public speaking encouraged him to proceed in his
studies with additional energy and vigor. The defect
in his enunciation (at school he went by the cogno-
men of 'Stuttering Jack Curran') he corrected by a
*regular system* of daily reading aloud, slowly, and with
strict regard to pronunciation, passages from his favorite authors. His person was short, and his appearance
ungraceful and without dignity. To overcome these
disadvantages he recited and studied his postures before a mirror, and adopted a method of gesticulation
suited to his appearance. Besides a *constant* attend-
ance at the debating clubs, he accustomed himself
to extemporaneous eloquence in private by proposing
cases to himself, which he debated with the same
care as if he had been addressing a jury."*

Mr. Macready, in the level part of the character
of Mordaunt, in the "Steward," and in some others,
has been said† to exhibit that very rare acquirement,
a perfectly unconstrained and graceful style of expression, accompanied by a cool, quiet, and uncon-

---

* Hogg's Weekly Instructor.        † Blackwood, 1819.

scious self-possession, in which the manners of a gentleman consist. This bearing, so indispensable in the speaker, is rarely to be acquired except by intercourse with good society. No closet theory will impart it so surely as the discipline of communication.

Men of brilliant rather than solid powers dazzle themselves and others with isolated thoughts, too little caring for coherency. In this way Hazlitt has told us that "an *improving* actor, artist, or poet, never becomes a great one. A man of genius rises and passes by these *risers*. A volcano does not give warning when it will break out, nor a thunderbolt send word of its approach." To this it is sufficient to reply, that the volcano is not the production of a moment, nor is the thunderbolt. The occasion of the display is sudden, but the collection of power, natural or human, is of slow growth.

---

# CHAPTER VI.

## TACT.

In matters not absolutely scientific, the principles of Method are more arbitrary and dependent upon the circumstances in which a speaker finds himself placed. We may abandon the order of nature and follow that of the understanding, where conviction can be more readily effected. This is the province of Tact. Method is straightforward procedure; Tact is adaptation. Method applies to general occasions; Tact to special.

The distinction between Method and Tact is illustrated in the following practical remarks of Paley: "For the purpose of addressing different understandings and different apprehensions, for the purpose of sentiment, for the purpose of exciting admiration of our subject, we diversify our views, we multiply examples. [This is Tact.] But for the purpose of strict argument, one clear instance is sufficient; and not only sufficient, but capable perhaps of generating a firmer assurance than what can arise from a divided attention." [This is Method.]

When an opponent urges an objection, one way of replying to it is by endeavoring to prove that the assertion contained in the objection is not true. Another alternative of which we may sometimes avail ourselves is, that if even the assertion be true, it is no objection to our position.

It sometimes happens that the argument advanced against us is really an argument in our favor. Tact discovers and avails itself of these advantages. Method arranges the materials, Tact applies the resources, of reasoning.

It is the judicious application of means that constitutes Tact. In journalism Tact is an indispensable requisite. The history of Mr. Murray's daily paper, the "Representative," published for six or eight months, about twenty years ago, is abundant proof that unlimited command of capital, first-rate literary abilities in every branch of knowledge, and the highest possible patronage, are all insufficient to establish a London morning paper without that commodity which alone lends practical value to the other three, and which is far more difficult to be procured than the three put together. What the princely fortune of

Mr. Murray, and his intellectual Titans of the "Quarterly," and all his regal and legal, and ermined and coroneted, and lay and clerical, and civil and military, friends could not obtain, was the simple but inestimable gift called Tact.*

Hamilton's "Parliamentary Logic" abounds in maxims which that experienced tactician had treasured up, observed, or invented during his public life. Many of these advices are utterly unworthy the imitation of an ingenuous man; but a few may be taken as illustrative of tact, good sense, and shrewdness:

State what you censure by the soft names of those who would apologize for it.

In putting a question to your adversary, let it be the last thing you say.

Distinguish real from avowed reasons of a thing. This makes a fine and brilliant fund of argument.

Upon every argument consider the misrepresentations which your opponent will probably make of it.

If your cause is too bad, call in aid the party: if the party is bad, call in aid the cause.†

Nothing disgusts a popular assembly more than being apprised of your intentions to speak long.

To succeed in a new sphere a man must take tact with him. In nine cases out of ten, method will miss the mark till tact has taught it adaptation. The House of Commons has often illustrated this opinion.

So many things have to be taken into account, that

* London Correspondent of the "Birmingham Journal."

† "If neither is good," adds Hamilton, "wound your opponent," which may be parliamentary, but I do not choose to recommend it.

nothing but experience can teach their management. Canning used to say, that speaking in the House of Commons must take *conversation* for its basis; that a *studious* treatment of topics was out of place. The House of Commons is a working body, jealous and suspicious of embellishments in debate, which, if used at all, ought to be spontaneous and unpremeditated.* Method is indispensable. Topics ought to be clearly distributed and arranged; but this arrangement should be felt in effect, and not betrayed in the manner. But above all things, first and last, he maintained that *reasoning* was the one essential element. Oratory in the House of Lords was totally different. It was addressed to a different atmosphere—a different class of intellects—more elevated, more conventional. It was necessary to be more ambitious and elaborate there.

"Fellows who have been the oracles of coteries from their birth; who have gone through the regular process of gold medals, senior wranglerships, and double foists, who have nightly sat down amid tumultuous cheering in debating societies, and can harangue, with an unruffled forehead and an unfaltering voice, from one end of the dinner table to the other; who, on all occasions, have something to say, and can speak with fluency on what they know nothing about, no sooner rise in the House than their spells desert them. All their effrontery vanishes. Commonplace ideas are rendered even more uninteresting by a monotonous delivery; and, keenly alive, as even boobies are, in those sacred walls, to the miraculous, no one appears more thoroughly aware of his unexpected and astounding deficiencies than

* See Note D, page 171.

the orator himself. He regains his seat, hot and hard, sultry and stiff, with a burning cheek and an icy hand; repressing his breath lest it should give evidence of an existence of which he is ashamed, and clenching his fist, that the pressure may secretly convince him he has not as completely annihilated his stupid body as his false reputation."*

How admirable a compendium is this of the history of rhetorical blockheads, who think that "in the great arena their little bow-wow" will be taken for "the loftiest war-note the lion can pour," just as if they were in their own small councils, and clubs, and societies! D'Israeli is said to have failed in this manner on the Spottiswoode business in the House of Commons; but afterward, as the world knows, he achieved brilliant distinction. Tact alone can teach a man to feel his way and measure the men opposed to him; it dictates judgment and effort, or *silence*.

Reputation and fortune are often made by Tact alone. The late Sir William Follett is an example. One of his obituary notices said: We do not, by any means, mean to say that at any period of his life he could be compared, as a scientific lawyer, (to scholarship he had no pretensions at all,) to Tindal, Maule, Patteson, Campbell; or, in the equity courts, to Pepys, Pemberton, or Sugden. Thus his professional position was attributable neither to the superiority of his professional knowledge nor to any talent above his cotemporaries. In Parliament he was not to be compared with Plunkett, Brougham, Sir William Grant, or Perceval. He possessed not the strong, eloquent, and condensed power of diction, joined to

* "Young Duke," by D'Israeli.

the closest and severest reasoning, of Plunkett; he had neither the stores of political, literary, and economical information, the versatility, the power of vigorous invective, nor of sarcasm, of Brougham; the calm, philosophic spirit of generalization of Grant; nor had he the dauntless daring and parliamentary pluck of Perceval. It must be admitted that he was neither an orator, nor a man of genius, nor a man of learning, apart from the *specialité* of his profession. He had neither passion, nor imagination of the fancy or of the heart. In what, then, lay his barristerial superiority? In his capability to play the artful dodge. His greatest skill consisted in presenting his case in the most harmonious and fair-purposed aspect. If there was anything false or fraudulent, a hitch, or a blot of any kind in his cause, he kept it dexterously out of view, or hurried it trippingly over; but if the blot was on the other side, he had the eye of the lynx and the scent of the hound to detect and run down his game. He had the greatest skill in reading an affidavit, and could play the "artful dodge" in a style looking so like gentlemanly candor, that you could not find fault.

I do not give this example as imitable, only as illustrative of Tact. Tact so employed may denote a very good lawyer, but a very indifferent man.

Those who had the pleasure of hearing Thom, the weaver poet, converse, know the Spartan felicity of expression which he commanded. His conversation was often a study in rhetoric. He told a story in the best vein of Scotch shrewdness. He was one day recounting an anecdote of Inverury, or old Aberdeen, to a coterie of listeners. The point of the story rested on a particular word spoken in fitting place.

When he came to it he hesitated as though at a loss for the term. "What is it you say under these circumstances," he asked: "not this, nor that," he remarked, as he went over three or four terms by way of trial as each was endeavoring to assist him: "Ah," he added, apparently benevolent toward the difficulty into which he had thrown them, "we say ——," for want of a better word. This, of course, was *the* word wanted; the happiest phrase the language afforded. He gained several things by this finesse; he enlivened a regular narrative by an exciting disgression, which increased the force and point of the climax. He created a difficulty for his auditors, for who, when suddenly asked, would be able to find a term which seemed denied to his happy resource? or, finding it, would have the courage to present it to such a fastidious epithetist? and he exalted himself by suggesting what appeared out of their power, and excited an indefinite wonder at his own skill in bringing a story to so felicitous an end, by the employment of a *makeshift* phrase. What would he have done if he could have found the right one? was naturally thought. This was tact. It was a case analogous to that given by Dickens in one of his early papers, where the President, at an apparent loss for a word, asks, "What is that you give a man who is deprived of a salary which he has received all his life for doing nothing, or, perhaps worse, for obstructing public improvement?" "Compensation!" suggests the vice. The case was the same, except that Thom was his own vice-president.

An instructive lesson in Tact is given in the preface of Thomas Cooper to his "Purgatory of Suicides." Those who know the variety of historic incidents which crowded for record in his career, wonder at the discretion with which he confines himself to the few which stand at the portal of his majestic poem, to inform you of its origin and design.

# PART II.

## ACQUIRED POWERS.

———— ◆•◆ ————

## CHAPTER VII.

### ORIGINALITY.

ORIGINALITY is reality. In reference to thought, it is the conception of the truth of nature in opposition to the truth of custom.

The material of which Originality is made has been discussed in previous chapters.* Its manifestation in literature has been well illustrated by the author of "Time's Magic Lantern,"† in a dialogue between Bacon and Shakspeare; an extract from which is to this effect:

"*Bacon.* He that can make the multitude laugh and weep as you do, Mr. Shakspeare, need not fear scholars. A head naturally fertile and forgetive is worth many libraries, inasmuch as a tree is more valuable than a basket of fruit, or a good hawk better than a bag full of game, or the little purse which a fairy gave to Fortunatus, more inexhaustible than all the coffers in the treasury. More scholarship might have sharpened your judgment, but the par-

---

* Logic of Facts, chaps. iv, v.

† A series of papers that appeared in "Blackwood" some years ago.

ticulars whereof a character is composed are better
assembled by force of imagination than of judgment,
which, although it perceive coherencies, cannot sum-
mon up materials, nor melt them into a compound
with that felicity which belongs to imagination alone.

"*Shakspeare.* My lord, thus far I know, that the
first glimpse and conception of a character in my
mind is always engendered by chance and accident.
We shall suppose, for instance, that I am sitting in a
tap-room, or standing in a tennis-court. The behavior
of some one fixes my attention. I note his dress, the
sound of his voice, the turn of his countenance, the
drinks he calls for, his questions and retorts, the
fashion of his person, and in brief, the whole out-
goings and in-comings of the man. These grounds
of speculation being cherished and revolved in my
fancy, it becomes straightway possessed with a swarm
of conclusions and beliefs concerning the individual.
In walking home, I picture out to myself what would
be fitting for him to say or do upon any given occasion, and these fantasies being recalled at some after
period, when I am writing a play, shape themselves
into divers manikins, who are not long of being
nursed into life. Thus comes forth Shallow and
Slender, and Mercutio, and Sir Andrew Aguecheek.

"*Bacon.* In truth, Mr. Shakspeare, you have observed the world so well, and so widely, that I can
scarce believe you ever shut your eyes. I too, although much engrossed with other studies, am, in
part, an observer of mankind. Their dispositions,
and the causes of their good or bad fortune, cannot
well be overlooked even by the most devoted ques-
tioner of physical nature. But note the difference of
habitude. No sooner have I observed and got hold

of particulars, than they are taken up by my judgment to be commented upon, and resolved into general laws. Your imagination keeps them to make pictures of. My judgment, if she find them to be comprehended under something already known by her, lets them drop and forgets them ; for which reason a certain book of essays, which I am writing, will be small in bulk, but I trust, not light in substance. Thus do men severally follow their inborn dispositions.

"*Shakspeare.* Every word of your lordship's will be an adage to after times. For my part, I know my own place, and aspire not after the abstruser studies : although I can give wisdom a welcome when she comes in my way. But the inborn dispositions, as your lordship has said, must not be warped from their natural bent, otherwise nothing but sterility will remain behind. A leg cannot be changed into an arm. Among stage-players, our first object is to exercise a new candidate until we discover where his vein lies."

In this mixture of observation and experiment, original information has its source. But the conventionalisms of society repress its manifestation. Jeffrey, in one of those passages marked by more than his ordinary good sense, has depicted its influence on young men :

"In a refined and literary community," says he, "so many critics are to be satisfied, so many rivals to be encountered, and so much derision to be hazarded, that a young man is apt to be deterred from so perilous an enterprise, and led to seek distinction in some safer line of exertion. His originality is repressed, till he sinks into a paltry copyist, or aims at distinc-

tion by extravagance and affectation. In such a state
of society he feels that mediocrity has no chance of
distinction; and what beginner can expect to rise at
once into excellence? He imagines that mere good
sense will attract no attention, and that the manner is
of much more importance than the matter, in a candidate for public admiration. In his attention to the
manner, the matter is apt to be neglected; and in his
solicitude to please those who require elegance of diction, brilliancy of wit, or harmony of periods, he is
in some danger of forgetting that strength of reason
and accuracy of observation by which he first proposed to recommend himself. His attention, when
extended to so many collateral objects, is no longer
vigorous or collected; the stream, divided into so
many channels, ceases to flow either deep or strong;
he becomes an unsuccessful pretender to fine writing,
and is satisfied with the frivolous praise of elegance
or vivacity."

The Rev. Sidney Smith left on record his opinion
of the influence of conventionality's cold decorum:
"The great object of modern sermons is to hazard
nothing;* their characteristic is decent debility, which
alike guards their authors from ludicrous errors, and
precludes them from striking beauties. Every man
of sense, in taking up an English sermon, expects to
find it a tedious essay, full of commonplace morality,
and if the fulfillment of such expectations be meri-
torious, the clergy have certainly the merit of not dis-
appointing their readers."

Emerson, above all men, has written the philosophy
of Originality: "Insist on yourself," says he, "never
imitate. Your own gift you can present every mo-

* See Note E, page 172.

ment, with the cumulative force of a whole life's cultivation; but of the adopted talent of another you have only an extemporaneous, half possession. The way to speak and write what shall not go out of fashion, is to speak and write sincerely. Take Sidney's maxim: 'Look in thy heart and write.' He that writes to himself writes to an eternal public."

## CHAPTER VIII.

### HEROISM.

WHAT has Heroism to do with Rhetoric? the reader will ask. Much. Courage in one thing, as we are told, does not mean courage in everything. A man who will face a bullet will not therefore face an audience. Heroism is the originality of action.

A cool, easy confidence is the source of daring. "Trust yourself; every heart vibrates to that iron string."* In one of those papers, rare in "Chambers's Journal," it is remarked: "There must, at all but extraordinary times, be a vast amount of latent capability in society. Gray's musings on the Cromwells and Miltons of the village are a truth, though extremely stated. Men of all conditions do grow and die in obscurity, who, in suitable circumstances, might have attained to the temple which shines afar. The hearts of Roman mothers beat an unnoted lifetime in dim parlors. Souls of fire miss their hour, and languish into ashes. Is not this conformable to what all

* Emerson.

men feel in their own case? Who is there that has
not thought, over and over again, what else he could
have done, what else he could have been? Vanity,
indeed, may fool us here, and self-tenderness be too
ready to look upon the misspending of years as anything but our own fault. Let us look then to each
other. Does almost any one that we know appear to
do or be all that he might? How far from it! Regard for a moment the manner in which a vast proportion of those who, from independency of fortune,
and from education, are able to do most good in the
world, spend their time, and say if there be not an
immense proportion of the capability of mankind
undeveloped.* The fact is, the bond of union among
men is also the bond of restraint. We are committed not to alarm or distress each other by extraordinary displays of intellect or emotion. Many struggle
for a while against the repressive influences, but at
length yield to the powerful temptations to nonentity.
The social despotism presents the fetes with which it
seeks to solace and beguile its victims; and he who
began to put on his armor for the righting of many
wrongs, is soon content to smile with those who smile.
Thus daily do generations ripe and rot, life unenjoyed,
the great mission unperformed. What a subject for
tears in the multitude of young souls who come in
the first faith of nature to grapple at the good, the
true, the beautiful, but are thrown back, helpless and
mute, into the limbo of Commonplace. O Conventionality, quiet may be thy fireside hours, smooth thy
pillowed thoughts, but at what a sacrifice of the right
and the generous, of the best that breathes and pants
in our nature, is thy peace purchased!"

* See Note F, page 173.

There is heroism in trusting yourself to events. That sagacity of which greatness is born puts its prowess to the test of experiment. In this lies the secret of the hero and the scholar; they do not *guess* their abilities, but *determine* them by enterprise and achievement. They *try*. My friend Mr. Storer, who was the wag of the Rhetoric class of which we were members when students, communicated to me the subjoined parody. As the soliloquy of a novice, it expresses with felicity the young speaker's doubts and fears:

To spout, or not to spout, that is the question:
Whether 'tis better for a shamefaced fellow,
(With voice unmusical and gesture awkward,)
To stand a mere spectator in this business,
Or have a touch at Rhetoric! To speak, to spout
No more; and by this effort, to say we end
That bashfulness, that nervous trepidation
Displayed in maiden speeches; 'twere a consummation
Devoutly to be wished. To read, to speechify
Before folks, perhaps to fail; ay, there's the rub;
For from that ill success what sneers may rise,
Ere we have scrambled through the sad oration,
Must give us pause: 'tis this same reason
That makes a novice stand in hesitation,
And gladly hide his own diminished head
Beneath some half-fledged orator's importance,
When he himself might his quietus make
By a mere recitation. Who could speeches hear,
Responded to with hearty acclamation,
And yet restrain himself from holding forth—
But for the dread of some unlucky failure—
Some unforeseen mistake, some frightful blunder,
Some vile pronunciation, or inflection,
Improper emphasis, or wry-necked period,
Which carping critics note, and raise the laugh,
Not to our credit, nor so soon forgot?
We muse on this! Then starts the pithy question:
Had we not best be mute and hide our faults,
Than spout to publish them?

Spout and publish them without hesitation. Had Raphael feared to daub, he had never been Raphael. Had Canova feared to torture marble, he had never been a sculptor. Had Macready feared to spout, he had never been an actor. If you stammer like Demosthenes, or stutter like Curran, speak on. He who hesitates to hesitate, will always hesitate.

---

# CHAPTER IX.

### PROPORTION.

BOMBAST is inflation; is turgid, dropsical language, great in parade, little in purport. It has its source in exaggeration, in want of proportion. A child catches at its coral and at the moon with the same expectation of clutching it. He has no idea of distance. The boy cuts a stick or trundles his hoop with as much exultation as the man defeats an enemy or wins his wife. The boy has no notion of relative value. As everything seems equally new, so everything seems equally important to him. This want of measure, innocent and healthy in youth, is the source of bombast in men.

"Man is a strange animal, but that complex animal, a public meeting, is stranger. Its vagaries are surprising, and baffle analysis. It always seems to have more force than sense. Two heads are better than one, but some hundreds of heads appear to be worse than none. Take any number of men, each of whom would listen to reason, be open to conviction, and resolute to see fair play all round; compound the honest men of sense in a public meeting, and the aggregate is headstrong, headlong, rash, unfair, and foolish. Tell any single man, *totidem verbis*, that there is nobody in the world like him, nobody so lovely and virtuous as his wife and daughters, and he will laugh in your face or kick you out of doors; but tell the aggregate man the same of his multitudinous self and family, he will vent an ecstasy of delight in 'loud cheers.'"* But only the uneducated imitate this delusion. The time will come when meetings no more than men will tolerate the collective nonsense.

The notorious defense of Thurtell some years since, which was so applauded for effectiveness by a portion of the press, is one of the most offensive exhibitions of vanity and wind-bag eloquence extant. Bombast is the language of vulgarity and villainy. Thurtell ought to have been condemned for his defense had he escaped from the penalty of his crime. Carelessness of assertion and wildness of accusation are to the English people extremely distasteful, as marking either a deficiency of intellect or a want of the love of truth.

Royalty has always been a patient and often a greedy recipient of egregrious adulation. The oratory addressed to James I. on his progress through Scotland was of no common cast. Officials who addressed him at the various towns at which he arrived, "put together Augustus, Alexander, Trajan, and Constantine. It was supposed that even the antipodes heard of his courtesy and liberality; the very hills and groves were said to be refreshed with the dew of his aspect; in his absence the citizens

* "Spectator."

6

were languishing gyrades, in his presence delighted
lizards, for he was the sunshine of their beauty. At
Glasgow Master Hay, the commissary, when attempting to speak before him, became like one touched
with a torpedo or seen of a wolf; and the principal
of the university, comparing his majesty with the
sun, observed, to that luminary's disadvantage, that
King James had been received with incredible joy
and applause; whereas a descent of the sun into
Glasgow would in all likelihood be extremely ill
taken. Hyperbole was not sufficient; the aid of
prodigies was called; a boy of nine years old harang-
ued the king in Hebrew, and the schoolmaster of
Linlithgow spoke verses in the form of a lion."*

The measure of a man's understanding lies in his
language. This he inevitably offers to all observers.
Besides just taste being outraged by disproportion,
he who is guilty of it loses the power of being impressive. We are told of Dante, whose potent use
of words has never been surpassed, that great and
various as his power of creating pictures in a few
lines unquestionably was, he owed that power to the
directness, simplicity, and intensity of his language.
In him "the invisible becomes visible," as Leigh
Hunt says; "darkness becomes palpable, silence
describes a character, a word acts as a flash of lightning which displays some gloomy neighborhood
where a tower is standing, with dreadful faces at the
window."†

"In good prose (says Frederic Schlegel) every
word should be underlined;" that is, every word
should be the right word, and then no word would

* Progress and Court of King James the First.—"Quarterly Review."
† "Athenæum," No. 1115.

be righter than another. It comes to the same thing, where all words are italics one may as well use roman. There are no italics in Plato, because there are no unnecessary or unimportant words." *

Declamation, which is assertion without proof, is disproportion in this sense, that it is a dogmatic enunciation, out of proportion with what is known by an auditory who reject the propositions announced. Nearly all Oriental eloquence is declamatory. Perhaps the Orientals are quicker to perceive or less exacting than Europeans, but the want of the reasons was felt among us, and Bishop Hooker supplied them sixteen centuries after.

Precision must be attained at any cost. If we do not master language, says Mr. Thornton, it will master us. An idle word, says the "*Daily News,*" has conquered a host of facts. We must keep watch and ward over words.

## CHAPTER X.

### STYLE.

Rousseau sways mankind with that delicious might (the power of words) as Jupiter does with his lightnings. This is John Müller's tribute to the style of Rousseau. It has recently been asserted among us that "style is, and always has been, the most vital element of literary immortalities. More than any other quality, it is peculiar to the writer; and no

* Guesses at Truth.

one, not time itself, can rob him of it or even diminish its value. Facts may be forgotten, learning grow commonplace, truths dwindle into mere truisms, but a magnificent or beautiful style can never lose its freshness and its value. For style, even more than for his wonderful erudition, is Gibbon admired; and the same quality, and that alone, renders Hume the popular historian of England in spite of his imperfect learning, the untrustworthiness of his statements in matters of fact, and the anti-popular caste of his opinions." * This is not greater praise than I should be inclined to award to masterly style, but this eulogy has the fault of making style to appear independent of sense. We value Hume for the grace and perspicuity of his narrative, and for those profound reflections which, whether founded on real or fictitious data, are equally full of wisdom. Method, perspicuity, brevity, variety, harmony, are indeed separable from sense, but no combination of such qualities will give life to a book without sense. They are but the auxiliaries of meaning, not the substitutes for it. Gilfillan has happily said that "the secret of perfect composition is manly wisdom, uttered in youthful language." Youthful language is simple and clear. These are its properties. We are nothing unless we are critical, and we are nothing unless we are clear. That criticism which destroys the power of pleasing must be blown aside, and so must that finesse of style which cannot be understood. Again, the truth is obvious that sense is the despot of style.

The "Dublin University Magazine" lately had this passage: "Boz has achieved a great thing—he has created a *style*. Perhaps I am wrong to say *created*,

* "Daily News," No. 499.

a term which implies independence of materials; whereas the singular circumstance in this case is, that by *careful study of previous styles*, by *imitation of them*, by more perhaps than imitation in the first instance, this author has produced out of *the heterogeneous elements* a compound essentially differing from all its component parts, and claiming, claiming justly, the high merit of being *original*. That such a result should follow such a course ought to encourage writers who aim at true celebrity to adopt this humble and painstaking initiatory system, which, though in other arts it has admittedly led to the grandest results, (in painting, for instance,) in literature has been too much overlooked and despised. Boz now stands alone in his style; he has had no models, he has no imitators, he will probably have no disciples." I should think Dickens has smiled at this violent attempt to make a literary alchemist of him, as one fusing all sorts of styles in his crucible of composition, and bringing out quite a new mixture. Present society has furnished him with materials; a patient and an accurate observation has gathered them; feeling, taste, and humor have combined them, and an unaffected simplicity has told them. I suspect that a happy nature and good sense have had more to do with Dickens's reputation than any amount of old styles, than Sterne or Sturm. Tindal said of Pitt's first speech, that it was more ornamental than the speeches of Demosthenes, and less diffuse than those of Cicero. That it should have been so often quoted, says Macaulay, "is proof how slovenly most people are content to think. It would be no very flattering compliment to a man's figure to say that he was taller than the Polish Count, (or Tom

Thumb,) and shorter than Giant O'Brien; fatter than *anatomie vivante*, and more slender than Daniel Lambert. No speaking can be less ornamental than that of Demosthenes, or more diffuse than that of Cicero."

Heldenmair lays it down as a maxim of education that freedom is the all-essential condition of growth and power. There can be no fervor while, in the language of Sam Slick, "Talk has a pair of stays, and is laced up tight and stiff." It is freedom which is the active element of all fresh and vigorous style. Dr. Gilchrist observes that "what one of the ancient philosophers said of laws may be truly said of rhetorical rules; they are like cobwebs which entangle the weak, but which the strong break through. The first rule of good composition is, *that the composer be free and bold.* Before a man can be a good thinker, or a good writer, he most be free and bold; he must be roused to noble daring; he must feel his whole soul rising in scornful indignation at the thought of having been for a day a blind follower of blind leaders, a slave of slaves, a member of the herd of creeping, crouching, servile minds. Can servile composers in the harness of rules, dreading the lash of criticism, limping upon quotations, with their eye upon precedents and authorities, create a style at once new and striking, yet just and proper? All real greatness is the offspring of freedom; there may be absurdity, folly, cant, hypocrisy, squeamish delicacy, finical politeness, sickly sentimentality, mawkish affectation in every possible fantastic form of fashion and variety; but there cannot be original, substantial excellence without intellectual independence, manly thinking and feeling."

As soon as a man understands a subject he is in a condition, so far as material goes, to write or speak about it. If he has also courage to write *himself* in his word, he may be said to have the materials and the strength to achieve originality. But let him not forget that fullness and freedom are both· blind ; and that without the lights of taste and perspicuity and brevity he may offend, bewilder, and tire.

Out of all a man may be able to say, taste (by which I chiefly mean a sense of utility) selects the most useful things which pertain to conviction and improvement.

An old woman, who showed a house and pictures at Towcester, expressed herself in these words: "This is Sir Richard Farmer; he lived in the country, took care of his estate, built this house and paid for it, managed it well, saved money, and died rich. *That* is his son; he was made a lord, took a place at court, spent his estate, and died a beggar!" A very concise, but full and striking account, says Dr. Horne. Here clearness and brevity are conspicuous; great qualities to master!

> As 'tis a greater mystery in the art
> Of painting to foreshorten any part
> Than draw it out; so 'tis in books the chief
> Of all perfections to be plain and brief.

Juniper Hedgehog wrote of the Bishop of Exeter: "What a lawyer was spoiled in that bishop! What a brain he has for cobwebs! How he drags you along through sentence after sentence—every one a dark passage—until your head swims !"* Character-izing with effect the darkness which prevails where perspicuity is absent.

* Jerrold's Shilling Magazine, No. 8. July, 1845.

Brevity and precision are oftener manifested among our French neighbors than among ourselves. The speeches made to mobs, the most hurried placards, abound in the felicities of condensation. Europe has for some time been agitated with communism. Few Englishmen could tell you what is meant by it. Yet nearly a century ago Morelly thus expressed it: "It is the solution of this excellent problem : to find a situation in which it shall be nearly impossible for man to be depraved or bad." We have never on this side the channel approached the felicity of this reply.

As a model of the old, simple, and manly Saxon tongue, the student may consult the writings of the author of the "Pilgrim's Progress." If all that Mr. Macaulay avers be true, the works of the Bedford tinman deserve special attention. The style of Bunyan, says Macaulay, is delightful to every reader, and invaluable as a study to every person who wishes to obtain a wide command over the English language. The vocabulary is the vocabulary of the common people. There is not an expression, if we except a few terms in theology, which would puzzle the rudest peasant. We have observed several pages which do not contain a single word of more than two syllables. Yet no writer has said more exactly what he wanted to say. For magnificence, for pathos, for vehement exhortation, for subtle disquisition, for every purpose of the poet, the orator, and the divine, this homely dialect, this dialect of plain working-men was sufficient. There is no book in our literature on which we would so readily stake the fame of the old unpolluted English language, no book which shows so well how rich that language is in its own proper

wealth, and how little it has been improved by all
that it has borrowed.

In the first edition of "Practical Grammar," the
author fell into this vagueness. If remarks had to be
made at the end of the statement, it was directed that
they should be neither " too strong nor too tedious."
But when he subsequently asked his class at the City
Mechanics' Institution, at what point of effectiveness
a man might be said to be *too strong*, it was agreed
that there was error somewhere. And the injunction
not to be "*too* tedious," was found to imply that we
might be tedious in some degree, which hardly seemed
desirable. Then it was asked, "What is Strength?"
Some answered, "Power." What was Power?
Some said, "Effectiveness." But it was soon felt
that these definitions left us like Swift's definition of
style, that it was the use of proper words in proper
places. What were proper words and proper places,
still remained open questions. So if power was
strength, and strength effectiveness, what was effectiveness was still unknown. It was finally agreed that
to be strong was to be just, and to avoid being tedious
was to be brief. We therefore agreed that "remarks
just and brief" were the proper characterization.
For what was just could never be *too* strong, and
what was brief could never be *too* tedious. From
which we also learned that the secret of the strength
of comment lay in just sentiments, and that tedium
was the tiresome progeny of prolixity.

:.

## CHAPTER XI.

### SIMILES.

PARACELSUS announced what Cogan reiterated, that "it is as necessary to know evil as good; for who can know what is good without knowing what is evil?" This principle of contrast is that upon which truth depends for its development and effect for its power. It is the principle on which similes are founded.

To preserve peace and to do good is a very old maxim of morality. Feltham thus enforces it: "When two goats on a narrow bridge met over a deep stream, was not he the wiser that lay down for the other to pass over him, rather than he that would hazard both their lives by contending? He preserved himself from danger, and made the other become debtor to him for his safety. I will never think myself disparaged either by preserving peace or doing good." This comparison elevates the sentiment, relieves its repetition from triteness, and gives it the freshness of truth.

Paine, whom I have heard Ebenezer Elliot describe as a great master of metaphor, said of a certain body in America, that at the very instant that they are exclaiming against the mammon of this world, they are nevertheless hunting after it with a step as steady as time, and an appetite as keen as death. The immutable insatiableness sought to be characterized is rendered much more evident by these similes. It will be observed that the contrast implied in similes is not absolute; it is the comparison of a lesser degree with a greater, which marks the idea to be enforced. This is seen in the saying of Dumont to the effect that " Both the Rolands felt convinced that Freedom could never flourish in France, and spring up a goodly tree, under the shadow of a throne." It is further seen in the remark of Mirabeau, who, when asked to counsel an obstinate friend, answered: " You might as well make an issue in a wooden leg as give him advice." The same principle is observable in the observation of Emerson at the soiree of the Manchester Atheneum, at which he spoke. Expressing the latent strength of Old England, he said she " had still a pulse like a cannon." The felicity of the simile was perfect. The same person, denoting the freshness of style of Montaigne, said the words, if you cut them, they would bleed. The " Cork Magazine " says that the preface of Thomas Davis to the speeches of Curran is, in some parts, as majestic as the orations which it prefaces; in others, displaying a wild pathos which " strikes upon the ear like the cry of a woman."

It does not appear to me to be necessary to enter into the usual enumeration of the various figures of speech specially set forth in rhetorics. Under the principle of comparison so wide a range of illustration is included as to be sufficient for the use of the rhetorician. Nothing, we are told, so works on the human mind, barbarous or civilized, as a new symbol. Metaphor is the majestic ground of enforcement, and its occupation is as extensive as its power. It is by this means the poverty of language is enriched by the eloquence of the universe, and the whole of inanimate nature admitted into society with man.

In Eastern lands they talk in flowers,
    And tell in a garland their loves and cares;
Each blossom that blooms in their garden-bowers
    On its leaves a mystic language bears.

Comparisons are implied by phrases.  An instance occurs in Newman's works, where he says: "Heresy did but precipitate the truths before held in solution." The allusion is chemical, but very happy.  Symbols expressed or implied were the weapons of Mirabeau. Contempt for the men-millinery of literature was never more forcibly expressed than in these words of his: "My style readily assumes force, and I have a command of strong expressions; but if I want to be mild, unctuous, and measured, I become insipid, and my flabby style makes me sick."  Dumont, a friend of Mirabeau's, recounting his own editorial experience in preserving brevity and a wise directness in his journal, says: "The most diffuse complained of our reducing their *dropsical* and *turgescent* expressions."

By some comparisons all the power of condensation is realized.  Grattan, comparing the Irish Parliament to a departed child, exclaimed: "I have sat by its cradle, and I followed its hearse."  There is here all the grandeur of eloquence and grief.

In the "Auditor," Lord Viscount Barrington was described as a little squirrel of state, who had been busy all his life in the cage, without turning it round to any human purpose.  The clearness attained by this simile needs no explanation.  Severity can be conveyed with equal ease, as instanced in Judge Haliburton's asseveration, that humility is the dress-coat of pride.

It is a trite remark, that men draw their symbols from those departments of science or life with which they are most familiar. The Greeks filled their language with geometrical allusions. Lieutenant Lecount, the well-known mathematician, having occasion to describe a wound, says: "One of the latest cases was a man with a *round* ulcer, about *two and a half inches in diameter*, on one side of his leg, and an *oval* one, *five inches by two and a half*, on the other side."*

When Mr. Mould, the undertaker in "Nicholas Nickleby," speaks of Shakspeare, it is as the theatrical poet who was *buried* at Stratford. But it matters not whence the similes are drawn, provided they are appropriate. In a sermon preached at Newgate after the escape of Jack Sheppard, the clergyman discoursed to this effect: "How dexterously did he pick the padlock of his chain with a crooked nail; burst his fetters asunder; climb up the chimney; wrench out an iron bar; break his way through a stone wall; make the strong door of a dark entry fly before him; reach the leads of the prison; fix a blanket to the wall with a spike stolen from the chapel; descend to the top of the turner's house; cautiously pass down stairs, and make his escape at the street door.

"I shall spiritualize these things. Let me exhort ye, then, to open the locks of your hearts with the nail of repentance; burst asunder the fetters of your beloved lusts; mount the chimney of hope; take thence the bar of good resolution; break through the stone wall of despair and all the strongholds in the dark entry of the valley of the shadow of death; raise yourselves to the leads of divine meditation; fix the blanket of faith with the spike of the Church; let yourselves down to the turner's house of resigna-

* "Midland Observer," March, 1844.

tion; descend the stairs of humility. So shall you come to the door of deliverance from the prison of iniquity, and escape from the clutches of that old executioner the devil, who goeth," etc., etc.*

The child when he first learns to speak will say anything, thinking he accomplishes much in continuing to talk. So with the public speaker when he first commences, and so with the early efforts of the young writer. He knows nothing of symbolic beauty or rhetorical proportion; he does not suspect that there are gaudy images and encumbering ornaments. When he first rises above the level of plain prose, he never knows when to descend to the earth; and instead of finding an elevation whence he can show his readers a wider landscape and new objects, he thinks he does enough by showing himself.

Prodigality of metaphors, like multitudes of superlatives, confound meaning. "It is an idle fancy of some," says Felton, "to run out perpetually upon similitudes, confounding their subject by the multitude of likenesses, and making it like so many things that it is like nothing at all."

The general rule to be observed is obvious. When we intend to elevate a subject, we must choose metaphors which are lofty or sublime. If our purpose is to degrade, the similes which sink the subject to contempt or ridicule are proper for employment. These are the two poles of tendency. A member of the Indiana Legislature has said: " Mr. Speaker—The wolf is the most ferocious animal that prowls in our western prairies, or runs at large in the forests of Indiana. He creeps from his lurking-place at the hour of mid-

* Volume of Trials of Criminals, printed at Leeds, 1809, for J. Davies, by Edward Baines.

night when all nature is locked in the silent embraces of Morpheus, and ere the portals of the east are unbarred, or bright Phœbus rises in all his golden majesty, whole litters of pigs are destroyed." Wanting sustainment, these figures end in the ridiculous.

## CHAPTER XII.

### PLEASANTRY.

I OFFER only a few suggestions on this subject. The happiest vein of pleasantry is needed to pen a suitable essay upon it. If men of wit and humor would analyze the sources of their inspirations, pleasantry might be taught as an art. And why not? Recreation is an element of health, a component of human nature, the third estate of life. It ought to have its professors and cultivators.

A comedian went to America and remained there two years, leaving his wife dependent on her relatives. Mrs. F——tt, expatiating in the greenroom on the cruelty of such conduct, the comedian found a warm advocate in a well-known dramatist. "I have heard," says the latter, "that he is the kindest of men, and I know that he writes to his wife every packet." "Yes, he writes," replied Mrs. F., "a parcel of flummery about the agony of absence, but he has never remitted her a shilling. Do you call that kindness?" "Decidedly," replied the author, "*unremitting* kindness." Here the wit turns upon words.

Goodrich relates a converse instance: "I once

heard of a boy who, being rebuked by a clergyman for neglecting to go to church, replied that he would go if he could be permitted to change his seat. 'But why do you wish to change your seat?' said the minister. 'You see,' said the boy, 'I sit over the opposite side of the meeting-house, and between me and you there's Judy Vicars and Mary Staples, and half a dozen other women, with their mouths wide open, and they get all the best of the sermon, and when it comes to me it's pretty poor stuff.'"

"Wit is the philosopher's quality, humor the poet's; the nature of wit relates to things; humor to persons. Wit utters brilliant truths, humor delicate deductions from the knowledge of *individual* character. Rochefoucault is witty, the Vicar of Wakefield the model of humor."*

English humor is frank, hearty, and unaffected. Irish light as mercury. It sets propriety at defiance. It is extravagant. Scotch humor is sly, grave, and caustic. Surely the analysis of Pleasantry is possible, and its cultivation practicable.

Many persons never think of pleasantry as an agent of relief in exposition, and of effect in many departments of enforcement. Some worry jokes to death. A man who runs after witticisms is in danger of making himself a buffoon.† Some speakers are so beset with the love of this display that they virtually announce to their audiences that the smallest laugh would be thankfully received. A degree of wit pertains to all topics. That which lies in our way is that which is relevant.

---

* Bulwer's Student.                    † See Note G, page 173.

# CHAPTER XIII.

## ENERGY.

ENERGY is the soul of oratory, and energy depends
on health. Dr. Samuel Johnson, with that strong
sense for which he was distinguished, once said, we
can be useful no longer than we are well. Of the
rhetorician it may as safely be said that he is effective
no longer than he is well. A variety of arts may be
pursued in indifferent health; feebleness only pro-
longs execution; in rhetoric it mars the whole work.
Even in the matter of efficient thinking health is
worth attention. The senses being the great inlets
of knowledge, it is necessary that they be kept in
health. It will be idle to conceal from ourselves that
the physical is the father of the moral man. "Morals
depend upon temperaments."*

The patience necessary for investigation cannot be
preserved with impaired nerves. Long-continued
wakefulness is capable of changing the temper and
mental disposition of the most mild and gentle, of
effecting a complete alteration of their features, and
at length of occasioning the most singular whims, the
strangest deviations in the power of imagination, and
in the end absolute insanity.

It may not be necessary, because Carneades took
copious doses of hellebore as a preparative to refuting
the dogmas of the Stoics, or because Dryden, when he
had a grand design, took physic and parted with
blood, that the searcher after truth should commence

* Edward Johnson—Life, Health, and Disease.

7

with an aperient; yet it will be useful that some attention be paid to the physiology of the

———intellect, whose use
Depends so much upon the gastric juice.

The public will remember the case of an ex-occupant of the woolsack who, after "six days' indisposition," attempted the annihilation of Lord Aberdeen on account of his Scotch Church Bill. The "Times," with some satire, expressed in reference to it much truth. "We recognize the deep interest of the public in Lord B.'s medicine chest. We pray him to take care of himself for all our sakes. We entirely enter into the feelings of a man who, after suffering six days under dyspepsia, bile, or otherwise, rushes into the House of Lords to avenge upon some minister the disarrangement of his system. The castigation of a secretary of state is an interesting incident in his disorder, a gratifying palliative of his discomfort, but it is, after all, in Epsom salts or quinine that the true and only effectual remedy must be found."*

Perhaps the lowest quality of the art of oratory, but one on many occasions of the *first importance*, is a certain robust and radiant physical health; great volumes of animal heat. In the cold thinness of a morning audience, mere energy and mellowness is inestimable; wisdom and learning would be harsh and unwelcome compared with a substantial man, who is quite a house-warming. I do not rate this animal life very high; yet, as we must be fed and warmed before we can do any work well, so is this necessary.† It often happens that you cannot come into collision with opinion without coming into col-

* "Times," June 29, 1843.                    † Emerson.

lision with persons. What would Danton have been without his cannon voice. When Mirabeau spoke, his voice was like the voice of destiny., He seemed as if moulded to be the orator of nature. The wise orator will as much attend to the exercise which gives him health, as to the exercise which gives him skill. We go to the oratorio to hear sublime sentiments set to the music of art; we go to the orator to hear them enforced by the music of nature. Oratory is the personal ascendancy of opinion. Without physical fascination it descends to mere eloquence of words. Intellect moves the scholar only. Oratory moves the illiterate to noble deeds.

When traveling expenses were the only payment I received for my lectures, I used to walk to the place of their delivery. On my walk from Birmingham to Worcester, a distance of twenty-six miles, it was my custom to recite on the way portions of my intended address. In the early part of my walk my voice was clear, and thoughts ready; but toward the end I could scarcely articulate, or retain the thread of my discourse. If I lectured the same evening, as sometimes happened, I spoke without connection or force. The reason was that I had exhausted my strength on the way. One Saturday I walked from Sheffield to Huddersfield to deliver on the Sunday two anniversary lectures. It was my first appearance there, and I was ambitious to acquit myself well. But in the morning I was utterly unable to do more than talk half inaudibly and quite incoherently. In the evening I was tolerable, but my voice was weak. My annoyance was excessive. I was a paradox to myself. My power seemed to come and go by some eccentric law of its own. I did not find out till years after that the utter exhaustion of my strength had exhausted the powers of speech and thought, and that entire repose instead of entire fatigue should have been the preparation for public speaking.

———————

# CHAPTER XIV.

### ELOQUENCE.

"THE histories of old times, and even of not very distant ones, acquaint us with the wondrous effects of eloquence upon whole multitudes, carried away to far crusades by the oratory of a hermit; and even upon grave political assemblies and parliaments, which an able speaker could twist, turn, and persuade according to fantasy, so that majorities hung upon his words. There is no such things now-a-days. Audiences are neither so pliable nor so soft; and eloquence, however mighty, fails in carrying convictions by storm. Perhaps this is the reason why so few public men of the present day fall into the mistake of striving or affecting to be eloquent.

"Persuasion, in fact, is now a long-winded and tedious task. The winning of an audience, of a party; the inculcating an idea, the disseminating it; the winning conviction first, and getting up the enthusiasm after, is now a slow work, almost like the dropping of a seed, and patiently waiting till it grows, in order to foster it, water it, protect its growth, and enjoy its expansion into the stem and the flower; such is the political eloquence of modern times. He who discovered it, and who practices it, is Richard Cobden."*

This is a fair history of modern eloquence; but it is hardly true that Mr. Cobden "discovered" it. He has been its greatest illustrator, but it has grown with the growth and commercial character of the nation. Long before Cobden's time, the magic fancy of Burke, the glittering sophistries of Pitt, the thundering declamation of Fox, were all alike founded upon the general and lasting truth of things—upon profound views—upon the inexhaustible resources of the understanding. The king of transcendentalists has said that "Eloquence must first be plainest narrative or statement; afterward it may warm itself until it exhales symbols of every kind, and speaks only through the most poetic forms; but at first and last it must still be, at bottom, a statement of facts. All audiences soon ask, ' What is he driving at?' and if this man does not stand for anything, he will be deserted."† This writer has given us the most eloquent version of eloquence extant. The substance of his views is as follows: " First, then, the orator must be a substantial person; then the first of his special weapons is, doubtless, power of statement; to have the fact and to know how to tell it. Next, is that method or power of arrangement which constitutes the genius and efficacy of all remarkable men. Next to this is the power of imagery. Nothing so works on the human mind, barbarous or civilized, as a new symbol. The power of dealing with facts, of illuminating them, of sinking them by ridicule or diversion of mind, rapid generalization, humor, wit, and pathos, all these are keys which the orator holds; yet these

* " Daily News," No. 522.      † Emerson.

foreign gifts are not eloquence, and do often hinder a
man from the attainment of it. To come to the heart
of the mystery, the truly eloquent is an excited man
with power to communicate his excitement. Arm a
man with all the talents just enumerated, so potent
and so charming, and he has equal power to ensnare
and mislead, as to instruct and guide you. A specta-
cle we may go round the world to see, is a man who,
in the prosecution of great designs, has absolute command of the means of representing his ideas, keeps
the grasp of a lion on his materials, and the eye of a
king to dispose them right, never for an instant light-
minded or insane. But, in the great triumph of the
orator, we must have something more; we must have
a certain reinforcing of the man from the events, so
as to have the double force of reason and destiny.
The eloquent man is not he who has beautiful speech,
but he who is inwardly and desperately drunk with
a certain belief, agitating and tearing him, perhaps
almost bereaving him of the power of articulation.
Then it rushes from him, in short abrupt screams, in
torrents of meaning. The possession of his mind by
the subject is so entire, that it insures an ardor of expressions which is the ardor of nature itself; and so
is the ardor of the greatest force, and inimitable by
any art. Add to this a certain regnant calmness,
which in all the tumult never utters a premature
syllable, and keeps the secret of his means and
method, and the orator stands before the people as
a demoniacal power, to whose miracles they have no
key. Youth should lay the foundation of eloquence,
not on popular arts, but on character and honesty.
Let the sun look on nothing nobler than he, let him
speak of the right, let him not borrow the language

of idle gentlemen or scholars, much less that of sens-
ualists, absorbed in money or appetite; but let him
communicate every secret of strength and good-will
communicated to his own heart, to animate men to
better hopes; let him speak for the absent, defend the
friendless and defamed, the poor, the slave, the
prisoner, and the lost. Let him look upon opposition
as opportunity; he is one who cannot be defeated or
put down. Let him feel that it is not the people who
are in fault for not being convinced, but he who cannot convince them. He has not only to neutralize
their opposition—that were a small thing—but to
convert them into apostles and publishers of the same
wisdom."

The only alteration I would make in this account
is this: Instead of making eloquence a thing of degree, which confounds eloquence with oratory, I
would mark the distinction. Eloquence belongs
merely to words, oratory to the passion which fires
them. The eloquence of intellect is that of speech,
and sense, and symbol; but the oratory which so
seldom greets the ears of men is the eloquence of the
man. The philosopher only reaches the scholar, the
orator reaches the mob. The philosopher talks the
rhetoric of the schools, the orator the language of
nature; he speaks heart words—that language which
is wide as the world, which reaches humanity, which
all nations understand, which the deaf and dumb
can feel—the language of gratitude, of gesture—that
which moves us on canvas, breathes on marble. It
is the burning word of passion. It knows no high,
no low, no rich, no poor, no citizen, no alien, no for-
eigner, no crime, no color. Savage and civilized,
learned and illiterate, (the accidents of condition,)

sink into insignificance when *man* speaks to man.
The orator penetrates to the equality of humanity. It
is in the equality of our common nature that a common purpose originates. He alone who penetrates
there inspires unanimity. It is when the multitude
are of one opinion that the orator's power is revealed;
that is the seal that nature stamps upon his genius.

It is said that one day when Massillon was preaching upon the Passion before Louis XIV. and all the
court, he so affected his hearers that everybody was
in tears, except a citizen, who appeared as indifferent
to what he heard as to what he saw. One of his
neighbors, surprised at such insensibility, reproached
him for it, and said to him, "How can you refrain
from weeping, while we are all bathed in tears?"
"That is not astonishing," answered the citizen, "I
am not of this parish." The eloquence which I have
endeavored to describe would have included this
man also in the general weeping. To say that a
touch of nature makes the whole world kin, is only
another way of saying, That "man is related to all
nature." Eloquence discovers this relation. In the
first remark, Shakspeare gives the effect, of which,
in the second remark, Emerson has assigned the cause.

With respect to passion, to which much importance
has been assigned, it will be useful to remark, that
though we must admit, with Lord Kames, that the
plainest man animated with passion affects us more
than the greatest speaker without it, we must keep in
view that the only passion tolerated among us is the
passion of conviction.* All the rest is, to Englishmen,
rant. The passion of conviction is modest, manly,
and earnest.

* See Note H, page 174.

# CHAPTER XV.

## PREMEDITATION.

THERE is every reason to believe that the greatest masters of oratory have been most sensible of the value of, and have most practiced premeditation. It is only the young would-be speaker who expects to be great without effort, or whose vanity leads him to impose upon others the belief that he is so, who affects to despise the toil of preparation. One of the biographers of Canning tells us that it is remarkable that, with his broad sense of great faculties in others, he was himself fastidious to excess about the slightest turns of expression. He would correct his speeches and amend their verbal graces till he nearly polished out the original spirit. He was not singular in this. Burke, whom he is said to have closely studied, did the same. Sheridan always prepared his speeches; the highly-wrought passages in the speech on Hastings's impeachment were written beforehand and committed to memory; and the differences were so marked that the audience could readily distinguish between the extemporaneous passages and those that were premeditated. Mr. Canning's alterations were frequently so minute and extensive that the printers found it easier to recompose the matter afresh in type than to correct it. This difficulty of choice in diction sometimes springs from *l'embarras des richesses*, but oftener from poverty of resources, and generally indicates a class of intellect which is more occupied with costume than ideas. But here are three instances which set all popular notions of verbal fastidiousness by the ears; for certainly Burke, Canning, and Sheridan were men of capacious talents; and two of them at least present extraordinary samples of imagination and practical judgment, running together neck and neck in the race of life to the very goal.

We owe the low state of oratory in this country, to a great extent, to the false contempt for "cut and dried speeches," till it has come to be considered a sign of weakness for a man to think before he speaks. Archbishop Whately has wisely cautioned young preachers against concluding that because the apostles spake well without premeditation, that others will speak so, unless, like the apostles, they are specially *inspired*.

Perhaps, although we use the term, we never have had oratory in England. There is an essential difference between oratory and debating; oratory seems an accomplishment confined to the ancients, unless the French preachers may put in their claim, and some of the Irish lawyers. Mr. Shiel's speech in Kent was a fine oration; and the boobies who taunted him with having got it by rote were not aware that in doing so he only wisely followed the example of Pericles, Demosthenes, Lycias, Isocrates, Hortensius, Cicero, Cesar, and every great orator of antiquity.*

It has been said by a popular writer that Demosthenes not only prompts to vigorous measures, but teaches how they are to be carried into execution. His orations are strongly animated, and full of the impetuosity and ardor of public spirit. His composition is not distinguished by ornament and splendor. It is an energy of thought, peculiarly his own, which forms his character and raises him above his species. He appears not to attend to

* "Young Duke," by B. D'Israeli.

words, but to things. We forget the orator and think of the subject. He has no parade and ostentation, no *studied* introduction; but is like a man full of his subject, who, after preparing his audience by a sentence or two for the reception of plain truths, enters directly on business.

Blair should have said Demosthenes had no *elaborate* exordiums. They were "studied," as is proved by their pertinency and fitness. Demades says that Demosthenes spoke better on some few occasions when he spoke unpremeditatedly.* Probably he spoke well in some of these instances, but it was the result of power acquired by premeditation. As a general rule, he who thinks twice before speaking once will speak twice the better for it.

When Macaulay was about to address the House of Commons, his anxious and restless manner betrayed his intention. Still he was regardless of the laugh of the witlings, and continued intent on his effort. This is the real courage that does things well; the courage that is neither laughed nor frowned from its purpose.

Macaulay spoke early in the evening, before the jarring of the debate confused him or long attention enfeebled his powers. Only the ignorant despise attention to minute details. When the great Lord Chatham was to appear in public he took much pains about his dress, and latterly he arranged his flannels in graceful folds. It need not then detract from our respect for Erskine, that on all occasions he desired to look smart, and that when he went down into the country on special retainers, he anxiously had recourse to all manner of innocent little artifices to aid his purpose. He examined the court the night before

* See Note I, page 175.

the trial, in order to select the most advantageous place for addressing the jury. On the cause being called, the crowded audience were perhaps kept waiting a few minutes before the celebrated stranger made his appearance; and when at length he gratified their impatient curiosity, a particularly nice wig and a pair of new yellow gloves distinguished and embellished his person beyond the ordinary costume of the barrister of the circuit.*

Amid the applause in this chapter bestowed upon premeditation, it would not be just to omit the ridicule with which it has been visited by the Rev. Sidney Smith: "It is only by the fresh feelings of the heart that mankind can be very powerfully affected. What can be more ludicrous than an orator delivering stale indignation and fervor of a week old? turning over whole pages of violent passions, written out in German text; reading the tropes and apostrophes into which he is hurried by the ardor of his mind, and so affected at a preconcerted line and page that he is unable to proceed any further?" True, "it is only by the fresh feelings of the heart that mankind can be very powerfully affected." But nature is always fresh, and he who reproduces nature will always affect. Macready never stabbed his daughter to preserve her honor; yet every man is moved at his Virginius. As Othello, Macready's "indignation" at Iago is thirty years old, yet we are as much affected by its intensity as on the first day when he displayed it. The speech of Antony over the dead body of Cesar was "written in German text" in the days of Elizabeth; it was "cut and dried" two hundred years ago; yet, whatever our satirical canon may

* Campbell's Lives of the Chancelors.

say to the contrary, it ceases not to affect us now. A great idea well expressed, or a deep feeling naturally portrayed, is "a thing of beauty and a joy forever."

## CHAPTER XVI.

### REALITY.

IT was said by Panchand that Mirabeau was the first man in the world to speak upon a question he knew nothing about. But Mirabeau had the confidence which enabled him to abandon himself to the reality of occasions, and he read the lessons they brought with them, while other men went to books; and, as reality is the most powerful teacher, he was wiser than the encyclopediasts.

I believe there are no difficulties in the moral or political world, no problem of events, which do not also bring their solutions with them, were we cool enough to read them; but we never trust ourselves to events; we do not believe what we see, or will not see what is before us. We make preconceived opinions, predetermined judgment, overrule new facts. We too often act the part of the man who is so much in love with his bark that he never ventures to sail in it. This is the course to be taken: scan the truth, and having learned it, trust to subsequent events to illustrate it.

In the premeditation which I have commended I do not mean to exclude extempore application of the faculties. An orator should go to the rostrum to announce conclusions, not to form them. In this I persist; but having laid the scene, I would leave him free to manage it as he pleased. Let him take advantage of the tide of feeling, temper, and exclamations of the meeting; but unless he is firm in a previous purpose, these things will take advantage of him and carry him away from his subject, instead of his carrying away the audience.

*Hic Rhodus; hic salta.** Do not wait for a change of outward circumstances, but take your circumstances as they are, and make the best of them. This saying, which was meant to shame a braggart, will admit of a very different and profounder application. Goethe has changed the postulate of Archimedes, " Give me a standing-place, and I will move the world," into the precept, " Make good thy standing-place, and move the world." This is what he did throughout his life.†

Abandonment to reality is the source of presence of mind, an indispensable element of oratorical greatness. It is storied that Frederic the Great being informed of the death of one of his chaplains, a man of considerable learning and piety, and determining that his successor should not be behind him in these qualifications, he told a candidate about to preach a trial sermon at the Royal Chapel that he would himself furnish him with a text from which he was to make an extempore sermon. The clergyman accepted the proposition. The whim of such a probationary discourse was spread abroad, and at an early hour the Royal Chapel was crowded to excess. The king arrived at the end of the prayers, and, on the candidate

* "Here is Rhodes; leap here."—*Old Fable.*
† Guesses at Truth. By two Brothers.

ascending the pulpit, one of his majesty's aids-de-camp presented him with a sealed paper. The preacher opened it, and found nothing written therein. He did not, however, in so critical a moment, lose his presence of mind; but turning the paper on both sides, he said: "My brethren, here is nothing, and there is nothing; out of nothing God created all things;" and he proceeded to deliver an admirable discourse upon the wonders of the creation. This man deserved the appointment.

A good converse story is told in Chambers's Scottish Jest Book, of a minister who had a custom of writing the heads of his discourse on small slips of paper, which he placed on the Bible before him, to be used in succession. One day, when he was explaining the second head, he got a little warm in the harness, and came down with such a thump upon the Bible with his hand that the ensuing slip fell over the edge of the pulpit, though unperceived by himself. On reaching the end of his second head he looked down for the third slip; but, alas! it was not to be found. "Thirdly," he cried, looking round him with great anxiety. After a little pause, "Thirdly," again he exclaimed; but still no thirdly appeared. "Thirdly," I say, my brethren," pursued the bewildered clergyman; but not another word could he utter. At this point, while the congregation were partly sympathizing in his distress, and partly rejoicing in such a decisive instance of the impropriety of using notes in preaching, which has always been an unpopular thing in the Scotch clergy, an old woman rose up and thus addressed the preacher: "If I'm no mista'en, sir, I saw thirdly flee out at the east window a quarter of an hour syne." It is impossible for any but a Scotchman to conceive how much this account of the loss of thirdly was relished by that part of the congregation which condemned the use of notes.

Before writing or speaking, it is of great service to try the matter over by telling it to a critical friend, or explaining it to some one utterly ignorant of it. By these trials of reality objections may be learned, impediments to conviction be discovered, and simplicity of enunciation acquired. If you have to speak of topics before thus maturing your power over them, supply a relay of telling points, so that when coherency fails you, you can have recourse to a striking thought. Few will discover its want of relevance. The majority always mistake brilliancy for eloquence. But remember, this expedient will only save you with the vulgar; the well-informed are not thus to be imposed on.

The neglect of the study of reality is, perhaps, nowhere so apparent as in the construction of controversial books. Authors satisfy themselves with inventing the arguments of their opponents, when the easiest and most satisfactory course is to extract the most powerful reasoning the other side has produced. By this course real objectors could be answered instead of imaginary ones. The neglect of this precaution was strikingly manifested in a work published some time ago entitled "Torrington Hall."

# CHAPTER XVII.

## EFFECTIVENESS.

EFFECTIVENESS lies in proportion. Not in the beauty of a pillar or the finish of a frieze, but in the command which the whole building has over the spectator; and not in the brilliance of a passage, but in the coherence of the whole, lies the effectiveness of a speech or a book.

Foremost in effectiveness stands purpose. Better say nothing than not to the purpose. Nothing should attract the main attention to itself. The chief merit of any part is its subserviency to the whole design. When parts are praised, a speaker is said to have brilliance; when the whole impresses, he is said to have power.

" The editor of Shelley's posthumous poems apologizes for the publication of some fragments in a very incomplete state, by remarking how much more than every other poet of the present day every line and word he wrote is instinct with beauty. Let no man sit down to write with the purpose of making every line and word beautiful and peculiar. The only effect of such an endeavor will be to corrupt his judgment and confound his understanding."[*]

A few generalities may be mentioned, attention to which will conduce to effectiveness. Avoid rant, study simplicity, abjure affectation, be natural. The natural voice is heard the farthest, and the natural affects the soonest. " The costly charm of the ancient

[*] Henry Taylor. Preface to Philip Van Artevelde.

tragedy, and, indeed, of all the old literature, is that the persons speak simply, speak as persons who have great good sense without knowing it."* Nothing astonishes men so much as common sense and plain dealing. Earnestness and simplicity carry all before them. On Thiers's first appearance in the French Chamber, he experienced an almost universally unfavorable reception, from certain personal peculiarities, over the effect of which he soon triumphed. In person Thiers is almost diminutive, with an expression of countenance, though intellectual, reflective, and sarcastic, far from possessing the traits of beauty. The face itself, small in form, as befits the body, is encumbered with a pair of spectacles so large, that when peering over the marble edge of the long narrow pulpit, called the tribune, whence all speakers address the Chamber, it is described as appearing suspended to the two orbs of crystal. With such an exterior, presenting something of the ludicrous, so fatal to the effect, especially in volatile France, M. Thiers, full of the impassioned eloquence of his favorite revolutionary orators, essayed to impart those thrilling emotions recorded of Mirabeau. The attempt provoked derision, but only for a moment. In his new sphere, as in the others he had passed through, he soon outshone competition. Subsiding into the oratory *natural* to him, *simple*, vigorous, and rapid, he approved himself one of the most formidable of parliamentary champions.

Bentham has made a wise remark on prolixity, which may teach the student a just use in the measure of words. "Prolixity," says Bentham, "may be where redundancy is not. Prolixity may arise not

* Emerson.

only from the multifarious insertion of unnecessary articles, but from the conservation of too many necessary ones in a sentence; as a workman may be overladen not only with rubbish, which is of no use for him to carry, but with materials the most useful and necessary, when heaped up in loads too heavy for him at once. The point is, therefore, to distribute the materials of the several divisions of the fabric into parcels that may be portable without fatigue. There is a limit to the lifting powers of each man, beyond which all attempts only charge him with a burden to him immovable. There is in like manner a limit to the grasping power of man's apprehension, beyond which if you add article to article, the whole shrinks from under his utmost efforts." "Too much is seldom enough," say the authors of "Guesses at Truth." "Pumping after your bucket is full prevents it keeping so."

Proportion of time as well as proportion of parts is essential, both for the sake of the speaker's strength, as well as the hearer's patience. Whitefield is reported to have said, that a man, with the eloquence of an angel, ought not to exceed forty minutes in the length of a sermon, and it is well known that Wesley seldom exceeded thirty. "I have almost always found," says another eminent preacher, "that the last fifteen minutes of a sermon an hour in length was worse than lost, both upon the speaker and congregation." There is practical wisdom in these remarks. A man who determines to speak but a short time is more likely to command the highest energy for his effort, and to speak with sustained power. Half an hour is time enough for immortality. Mirabeau achieved it by efforts of less duration.

Here it may be observed that a man who intends to be brief and comprehensive will seldom need notes to assist him. In cases where time cannot be commanded to master the subject in the memory, notes are better than the risk of anxiety or forgetfulness. Generally speaking, a subject deeply felt and fully understood will make itself a place in the memory.

The chief quality in the success of the late Sir William Follett consisted in his confining himself to what he understood. This was the basis on which his tact rested. He knew where his strength lay, and kept there. Of the "Lowell Offering," published by Knight some time since, the "Times" said: "It is the production of factory girls in Lowell, the American Manchester, and we much doubt if all the duchesses in England could write as much and so seldom offend against good taste. The secret of these girls' success in writing arises from their writing only about what they know—common life and their own affairs." He who seeks any kind of effectiveness will do well to remember the incidental lesson conveyed in these words. A frequent cause of failure with young lecturers, is neglecting to find a point of common understanding between themselves and their auditors. They do not comprehend the philosophy of exordium. Much rhetorical wisdom may be gathered from the mathematician's example. We know that the geometer would in vain reason with others unless axioms were previously agreed upon for reference. So with an audience. If they do not agree with the speaker as to the premises from which he reasons, the audience have no standard by which they can test his conclusions. Hence, though he may confound them, yet he will never convince them.

It is in this sense that those who would improve the public must "write down" to the public. They may, and they ought to elevate the public by their sentiments, but they must found their reasoning on what the populace understand and admit, or they reason in vain. The people must be taken at what they are, and elevated to what they should be.

Young men, poetical from ardor and enthusiastic from passion rather than principle, will often rush from libraries crammed with lore, with which nobody else is familiar, and pour out before an audience what the speaker believes to be both sublime and impressive, but which his hearers cannot understand. They grow listless and restless, and he retires over-whelmed with a sense of failure. A. B., a young friend of considerable promise, thus failed in my presence. I endeavored thus to divert his despondency.

"Failures," I urged, "are with heroic minds the stepping-stones to success."

"Why have I not succeeded?" he asked; "I can never hope to say better things of my own than I said to-night of others."

"The cause of your non-success is obvious; you commenced by addressing your auditors as men, and you left them as children.

" A young preacher who had ascended the pulpit with great confidence, but who broke down in the middle of his sermon, was met by Rowland Hill as he was rushing from the pulpit. ' Young man,' said Rowland, ' had you ascended the pulpit in the spirit in which you descended, you would have descended in the spirit in which you ascended.' Something of this kind will explain your case. In your exordium you should address your auditors as though they were children, state your arguments as though they were learners, and in your peroration only assume them to be men. On the threshold of a new subject men are as children; during its unfoldment they are learners : only when the subject is mastered are they as men with manhood's power to execute their convictions. Had it struck you that probably no man of your audience was familiar with the habits of society in the days of Spenser's 'Faery Queene,' or with the high and mystic imaginings of the solitary Paracelsus, would not the thought have caused you to recast your whole lecture? Take care that you do not render yourself amenable to the sarcasm of Swift, who, when Burnet said, speaking of the Scotch preachers in the time of the civil war, 'The crowds were far beyond the capacity of their churches, or the reach of their voices,' Swift added, 'And the preaching beyond the capacity of the crowd. I believe the church had as much capacity as the minister.'"

The error of A. B. became evident to him. It is an error that many perpetually commit. In courts of equity the judges first distinguish by their approval those young barristers who unfold a case with simplicity, and make lucid the points at issue. Auditors are the judges in popular assemblies, and their first applause is bestowed on the clear-headed speaker.

Another source of failure is, that the young lecturer is too little impressed with the wide application of the philosophy of controversy. The discipline of debate should enter into every oration.

It is for this reason that speaking requires to be in some degree verbose. In writing we may be brief, suggestive, and epigrammatic, because each word remains to be pondered over; but that which falls on the ear not being so permanent as that which falls on paper, fullness and many-lighted treatment is indispensable.

The "Encyclopedia Metropolitana" has the following practical synopsis of the leading characteristics which conduce to Effectiveness: "As regards the style which speakers should use for the public, it is clear that a style *too terse* is unintelligible to the majority; while the remedy usually adopted, that of using a prolix and amplifying mode of expression, is repugnant to the public, who never fail to desert a speaker who employs it. The better plan is to use brief and terse sentences, and often repeat the same idea, not by a mere substitution of terms, but by a different arrangement of the members, reversing the premises, or conclusion, etc., never forgetting in the repetition always to use terse sentences. Burke is for this an admirable model.

" While it is always preferable to use short sentences, it must not be supposed that long sentences are always to be avoided. Long sentences, with a proper arrangement of their members, so that the audience may know what is aimed at, and not be compelled to reread, or call back to memory a sentence just uttered, are by no means obnoxious. If they induce trouble, by requiring a second reference, they cause ambiguity, because readers and auditors will not willingly give themselves this trouble. It is a common fault with authors to suppose a clause intelligible because on *their* reading it appears to suit;

but they forget that when they peruse it they know what is coming, which is more than can be expected of an audience. Hence it frequently happens that the best read and the best informed are frequently the worst expounders of their particular subjects of thought and study.

"In laying before the public any exposition, it is absolutely essential to avoid all nice distinctions that please, and indeed are necessary to a discourse in the closet. The oration is similar to a large picture to be viewed at a distance, where nice lines are unseen, or perhaps annoying, while broad, nay, sometimes vulgar strokes are seen, admired, and consequently effective.

"In preparing for the press, as the style was in the former case reversed from the nicety of an essay, it must be again returned to its original propriety.

"As regards delivery, it is not advisable to adopt any system of studied action, modulation of voice, or mimicry of others, but merely to thoroughly understand the subject; and reading or speaking, according to sense, allow nature to modulate the voice in her own way, which will inevitably be the best.

"In speaking, it has often been a matter of deep and curious consideration that a person will explain his views to a single individual in such terms as to force conviction in many instances, and where he fails the exposition would be just such a one as would please an audience. It is notorious that what will not convince one or two will be most effecitve on many persons; yet while he can succeed in the more difficult task with one or two, when he comes before an audience he is totally abashed, and cannot utter two consecutive sentences with propriety, energy, or sense. An analysis proves this bashfulness to be concomitant with other phenomena : 1. The increased liveliness of sympathy with numbers ; 2. The constant and free operation of this sympathy thus lively throughout the entire audience. The bashfulness of a speaker may therefore be attributable to intricate action and reaction of these several sympathies. There is, 1. The sympathy of the speaker with the audience ; 2. The fact that the speaker knows how each individual sympathizes with him ; and, 3. The knowledge of the speaker of the great sympathy existing between all the members of the audience.

"It is therefore necessary that the speaker should endeavor to lose sight of himself in the audience, and be guided and inspired wholly by the subject, having full confidence in his views and in the necessary relations of things, to render an exposition so attempted perfectly successful. This is the reason that vulgar speakers so frequently succeed. Their very eccentricities and vulgarities show the honesty and earnestness of purpose, and it is that that never fails to prosper."

## CHAPTER XVIII.

### MASTERY.

IT is truly held by great teachers that the most useful lesson the young thinker has to master is to learn one thing at a time. Experience tells us that it is also the most difficult. He is initiated into the art of thinking (power of consecutiveness is the principal sign of this art) who can think of one thing at a time; and he is *master* of the art who can think of *any* one thing when he pleases. That which distracts and discourages the young student is confounding the steps of progress with the results and displays of perfection. He confounds the elements of an art with the refinement of its mastery. Let him observe the gradations between incipient efforts and remote excellence, and the perplexity is cleared up, the difficulty surmounted, the discouragement dissipated.

When Dr. Black had a class of young men at the Reform Association, he disciplined them in rhetoric by causing each to marshal his discourse on a chosen theme under certain heads. These heads once gone over, he required them to be spoken upon by inversion, beginning probably with the peroration, continuing with the argument, taking afterward the statement or other division belonging to the theme, and ending with the exordium. Not until a member could speak equally well on any one head, and in any order, was he deemed master of his subject.

Professor de Morgan, who is considered the greatest of our mathematical teachers, remarks, in a paper which he furnished to Dr. Lardner's Geometry, that to number the *parts* of propositions is the *only* way of understanding them. Indeed, all great teachers admit that to identify *details* and grasp the *whole* are the two indices of proficiency.

Margaret Fuller relates how backwoodsmen of America, whom she visited, would sit by their log fire at night and tell "rough pieces out of their lives." This disintegration of events by men strong of will and full of matter, in order to set distinct parts before auditors, is a sign of that power which we call mastery. The ability of the backwoodsman would be natural ability; but all ability is the same in nature, though different in refinement. Ability is always power under command.

A barrister will occasionally state a complex case to the jury before him, beginning with the simplest circumstance, continuing with the more difficult, arranging the facts in such order that the series throws light on the most obscure, that the whole case may be fully understood. When he feels this to be accomplished he returns, recapitulates, extracts those points that are to have most weight and puts them before the attention in the most prominent and forcible manner, and if his brief will afford it, like Fitzroy Kelly, he sheds tears to make his rhetoric pathetic. Without this power of statement, analyzation, and enforcement of special facts at will, a man is not master of his subject; his subject is rather master of him.

In learning grammar, the parts of speech have first to be distinguished: nouns, verbs, descriptives. When these can be identified instantly, and in any order; when their signs are evident on cursory inspection, parsing is surmounted. When the inflections of these words are as readily perceived, another stage of progress is insured. When the subject, attribute, and object of a sentence are readily known, a third point is attained. There is a natural order of speech—the order of the understanding, the order in which the subject is placed first, the affirmation second, the object last. When these positions can be transposed with ease, and the sense preserved, an additional portion of power is attained. When compound sentences can be broken up into short ones, and distinct fragments of meaning expressed one by one, the power of perspicuity is acquired. When the different circumstances in any narrative can be taken in at a glance, and the speaker or writer can fix upon those which are most likely to arrest attention and arrange them so as to produce this effect without losing the thread or coherence of truth, the power of impressiveness is reached. After this comes the ability to put short clauses first, longer ones next, and the lengthiest last, so as to fill the ear without marring the meaning or weakening the force. When this can be done the power of elegance is possessed. When propositions can be stated with perspicuity, supported by cogent facts, and arranged with transparent method; when the enunciation is distinct, manly, and sonorous, when similitude or imagery can be introduced, illuminating the subject by the light of wit, sinking it by ridicule or elevating it by symbol, thrilling by pathos, or irresistibly impressing by rapid condensation; when a speaker can employ these weapons at pleasure, holding them at command with the grasp of a lion, and disposing them with the absolute will of a king, he has reached the summit of the rhetorical art; and if animated with a sublime purpose may influence, like Demosthenes or Mirabeau, the destinies of men.

Besides these there are other signs of mastery. Whewell thinks that we are never master of anything till we do it both well and unconsciously. But there is no test of proficiency so instructive as that put by George Sand into the mouth of Porpora, in her novel of Consuelo. When Consuelo, on the occasion of a trial performance, manifests some apprehension as to the result, Porpora sternly reminds her, that if there is room in her mind for misgiving as to the judgment of others, it is proof that she is not filled with the true love of art, which would so absorb her whole thoughts as to leave her insensible to the opinions of others ; and that if she distrusted her own powers it was plain they were not yet her powers, else they could not play her false. Porpora suggested the most instructive sign of mastery. The true love of art, like the perfect sense of duty, casteth out fear. And when study and discipline have done their proper work, failure is impossible ; we do not tremble at the result of the trial of our powers ; we are rather anxious for the opportunity and quite confident as to the result.

# PART III.

## APPLIED POWERS.

———◆•◆———

## CHAPTER XIX.

### CRITICISM.

ASSUMING that the various principles discussed in this treatise are practical and relevant, the application of them to the judgment, to literary and oratorical efforts, will be Criticism. For instance, after what has been said under the head of Effectiveness, the assenting reader will be prepared to pronounce that no work, consisting of many pages, should have detached and distinguishable beauties in every one of them. No great work indeed should have many beauties; if it were perfect, it would have but one, and that but faintly perceptible, except on a view of the whole. After what has been said in reference to the individuality resulting from Method, the reader of the works of the facetious American satirist, Paulding, will be able to decide to what extent he has the fault, in common with some others, of labeling his characters, gay, sedate, or cynical, as the case may be, with descriptive names, as if doubtful of their possessing sufficient individuality to be otherwise distinguished. If a hero cannot make himself known in his action and conversation, he is not worth bringing

upon the boards. The student who coincides with
what has been explained relative to Brevity, will, on
reading such a passage as this, " Nicias asked merely
for quarter for the miserable *remains* of his troops
*who had not perished* in the Asinarius, or upon its
banks,"* be at no loss in discovering the superfluous
information given, that Nicias asked for quarter for
those who " had not perished." No general asks for
quarter for those who have. The same writer tells
us that " discipline yielded to the pressure of necessity. They hurried down the steep in confusion and
without order, and trod one another to death in the
stream." Necessity is all " pressure," and it is not
necessary to specify the essence of a thing as opera-
tive. It is needless to tell us that men all " in confusion " " were without order."

When we discover a number of emphatic words
employed, we know the writer or speaker has no
consciousness of measure. He either has no strength
or he does not know where it lies. " When Rigby,"
says D'Israeli, " was of opinion he had made a point,
you may be sure the hit was in *italics*, that last resource of the forcible feebles."

To tell your feelings on reading a book is one way
of criticising its beauties. This rule was suggested to
Gibbon on reading Longinus. The appeal to nature
is here, as elsewhere, the purest guide.

One can only conceive of Hamlet by tracing out
men. Brutus has first to be found in society. He
who has never seen the majesty of a noble nature will
hardly conceive it well. How can we test the orator's skill, or player's art, but by rules founded by
ourselves on observation?

* Mayor's History of Greece, chap. xi.

"It belongs," says Schlegel, "to the general philosophical theory of poetry and the other fine arts, to establish the fundamental laws of the beautiful. Ordinarily, men entertain a very erroneous notion of Criticism, and understand by it nothing more than a certain shrewdness in detecting and exposing the faults of a work of art." In the search for the beautiful, he continues, "everything must be traced up to the root of human nature. Art cannot exist without nature, and man can give nothing to his fellow men but himself. The groundwork of human nature is everywhere the same; but in our investigations we may observe, that throughout the whole range of nature there is no elementary power so simple, but that it is capable of dividing and diverging into opposite directions. The whole play of vital motion hinges on harmony and contrast."*

It would be treason to truth, an affectation of philanthropy, systematically to conceal primary errors, or gloss over influential faults. It will ever be the province of Criticism to notice such in the spirit of improvement. But at length the principle has been established in literature, that perfection is better advanced by the applause of excellence than by the eternal descantation on defects. Human nature has been analyzed, and it is found that more is to be gained by appealing to the sentiment of the beautiful than by exciting the horror of deformity. This is now Criticism's admitted canon; demonstrated beyond the power of prejudice to distort, or of willfulness to neglect. This principle is not, or should not be, understood as warranting the reviewer in conniving at error, but only as making his chief province

* Dramatic Art and Literature, chap. i.

to be the genial recognition of artistic truth. Criticism still keeps watch and ward in the towers of Truth, that no enemy from the camps of Error shall steal into its dominions; but it is ever anxious to welcome and to admit all followers of Progression, even though they may not exactly possess society's accredited passport.

---

# CHAPTER XX.

### DEBATE.

DEBATE is a great advantage, and when you win a sincere and able man to discuss with you, enter upon the exercise with gratitude. Your opponent may be the enemy of your opinions, but he is the friend of your improvement. The more ably he confronts you, the more he serves you, if you have but the wisdom to profit by it. The gods, it is said, have not given to mortals the privilege of seeing themselves as others see them, but by a happy compensation in human affairs it is given to candid friends to supply what fate denies: and though candor does not imply infallibility, it always includes instruction; it affords that indispensable light of contrast which enables you to discover the truth if hidden from you, or to display the truth if you possess it.

A good writer, says Godwin, must have that ductility of thought that shall enable him to put himself in the place of his reader, and not suffer him to take it for granted, because he understands himself, that every one who comes to him for information will understand him. He must view his phrases on all sides, and be aware of all the senses of which they are susceptible. But this facility can nowhere be so certainly acquired as in debate, which is evidently a discipline as serviceable to the writer as to the speaker.

All investigation should commence without prepossession and end without dogmatism. Each disputant should be more anxious to explain than to defend his opinion.

As an established truth is that which is generally received after it has been generally examined in a fair field of inquiry, it is evident that though truth may be discovered by research, it can only be established by debate. It is a mistake to suppose that it can be taught absolutely by itself. We learn truth by contrast. It is only when opposed to error that we witness truth's capabilities, and feel its full power.

Oral investigation claims especial attention, because to a great extent it insures that its results shall be carried into practice. The pen develops principles, but it is the tongue that chiefly stimulates to action.

Discussion after public addresses would be of great public value. The discipline, to both speaker and hearers, would be greatly salutary. The argument against it, that it would lead to strife and discord, is the very reason why it should be practiced. Men are very childish intellectually while in that state in which debate must be prohibited. If they be children, train them in the art of debate until they are translated into men.

To admit debate after an address, it is said, enables factious individuals to destroy the effect of what has been said. When unanimity of opinion comes, discussion will fall into disuse; but till it does come, (and debate alone can bring it) discussion must be borne. It is the fault of the lecturer if any one is able to destroy the effect of his lecture.

As a general rule, discussions, set and accidental, are good. A twofold reality by their means is brought to bear on the public understanding, more exciting than that of any other intellectual agency. An opinion that is worth holding is worth diffusing, and to be diffused it must be thought about; and when men think on true principles they become adherents; but only those adherents are worth having who have thought on *both* sides, and discussion alone makes them do that well. True, men may *read* on both sides, but it seldom happens that men who are impressed by one side care to read the other. In discussions they are obliged to hear both sides. If men do read both sides, unless they read a "Discussion," they do not find all the facts on one side specially considered on the other. In a discussion read, unless read at one sitting, the strength of an impression and the clearness of the argument on one side is partly lost before the opponent's side is perused. But in an oral debate, the adaptation of fact to fact is complete as far as it perhaps can be; the *pro* and *con* are heard successively, the light of contrast is full and clear, and both sides are weighed at the same time when the eye is sharply fixed on the balance. It matters not whether the disputants argue for victory or truth. If they are intellectual gladiators so much the better. The stronger they are the mightier the battle and the more instructive the conflict. It is said that people come out of such discussions as they go into them; that the same partisans shout or hiss on the same side all through. This is not always true, and no matter if it is. The work of conviction is often done, though the audience may not show it. They may break your head, and afterward own you were right. Human pride forbids the confession, but change is effected in spite of pride. But if an audience remain the same at night, they will not be the same the next morning. I rather like to contemplate that conviction which is *begun* in discussion, not *ended* there. He who hastily changes is to be suspected of weakness or carelessness. The steady and deliberate thinker who takes time to consider is the safest convert.

If you invite opposition do it with circumspection. Never debate for the sake of debating. It lowers the character of debate. The value of free speech is too great to be trifled with. Seek conflict only with sincere men. Concede to your opponent the first word and the last. Let him appoint the chairman. Let him speak double time if he desires it. Debate is objected to as an exhibition in which disputants try to surprise, outwit, take advantage of, and discomfit each other. To obviate this objection explain to your opponent the outline of the course you intend to pursue, acquaint him with the books you shall quote, the authorities you shall cite, the propositions you shall endeavor to prove, and the concessions you shall demand. And do this without expecting the same at his hands. He will not now be taken by surprise. He will be prewarned and prearmed. He will have time to prepare, and if the truth is in him it ought to come out.

If you feel that you cannot give all these advantages to your opponent, suspect yourself and suspect your side of the question. Every conscientious and decided man believes his views to be true, and if consistent, he believes them to be impregnable. Neither in minutes, months, or years are they to be refuted. Then a man so persuaded may despise petty advantages, and enable his opponent to arm himself beforehand.

In another particular discussions were esteemed unsatisfactory. When statement and reply have been made, then came the reply to the reply, and then the reply to that, till the cavil seemed endless, perplexing, and tiresome.

Now the object of discussion is not the vexatious chase of an opponent, but the contrastive and current statement of opinion. Therefore endeavor to select leading opinions, to state them strongly and clearly; and when your opponent replies, be content to leave his arguments side by side with your own for the judgment of the auditors. In no case disparage an opponent, misstate his views, or torture his words, and thus, for the sake of a verbal triumph, produce lasting ill-feelings. Your sole business is with *what* he says, not *how* he says it, nor *why* he says it. Your aim should be that the audience should lose sight of the speakers and be possessed with the subject, and that those who come the partisans of persons shall depart the partisans of principles. The victory in a debate lies not in lowering an opponent, but in raising the subject in public estimation. Controversial wisdom lies not in destroying an opponent, but in destroying his error; not in making him ridiculous so much as in making the audience wise.

Debate requires self-possession, a power to think on your legs. But even in debate, the victory is oftener with the foregone than with the impromptu thinker. A man who knows his subject well will be forearmed.

He alone can distinctly see the points in dispute, and the nature of the proof or disproof necessary to settle the question.

At the threshold of controversy it is well to define all leading terms, which should never be used in any other than the settled sense. A common standard of appeal should be agreed upon. The question at issue should be stated so clearly that it cannot possibly be misunderstood. No opponent should be accepted whose sincerity you cannot assume, as it must never be questioned in debate. Find no fault with his grammar, manner, intentions, tone, whatever may be the provocation. Attend only to the matter. Hear all things without impatience and without emotion. Let your opponent fully exhaust his matter. Encourage him to say whatever he thinks relevant. Many persons believe in the magnitude of their positions because they have never been permitted to state them to others; and when they have once delivered themselves of their opinions, they often find for the first time how insignificant they are. There are some persons whom nobody can confute but themselves. When you distinguish such your proper business is to let them do it. Learn to satisfy yourself and to present a conclusive statement of your opinions, and when you have done so, have the courage to abide by it. If you cannot trust your statement to be canvassed by others; if you feel anxious to add some additional remark at every step; if reply from your opponent begets reply from you, suspect your knowledge of your own case and withdraw it for further reflection. Master as completely as you can your opponent's theories, and state his case with the greatest fairness, and if possible state it with more force against yourself

than your opponent can. The observance of this rule
will teach you two things, your opponent's strength
or weakness, and your own also. If you *cannot* state
your opponent's case you do not know it, and if you
do not know it you are not in a fit state to argue
against it. If you *dare not* state your opponent's case
in its greatest force you feel it to be stronger than
your own, and in that case you *ought not* to argue
against it.

The course here suggested will be as useful to truth
as to the disputant. Great prejudice may often be
disarmed by thus daring it. In this manner Gibbon
delivered his argument in favor of an hereditary monarchy. "Of the various forms of government which
have prevailed in the world, an hereditary monarchy
seems to present the fairest scope for ridicule. Is it
possible to relate, without an indignant smile, that
on the father's decease, the property of a nation, like
that of a drove of oxen, descends to his infant son, as
yet unknown to mankind and to himself, and that the
bravest warriors and the wisest statesmen, relinquish-
ing their natural right to empire, approach the royal
cradle with bended knees and protestations of invio-
lable fidelity! Satire and declamation may paint
these obvious topics in the most dazzling colors,
but our serious thoughts will respect a useful
prejudice that establishes a rule of succession independent of the passions of mankind; and we shall
cheerfully acquiesce in any expedient which deprives
the multitude of the dangerous, and indeed the ideal
power of giving themselves a master." We often
hold an opinion from the belief that those who dis-
sent from it do not know its full bearings as we do
or they would be of our opinion too; but when, as

in the case of Gibbon, we arc instructed that our opponent perfectly understands our case, and states its strongest points, we feel that justice has been done to us, and we are the more disposed to acquiesce in an adverse judgment come to after we have been fully heard.

What Dr. Paley has delineated with respect to a written controversy is not inapplicable to an oral debate. The fair way of conducting a dispute is to exhibit one by one the arguments of your opponent, and with each argument the precise and specific answer you are able to give it. If this method be not so common, nor found so convenient as might be expected, the reason is because it suits not always with the designs of a writer, which are no more perhaps than to make a *book*; to confound some arguments, and to keep others out of sight; to leave what is called an impression upon the reader, without any care to inform him of the proofs or principles by which his opinion should be governed. With such views it may be consistent to dispatch objections, by observing of some " that they are old," and, therefore, like certain drugs, have lost, we may suppose, their strength; of others, that " they have long since received an answer;" which implies, to be sure, a confutation; to attack straggling remarks, and decline the main reasoning as " mere declamation;" to pass by one passage because it is " long-winded," another because the answerer " has neither leisure nor inclination to enter into the discussion of it;" to produce extracts and quotations which, taken alone, imperfectly, if at all, express their author's meaning; to dismiss a stubborn difficulty with a " reference," which, ten to one, the reader never looks at; and, lastly, in order to give the whole a certain fashionable air of candor and moderation, to make a concession or two which nobody thanks him for, or yield up a few points which it is no longer any credit to maintain.

It will be evident that this minuteness of reply could not be undertaken without reference to the importance of the question at issue and the abilities of the opponent. Such elaborate pains belong only to great occasions.

It is not necessary always to demonstrate the validity of a given position. To show the impotence of the opposite is often quite sufficient.

It is recorded in the historical memoirs of Curran, that his general practice as a lawyer, when engaged for the defense, was rather to rely on the weakness to which he could reduce the case of his opponents than on the strength of his own, except on very peculiar occasions.

Be very careful of generalization; utter no wholesale censure. It will nearly always be wrong. Classify the partisans of opinions which you confute. You will reduce your opponents, and gain in justice and force; for when you confound objectors together, you outrage all and convince few. If you *can* distinguish classes, address but one class at a time.

Upon the general rules proper for conducting a debate it is hardly possible to enter. Even public meetings in this country are conducted on the crudest principles. If men were commonly intelligent, and many were disposed to take part in public meetings, it would be impossible that any business could be transacted under several days. The assumption that *every* man has a right to be heard, could not be acted upon if half who usually attend public meetings were to enforce that "right."

When a speech or lecture is debated, each disputant expects to occupy the same time as the speaker, which often prevents more than one being heard in reply. But a short time for several might be fixed, and thus combine discipline with disputation. Brevity of time would induce directness and brevity of speech; it is not the work of any one speaker, but the work of many to attack the whole lecture, and each should select a leading point, and ten minutes would afford time for a very effective objection if one could be raised.

At public meetings, where many opposing parties often struggle to be heard, confusion, delay, and ill-feeling might be obviated by each party preappointing a representative of ability, in whom confidence could be reposed, to speak on their behalf, and by those calling the meeting being made acquainted with, and consenting to the arrangement, the views of half a dozen parties could be advocated, where the views of one are heard but inadequately and impatiently now.

---

## CHAPTER XXI.

### LAWS OF PERSONALITIES.

The first problem that has to be solved by the people is one of fraternization. If we wait till unity of opinion on all points is created before we co-operate together, reforms will be delayed for ages.

The only mode whereby public success can be achieved in our day is by the union on general points of men differing on infinite particulars. But personalities constitute a serious danger. The only way to disarm them is to brave them. To court personalities is fatal to union; to shun them, fatal to reputation. The friends of a cause ought to be able to dare all opinions, and all opinions might be dared by those in the right. There can be no quarrel unless *two* parties engage in it, and it is always in the power of one party to prevent it by refusing to be a party to it. No man can quarrel with another without that other's consent. Hence the veto of peace and amity is always in the hands of one of the disputants. It is often a duty to notice individual error. It is often indispensable. But the execution of such a duty would not be so distasteful to the public as it now is, were it not for the unskillful manner in which it is generally done. If, when objections to a public man must be made, they were well selected and singly urged, without ill-will, and when once presented left as a public warning, the practice would be felt to be useful and tolerable. Instead of this course a miscellaneous fire is extended to every imaginable peccadillo, and conjectures called in when facts are exhausted, until what was, or should be, intended as a public lesson becomes a gratification of private resentment. When retaliation usurps the desire to improve another the contest sinks into personalities.

I have often sent pupils out together in pairs to talk with all deliberation and caution, and to note how many expletives they employ, how many errors they commit, how insequential are their thoughts, and how inexact their language. Indeed, how few men have disciplined themselves in these respects! How few ready, florid writers or speakers are precise! How few men have the power of being coherent! How much is said which is never meant, even by those who are most careful! How few ever acquire the habit of thinking before they speak! Passing from common life, let the experience of the bar and the closet be heard. Does not the shrewd lawyer, whose whole life is one long, laborious study of accuracy, perpetually find the Act of Parliament upon which many have labored open to three or four interpretations? And does not the philosopher daily regret the vagueness of human language? Then on what principle of good sense can we, without most patient deliberation, hurl at each other obnoxious epithets?

What eloquence is more touching than that of a simple tale of actual wrong! The very absence of passion gives it force. The dispassionateness of its relation infuses the air of truth. The presence of passion leads us to suspect the partisan, and invective is felt to be the twin brother of exaggeration. Strength is always calm in battle. Truth imparts repose; the suffrage of mankind is always on the side of dignity. Disputants instinctively bear out the truth of all this. When a man feels that he has a strong case, we have therefore no excitement, no self-returned verdict. A man who thinks he has a clear case always feels he may safely leave it to the judgment of others. No barrister makes a long speech to the jury when the evidence is all on his side. Fitzroy Kelly never sheds tears except when he has a Tawell to defend.

All which should be done for the adjustment of a difference is, that a man should quietly understate his case, that he should make no material assertion unaccompanied by the proof, that he should make the fairest allowance for his rival's excitement, put the best possible construction on his words and acts, and leave the matter there. All whose suffrages are worth having will make the proper award on his side without further trouble on his part. The reason of so many departures from this rule is the want of courage or the want of sense. It is a common opinion, that if a man does not bluster and retort, he is deficient in spirit. It is this apprehension which betrays weak men into violence, and to prove themselves independent they become rude and insolent, and mistake the part of the bravo for that of the hero. But a man of disciplined intelligence knows that courage always pursues its own resolute way without noise or ostentation, firmly preserves its independence, stands immovable in frankness and kindness corrects misrepresentation, repairs any injury it may have done, silences slander with the truth, and goes on its way. No wise man answers a fool according to his folly. He shows that it *is* folly, and abandons it to die by its own hands.

A few years ago a couple of Dutchmen, Von Vampt and Van Bones, lived on friendly terms on the high hills of Limestone. At last they fell out over a dog. Von Vampt killed Van Bones's canine companion. Bones, choosing to assume the killing to have been intentional, sued Vampt for damages. They were called in due time into court, when the defendant in the case was asked by the judge whether he killed the dog. "Pe sure I kilt him," said Vampt, "but let Bones prove it." This being quite satisfactory, the plaintiff in the action was called on to answer a few questions, and among others he was asked by the judge at what amount he estimated the damages. He did not well understand the question, and so, to be a little plainer, the judge inquired what he thought the dog to be worth? "Pe sure," replied Bones, "the dog was worth nothing; but since he was so mean as to kill him, he shall pay de full value of him." How many suits have occupied the attention of courts, how many contests have engaged the time of the public, and have been waged with virulence and invective, having no more worthy difference than that of Von Vampt and Van Bones!"

At every step, however, we are admonished how conscientiously a man can be in the wrong. Many enter the quagmire of recrimination as a matter of duty rather than taste. The question is commonly put, "Ought we not to state all we know to be true?" I answer, no; unless it can be shown to be useful. Every man knows a thousand things which are true, but which it would profit nobody to hear. When we essay to speak the rule is imperative that we speak the truth, absolutely and truly the truth, if one may write so paradoxically; but of *what* truth we will communicate, good sense must be the judge, utility the measure. If all truth must be published without regard to propriety, William Rufus, who drew a tooth per day from a rich Jew's head to induce him to tell where his treasures were concealed, was a great moral philosopher. "Well, but what a man believes to be true and useful may he not state?" will be inquired of me. I answer, no;

unless he can *prove* it. If every man stated his *suspicions*, no character would be safe from aspersion; society would be a universal school for scandal. Suspicion is the food of slander. What public man is at this hour safe from it? There is already more actual evil in existence than the virtuous are likely soon to correct; and little necessity exists for suspicion to supply hypothetical cases. "But to bring the question to the point," observes the reader, "if two disputants have respectively 'proved' the fitness of the epithets they have mutually applied, are they not justified in having used them?" I answer, avoid it as often as possible. It is the complainant usurping the province of the jury and the judge. It is the vice of controversy that each disputant will unite the offices of witness, jury, and judge, give his own evidence, return his own verdict, and pronounce the sentence in his own favor. A function which no man would tolerate in a court of justice every controversialist exercises with an inflexible will. It is this which has been the real "disgrace" of religious, political, and literary discussions. That precaution which the wisdom of the lawyer has taken against human frailty is not lightly to be set aside. Lawyers are the philosophers of disputes, and have wisely taken out of the hands of interest, petulance, and passion the power of deciding upon their own case. Yet disputants will do that unhesitatingly, with regard to each other, which in a court of justice would long engage the anxious and earnest attention of twelve disinterested, dispassionate, and patient men.

The first principle which should actuate all human intercourse, public or private, is that of aiming at the improvement of each other. This neither passion

nor interest should obscure. Yet how often do men
come into the field, not as true friends who have
differences to adjust, but as adversaries bent on each
other's destruction? Those who would decry a duel
in the usual way, will yet fight a duel on paper. We
have nothing to do with our neighbor as his evil
genius; we ought, like Rudolph, to be the providence
of our friends. The people boast how far they are in
advance of the government, but in respect of etiquette
they are far behind. Even despotic states admit, in
theory, that the punishment of criminals is in itself
indefensible malignity; that only so far as the brute
ignorance of others renders it necessary as an example, ought it ever to be attempted. The improvement and not the mortification in person or character
is that at which jurisprudence and well understood
justice now aim. Disagreement is a contingency of
human nature, from which it will never be freed until
men are cast in one monotonous mould. Differences
are in themselves as natural and as innocent as varia-
tion in form, color, or strength. It is the manner in
which those who differ seek to adjust their differences
that constitutes any disgrace there may be in any
case. Unless we have boasted of philosophy in vain,
we ought never to take up arms against an enemy
without at the same time keeping his welfare in view,
as well as our own defense. Before the genius of
this aphorism the prosaic commonplaces of life dissolve; man rises to nobility. To consult the welfare
of friends is kind, obliging, amiable; but the publi-
cans do even the same. To promote the welfare of
enemies, to do good to those who hate us, is generous.
Higher than Brutus, we walk the platform with
Coriolanus. Our true business is not with good and

10

bad men, but with fair or unfair, right or wrong conduct. We ought never to disparage, never to impute evil intentions, and in the strongest cases leave the way open for explanation and reconciliation. We may be firm, and yet fraternal; manly, and yet kind!

Locke called his opponents "irrational," Addison "miscreants," Dr. Clarke "crazy," Paley "insane," and Sir Walter Scott makes Sir Everard Waverly class "rakes, gamblers, and *whigs*" together. These are the mere expletives of polemical and political partisanship, the commonplace effervescences of passion, old as ignorance, universal as vulgarity. They have no novelty, no originality. The elegant contrast of controversy lies in contrast of argument; this is ever fresh and instructive. All recrimination being common to both disputants will in time, like the common quantities in an algebraic equation, be struck out of disputes as only making more difficult the finding of the true result. If any epithets are retained in use they will be confined to error rather than showered on the erring, and the limit of their application will exclude personal disparagement.

Our reformers disagree not about reforms, but modes of advocacy. I think it can be shown that our government seldom if ever pass laws against purpose, but against extravagance of language, in which passion, or hate, or unskilfulness express that purpose. Passion and hate may be founded in sincerity, but not in wisdom; and were men rhetorically wiser they might aim at more and accomplish more than they now can.

It admits of demonstration that the progress of reform is mainly hindered among us by a few metaphysical mistakes. The diatribes respectively hurled by rich and poor against each other arise in an error of generalization. Both mean the truth, but they express more than the truth, and out of this error come division and ill-will.

Generalizations in science have to be stated circumspectly and with qualification. A generalization finds a resemblance in perhaps one point only, and that resemblance probably in only the majority of a class. If you accuse in exact language a class of stones possessing a certain property which is not possessed by all, the exceptional stones will not be scandalized as the same number of men would whom you happened to include in a carelessly-worded, disparaging general assertion. It is of no use that you say to the person whom you have wrongly accused: "O I did not mean you; I meant to allow that there were exceptions." Men naturally suspect that he who is incapable of speaking with accuracy is incapable of thinking with accuracy, and if they acquit you of incapacity they convict you of carelessness.

Facts make up accusative propriety; and if the facts are not absolutely universal—and with grades of human character they never are—the application of accusation must always be *special*.

It is a wise maxim in jurisprudence, that ten guilty men had better escape than that one innocent man should suffer. So with rhetorical and public judgments. The one innocent man condemned will do both judge and justice more harm than the ten guilty who escape.

Men live on good opinion to a great extent. When therefore you take away a man's good name you take away that which is in many cases the basis of self-respect. In the advocacy of a good cause, then, let us beware how we proceed with personalities, lest we undo in one direction what we seek to do in another.

A. de Morgan, in his reply to Sir W. Hamilton, in their recent discussion on the origination of Formal Logic, makes these useful remarks: " In the day of swords it was one of the objects of public policy to prevent people from sticking them into each other's bodies on trivial grounds. We now wear pens; and it is as great a point to hinder ourselves from sticking them into each other's characters without serious and well-considered reasons. To this end I have always considered it as one of the first and most special rules that *conviction* of the truth of a charge is *no sufficient reason for its promulgation.* I assert that no one is justified in accusing another *until he has his proof ready;* and that in the interval, if indeed it be right that there should be any interval between the charge and the attempt at substantiation, all the leisure and energies of the accuser are the property of the accused."

Thomas Cooper, D.D., Bishop of Winchester, in 1589 issued a pamphlet with this title: " An Admonition to the People of England : wherein are answered not onely the slaunderous vntruethes, reproachfully vttered by Martin the Libeller, but also many other Crimes by some of his broode, objected generally against all Bishops, and the chiefe of the Cleargie, purposely to deface and discredite the present state of the Church."

Even the Bishop of Exeter would not now, in 1849, think of inditing such a title-page against his most decided opponents. It is not that truth and falsehood or right and wrong have changed, but that good taste and private justice are in the ascendant. We no longer (in good society) attack the motives, but the principles of men.

Let us apply the rule we have been illustrating to Parliamentary controversies. If every member were to say what is true or what he believes to be true of another, our legislative assemblies would soon come to resemble those of the United States, in one of which, not long ago, a member in audience being tired in listening to the member in possession of the house, got up and said: " Mr. Speaker, I should like to know long that there blackguard is to go on tiring me to death in this manner?" The Irish House of Commons, before the Union, furnishes a specimen of what must happen if sentiments are to be expressed without rule : "I will not call him *villain*, because he is chancelor of the exchequer ; I will not call him *liar*, because he is a privy counselor ; but I will say of him that he is one who has taken advantage of the privilege of this house to utter language to which, in any other place, my answer would have been a blow." Such were the expressions used by Mr. Grattan toward Mr. Corrie, and a duel was the immediate result. We endeavor to keep clear of this blackguardism ; not because it is unimportant whether a man lies or not, but because we have learned the good sense of not impugning integrity upon suspicion ; and when we can impugn it on fact we need no harsh words ; the fact is the severest judgment.

De Morgan, whom I have just quoted, relates that the late Professor Vince was once arguing at Cambridge against dueling, and some one said, " Well, but professor, what could you do if any one called

you a liar?"  "Sir," said the fine old fellow in his
peculiar brogue, "I should tell him to pruv it; and
if he did pruv it, I should be ashamed of myself; and
if he didn't, *he* ought to be ashamed of himself."

The obvious laws we should impress on all who .
controvert, seem to be these :

1. To consult in all cases the improvement of those
whom we oppose, and to this end argue not for our
gratification, or pride, or vanity, but for their enlightenment.

2. To invert the vulgar mode of judgment, and
not, when we guess at motives, guess the worst, but
adopt the best construction the case admits.

3. To distinguish between the personalities which
impugn the judgment, and those that criminate character, and never to advance accusations of either kind
without distinct and indisputable proof; never to assail
character on suspicion, probability, belief, or likelihood.

4. To keep distinct the two kinds of personalities,
never mixing up those which pertain to character
with those which pertain to judgment.

5. To never meddle with either, unless some public
good is to come out of it.  It is not enough that a
charge is true; it must be *useful* to prefer it, before a
wise publicist will meddle with it.

6. To dare all personalities ourselves; to brave all
attacks ; to defy the judgment of mankind, and when
we are assailed, unfailingly to respect ourselves, and
keep in view the betterance of him whom we oppose,
rather than our own personal gratification.*

* For an enlarged consideration of this question see articles (Nos.
20 and 24 of the "People's Press") entitled the "Philosophy of
Personalities," where I have treated of their introduction into public
parties.

Were the errors discussed in this chapter confined to the vulgar, we might confide in the spread of ordinary intelligence to dissipate them. But it is otherwise. Who would have expected to have found the "sweetest and most genuine poetess of the age," C. B., writing in the *Athœnum* a letter of anger, reproach, and condemnation of Mr. Howitt, for having written something which she confesses she had "never read." Literary etiquette seems to have received no improvement with time. Hazlitt, Byron, Southey, and other luminaries of literature, sink to the level of the meanest of mankind when they are found engaged in the adjustment of their differences. When turning over the periodicals of their times, one is amazed at the flood of vituperation, the envy, jealousy, and miserable disparagement of each other. Yet if all this littleness exists, better that it be expressed, that one may see what our gods are made of. Rudeness is healthier than hypocrisy, and therefore the policy which conceals rankling malignity is more pernicious than the display of it. Let it be avowed until men are convinced that it is unreasonable. Leigh Hunt has the credit of having prophesied long ago that the old philosophic conviction would revive among us as a popular one, that recrimination, denouncements, and threats should be put an end to, and the perception prevail that the errors of mankind arise rather from the want of knowledge than the defect of goodness. But what is the history of modern parties? Has not recriminative error broken up the best of them into miserable sections? "Stupidity" can be informed, "ignorance" can be enlightened; but the "collision of interest and passion, and the perversities of self-will and self-opinion" destroy all before them.

What hope is there of the improvement of the uneducated, while those who should know better perpetuate the infectious example? Men whose names it is needless to cite, and whom, prior to experience, I could not have believed to be unconscious of the fact, I have found unaware that simplicity in the expression of passion is the lesson of nature and of genius, and the greatest discovery of rhetorical experience. It is, however, clear that there is no hope for the efficient progress of the order of industry while their natural leaders and exemplars depart from that propriety which alone is strength.

The necessity of enforcing this most practical part of rhetoric, (the rhetoric of dispute,) which is taught in no Mechanics' or Literary Institution, is evidenced in the discouraging fact that an impartial, impersonal, and dispassionate tone is almost fatal in newspaper and periodical literature. We address a populace to whom nothing that is just seems spirited. We must be offensively personal or we are pronounced tame. Unless we are rancorous we are not relished. The reason is that most men, when stung by a sense of injury, are naturally precipitated from extreme to extreme. Their opinions, when sincere, "are not produced by the ordinary law of intellectual births, by induction or inference, but are equivocally generated" by the heat of fervid emotion, wrought upon by some sense of unbearable oppression.

So it ever is with the intellectually undisciplined, of whatever class; they believe all strength manifests itself in spasms, that truth is a descendant from the furies, that no man can be brave who does not bluster, nor have enthusiasm if he do not write in hysterics. But I quit this subject, repeating the fine language of one whom I have several times quoted : " Defect in manners is usually the defect of fine perceptions. . . . A beautiful behavior is better than a beautiful form : it gives a higher pleasure than statues or pictures. It is the finest of the fine arts. . . . The person who screams, or uses the superlative degree, or converses with heat, puts whole drawing-rooms to flight. If you wish to be loved, love measure. . . . Coolness and absence of heat and haste indicate fine qualities. A gentleman makes no noise : a lady is serene. . . . Let us leave hurry to slaves. The compliments and ceremonies of our breeding should signify, however remotely, the grandeur of our destiny."

---

# CHAPTER XXII.

## QUESTIONING.

The Socratic method of disputation or artful questioning, (of which Zeno, the Eleatic, was the author,) by which an opponent is entrapped into concessions, and thus confuted, is rather fit for wranglers and sophists than reasoners. There is too much reason to believed that Socrates condescended to this course often at the expense of ingenuousness. It is said in his defense that he did it not as the sophists, for the sake of confounding virtue, but for the purer purpose of confounding dexterous vice. It is, however, beneath the dignity of a reasoner to *betray* his opponent into the truth.

Questioning, however, is an essential instrument. A high authority, Dr. Arnold, has put this in a useful light : " An inquiring spirit is not a presumptuous one, but the very contrary. He whose whole recorded life was intended to be our perfect example, is described as gaining instruction in the temple by hearing and asking questions ; the one is almost useless without the other. We should ask questions of our books and of ourselves, what is its purpose, by what means it proceeds to effect that purpose, whether we fully understand the one, whether we go along with the other. Do the arguments satisfy us ? do the descriptions convey lively and distinct images to us ? do we understand all the allusions to persons or things ? In short, does our mind act over again from the writer's guidance what his acted before ? do we reason as he reasoned, conceive as he conceived, think and feel as he thought and felt ? or if not, can we discern where and how far we do not, and can we tell why we do not ?

Questioning has also a place in rhetoric as well as in research. Frankly conducted, it is a mode of conviction without offense. To whatever an opponent urges, with which we do not agree, of course we have some objection. Put this objection incidentally, and ask it as a question, what answer can be given to it ? This is a good conversational mode of debate, where the improvement of an opponent, rather than a triumph over him, is the object. It is not showy, but it is searching.

In a similar way confidence may be acquired by diffident speakers. A novitiate conversationalist is shy of taking part in debating a topic lest he should not be able to sustain himself. To such I have said : Put your argument in the form of an objection which some would urge, and beg some one of the company to tell you what he would say in reply. If to this answer you have an objection further, put that also in the querist form; for a man will be able to ask a question who would never be able to make a speech. By this easy means the most diffident may get into conversation; and when once excited will speak freely enough, perhaps too freely. A coward will fight when he grows warm in strife.

This method has another advantage : by this means a novice learns the best answers which the company can give to his own argument, and thus, without risk of exposure, he learns their weakness or finds out their strength. He has also taken the guage of his opponents' powers, and can, if he sees well, match himself against them.

————•————

## CHAPTER XXIII.

### REPETITION.

THE reformer who comprehends his mission attempts the discipline of the people in nobler views. Only great natures are heroic by instinct. But it is not more true that all men are eloquent sometimes than that all men are noble sometimes; but few continue so, for want of the influence of suitable circumstances to nourish and sustain the feeling. Every man is great when he lays down Pluturch, but the feeling dies away in the contact with the lower life of cities. To remedy this the reformer has recourse to reiteration.

In introducing a new topic to an auditory a wise speaker repeats the same sentiment and argument in many different forms of expression, each in itself brief, but all together affording such an expansion of the sense to be conveyed, and detaining the mind upon it, as the case may require. Care must be taken that the repetition may not be too glaringly apparent; the variations must not consist in the mere use of other synonymous words, but what has been expressed in appropriate terms may be repeated in metaphorical; the antecedent or consequent of any argument or the parts of an antithesis may be transposed, or several different points that have been enumerated presented in a varied order.

It is given to reiteration to accomplish that which is denied to power. The reputation of Robespierre, now breaking a little through clouds of calumny denser and darker than ever before obscured human name, is a striking illustration of the omnipotence of repetition. The most eloquent of its vindicators has thus sketched his triumph:

"Still deeper in the shade, and behind the chief of the National Assembly, a man almost unknown began to move, agitated by uneasy thoughts, which seemed to forbid him to be silent and unmoved; he spoke on all occasions, and attacked all speakers indifferently, including Mirabeau himself. Driven from the tribune, he ascended it next day; overwhelmed with sarcasm, coughed down, disowned by all parties, lost among the eminent champions who fixed public attention, he was incessantly beaten, but never dispirited. It might have been said that an inward and prophetic genius revealed to him the vanity of all talent and the omnipotence of a firm will and unwearied patience, and that an inward voice said to him: 'These men who despise thee are thine; all the changes of this revolution, which now will not deign to look upon thee, will eventually terminate in thee, for thou hast placed thyself in the way like the inevitable excess, in which all impulse ends.' "

---

# CHAPTER XXIV.

## POETRY.

Such proverbs as "poets are born and not made," have encouraged the notion that inspiration does everything for the poet and art nothing; whereas inspiration gives him the idea, and art enables him to express it. It is very probable that "creative" capacity is an element in the poetic nature which art does not make, but educates only. Yet experience teaches us that decided poetic power sometimes sinks into the commonplace, and that that which has been pronounced mediocre has been cultured into excellence. We therefore ought to pause before treating so disdainfully, as is the fashion, the humble versifiers who from time to time solicit the world's notice. Certainly Byron's "Hours of Idleness" were as weak a specimen of the poetic as patrician or plebeian fancy ever concocted. It gave no sign of that fierce power which was afterward evoked from the same pen. Both Burns and Elliott have been greatly indebted, perhaps as much indebted, to art as to their ideas for the distinction which attaches to their names. Many a name of note now might be cited whose infantile genius was rocked in the cradle of doggerel.

Between rhyme and poetry there is a great gulf, which patient study alone may bridge over. Some of the intermediate steps may be indicated. The gradations may be explained, which, though all may not be able to pass through, all may be able to understand and determine their own position in reference to them.

A Sunderland candidate for Parnassian laurels lately presented the public with the following very A-B-C effort:

> Two gentlemen dined at my house,
>    For breakfast they had some ham;
> Says I, "Are you going to Hartlepool?"
>    "O yes," says they, "we am."

Even the rudest kind of verse should have some qualities not found in prose. What poetry is it is not easy to define satisfactorily. But this is agreed upon, that whatever is called poetry ought to contain an idea or ideas above the level of prose, and such as cannot be so well expressed in prose. Now ordinary prose, if tolerable, is grammatical, but the verse above quoted has not this quality. In verse the corresponding terminations of lines should rhyme; this rule is also neglected. Corresponding lines should have the same number of syllables in them; that is, should have the same measure, the same quantity of accented and unaccented sounds. The versifier we have cited seems innocent of any such requirement. Indeed, the majority of those who publish rhymes never have paid the least attention to these essential elements of verse. Many, indeed, have never heard that there are such elements. Most of the rejected "poetry" sent to periodicals and newspapers is of this class; for persons who understand the mechanical part of poetry frequently know what they are about, know their own powers, and do not send out productions which have not some stamp of excellence upon them.

A young mind of any force or emulation commonly takes to the experiment of verse. The exercise should always be encouraged and criticised. In this way the new thinker may learn the power of words agreeably, and the nature of elevated ideas. He will consult dictionaries of synonyms. So much the better. The habit will increase his knowledge. He will keep what he acquires, because he will get it when he wants it. Turn his ambition to useful account. If you cannot make him a poet, you may make him a grammarian, a linguist, and a thinker, and save him from making himself ridiculous by teaching him the difference between prose, rhyme, verse, and poetry. Let it be understood that "all persons may rhyme, but that it is given only to few to compose thoughts; the first requisites of which are, that they be new, striking, and beautiful, and for the expression of which it is further necessary that there be gifts and acquirements of language infinitely above those required for common purposes."*

We may usefully trace the distinctions suggested a little further. Mere rhyme often assists the memory, and if nervous, it may better strike the understanding than prose. Of this quality are some old lines on Feasting and Fasting, beginning thus:

* "Chambers' Journal," No. 21, 1844.

> Accustom early in your youth
> To lay embargo on your mouth;
> And let no rarities invite
> To pall and glut your appetite;
> But check it always, and give o'er
> With a desire to eating more ;
> For where one dies by *inanition*,
> A thousand perish by *repletion*.*

Old Dr. Johnson had not a fine ear, and he judged the artistic quality of poetry chiefly by the calculation of syllables. He was a poet himself, but was chiefly distinguished for his power of making verse. His knowledge of literary art and his manly sense have given an elevation to his productions which have won for them distinction, and which show how good sense will command respect where imagination is wanting. I quote his Prologue spoken by Garrick at the opening of the Theater Royal, Drury Lane, because, as well as illustrating his powers, it illustrates the topics of this book:

> When learning's triumph o'er her barbarous foes
> First reared the stage, immortal Shakspeare rose.
> Each change of many-colored life he drew,
> Exhausted worlds, and then imagined new :
> Existence saw him spurn her bounded reign,
> And panting Time toiled after him in vain.
> His powerful strokes presiding truth impressed,
> And unresisted passion stormed the breast.
>
> Then Jonson came, instructed from the school,
> To please in method, and invent by rule ;
> His studious patience and laborious art
> By regular approach essayed the heart.
> Cold approbation gave the lingering bays,
> For those who durst not censure, scarce could praise;
> A mortal born, he met the general doom,
> But left, like Egypt's kings, a lasting tomb.

---

* E. Roynard, M. D., 1750.

The wits of Charles found easier ways to fame,
Nor wished for Jonson's art, nor Shakspeare's flame.
Themselves they studied—as they felt, they writ—
Intrigue was plot, obscenity was wit.
Vice always found a sympathetic friend;
They pleased their age, and did not aim to mend;
Yet bards like these aspired to lasting praise,
And proudly hoped to pimp in future days.
Their cause was general, their supports were strong,
Their slaves were willing, and their reign was long;
Till shame regained the post that sense betrayed,
And virtue called oblivion to her aid.

Then, crushed by rules, and weakened as refined,
For years the power of tragedy declined;
From bard to bard the frigid caution crept,
Till declamation roared while passion slept;
Yet still did virtue deign the stage to tread,
Philosophy remained though nature fled;
But forced, at length, her ancient reign to quit,
She saw great Faustus lay the ghost of wit;
Exulting folly hailed the joyous day,
And pantomime and song confirmed her sway.

Hard is his lot that here by fortune placed,
Must watch the wild vicissitudes of taste;
With every meteor of caprice must play,
And chase the new-blown bubbles of the day.
Ah! let not censure term our fate our choice,
The stage but echoes back the public voice;
The drama's laws the drama's patrons give,
For we that live to please, must please to live.

Then prompt no more the follies you decry,
As tyrants doom their tools of guilt to die;
'Tis yours this night to bid the reign commence
Of rescued nature and reviving sense;
To chase the charms of sound, the pomp of show,
For useful mirth and salutary woe;
Bid scenic virtue form the rising age,
And truth diffuse her radiance from the stage.

This prologue has wit, energy, and striking sense;
but Johnson's want of fancy is more evident in his

"Death of Charles the Twelfth," which has his perfect force, but at the close only rises into the poetical. The last two lines have the true genius of poetical inspiration :

> On what foundation stands the warrior's pride,
> How just his hopes, let Swedish Charles decide ;
> A frame of adamant, a soul of fire,
> No dangers fright him, and no labors tire ;
> O'er love, o'er fear, extends his wide domain,
> Unconquered lord of pleasure and of pain ;
> No joys to him pacific scepters yield,
> War sounds the trump, he rushes to the field.
> Behold surrounding kings their power combine,
> And one capitulate, and one resign.
> Peace courts his hand, but spends her charm in vain.
> "Think nothing gained," he cries, "till naught remain,
> On Moscow's walls till Gothic standards fly,
> And all be mine beneath the polar sky."
> The march begins in military state,
> And nations on his eye suspended wait.
> Stern famine guards the solitary coast,
> And winter barricades the realm of frost :
> He comes—not want and cold his course delay—
> Hide, blushing glory, hide Pultowa's day !
> The vanquished hero leaves his broken bands,
> And shows his misery in distant lands ;
> Condemned a needy suppliant to wait,
> While ladies interpose and slaves debate.
> But did not chance at length her error mend ?
> Did no subverted empire mark his end ?
> Did rival monarchs give the fatal wound ?
> Did hostile millions press him to the grounds ?
> His fall was destined to a barren strand,
> A petty fortress and a dubious hand.
> *He left a name at which the world grew pale,*
> *To point a moral, or adorn a tale.*

Johnson was a mechanical poet. Allan Cunningham, speaking of Chevy Chase, a genuine poem, which Sir Philip Sidney said fell on his ears like the sound of a trumpet, suggests to us the highest elements of poetry. "'Chevy Chase' and 'Sir Andrew Barton' are history and truth: but history excited, elevated, and inspired: truth all life, spirit, and heroism." "Poetry," says Gilfillan, is "thought on fire." It is in its impassioned truth that we feel its presence; it is for the beauty of ideas, distinct from the beauty of things, that we admire it.

Personification is the soul of poetry. In few of our modern writers is this quality more remarkable than in Douglas Jerrold, whose writings are characterized by the omnipresence of personification. Bulwer presents more of the appearance of personification in his writings, but Jerrold more of the reality. Bulwer's personifications seem often to be artificial, and suggested by capital letters, while Jerrold's are presented in deep-set, finished pictures. Many are the attributes of poetry, but its grandest power is personification. *It* peoples the world of fancy and thought with new forms; it individualizes sentiments; it adds to our intellectual acquaintances. How dim and indefinite are our impressions of the past! but in the hands of Bryant what a majestic entity it becomes in that poem beginning:

> Thou unrelenting Past!
> Strong are the barriers round thy dark domain,
> And fetters sure and fast
> Hold all that enter thy unbreathing reign.

What a splendid ideality is in this poem realized! What multitudinous forms are bodied forth! It is like the revelation of eternity, and the mind trembles and thrills as on the verge of a new world.

Poetry is found in various states, sometimes in the invocation of historic names, in allusions, in illustrations, in similes, sometimes in intensity of language, and sometimes in intensity of feeling.

Poetry is often found independent of the verse it forms, as gems are found unset. "We would define poetry to be that mode of expression by which intensity of feeling on any subject is conveyed from one mind to another. Of course the more just, the more striking the mode of expression, the more complete and rapid will be the communication; hence, and still more because many persons have not courage to dive beneath a rough surface, it is desirable that the poet should be able to clothe his thoughts in mellifluous language. But words are not poetry. Witness the beautiful idea of Professor Heeren: "Persepolis rising above the deluge of years." This, being a translated passage, is not dependent upon phraseology for its beauty. But who does not feel its exquisiteness, picturing at once the almost miraculous stability of those thread-like columns which the intemperate policy of Alexander failed to overthrow, and the vague, shapeless uncertainty which clouds the period to which their erection is attributed? The whole passage forms a most poetically drawn picture.

"Again: 'Time sadly overcometh all things, and is now dominant, and sitteth upon a sphinx, and looketh unto Memphis and old Thebes; while his sister, Oblivion, reclineth semi-somnous on a pyramid, gloriously triumphing, making puzzles of Titanian erections, and turning old glories into dreams. History sinketh beneath her cloud. The traveler, as he paceth amazedly through those deserts, asketh of her,

Who builded them? and she mumbleth something,
but what it is he knoweth not.'

"Is not this poetry? and yet how quaint, almost
inharmonious is its structure. Compare it with the
famous simile in Pope's Homer, beginning,

Thus, when the moon, refulgent lamp of night.

Will this passage, replete with the most gorgeous
epithets, and clothed in the most harmonious verse,
bear a comparison with the strangely appareled
poetry of Sir Thomas Browne? It is not our ear
which prompts the verdict; it is our innate feeling
of truth and beauty. If thus poetic genius can exist
independent and despite of phraseology, may we not
suppose it to be given (we do not say in a high degree) to multitudes of those whom the world would
never accuse of being poets? Our daily experience
confirms this. We have heard a servant describe
scenery with a beauty of feeling and an imagery
which was true poetry; and we hear a child talk
poetry to her doll. Facility of illustration is an attribute of poetic genius we have met with in a
laborer."*

An instance of the highest form of poetry is Blanco
White's great Sonnet to Night, which is perhaps the
distinctest addition to human speculation which the
genius of the thinker has ever made. It happens,
also, to be one of the most accomplished efforts of
Elocution to deliver it well. It requires great and
varied power, and the last line is remarkable for the
distinctness of enunciation required:

* "Sharpe's Magazine," No. 25, 1846.

Mysterious Night! when our first parent knew
   Thee from report divine, and heard thy name,
   Did he not tremble for this lovely frame,
This glorious canopy of light and blue?
Yet, 'neath a curtain of translucent dew,
   Bathed in the rays of the great setting flame,
   Hesperus with the host of heaven came,
And lo! creation widened in man's view.
Who could have thought such darkness lay concealed
   Within thy beams, O Sun? or who could find,
While fruit, and leaf, and insect stood revealed,
   That to such countless orbs thou mad'st us blind?
Why do we, then, shun *death* with anxious strife?
If Light conceals so much, wherefore not Life?

The previous discovery of Truth is implied by Rhetoric, which is the art of communicating Truth; and of all the forms of the enforcement of Truth, Poetry is the highest. All the powers of language, all the graces of literature, all the resources of genius, and nature, and feeling are employed to illustrate that splendor of expression, that harmony of thought, which, wedded to harmony of time and sound, men call Poesy.

# NOTES..

## A.—See page 27.

OUR author is quite liable to be misunderstood in this allusion to the "theater." Judging from many passages of his book, and indeed from its whole tenor, nothing could have been further from his intention than to present our modern theater as a model for pulpit speaking. At the present day the pulpit, in comparison with the theater, will suffer only in one particular, in its *ease* or *naturalness*. Though we can hadly be said to have any modern theater where anything like true eloquence is found, yet its highest excellence is its adaptation of utterance to the thought or sentiment. This quality of speaking, wherever it is acquired, on the stage, at the bar, or in the pulpit, effectually establishes entire freedom from monotone and tone. In this respect we have no doubt the speaking of the stage excels both that of the bar and pulpit. This, too, is doubtless its solitary redeeming quality, as well as the secret of its attraction and power. Nature loves herself, and delights to be portrayed in her own undisguised simplicity, but turns away in disgust whenever she is caricatured. This, it may be, is an important point at which the pulpit fails; it is prosy, monotonous, and is rendered thereby not unfrequently repulsive. To deviate in the least from the beaten track in intonation, accent or emphasis, is thought unclerical, and hence most carefully avoided. Thus our Gospel minister plods on, content with an exact cold logic, reposing in a dead orthodoxy. Here lies the fatal plague-spot on sacred eloquence, the tones of which are sepulchral, and the touch of which is paralyzing to the warm and gushing heart of humanity. These clergymen "are solid men," but emotionless as a frozen ocean! This, doubtless, is what was in our author's mind, though left unamplified. We cannot suppose he would have introduced into the pulpit anything akin to the low buffoonery of mountebanks, which at the present day chiefly gives character to the theater. For it is already noticeable, that with a few who are aiming to be

" star preachers," we have a disgusting imitation of the tragedian style in grotesque action and intonations, but so entirely destitute of its naturalness as to make it superlatively ridiculous. Such is the usual result of attempts at copying or adopting the style of others— the defects only will appear. Copyists will invariably fall below the original, which should lead a public speaker to avoid the practice as he would the open grave of his success.

Clergymen are supposed to be men of sufficient sense and good taste to discover in the world of literature around them, what is and what is not adapted to their profession. Why not appropriate, then, the former and exclude the latter ?

---

## B.—See page 34.

Hamlet says to his players :

"Speak the speech, I pray you, as I pronounce it to you, trippingly on the tongue ; but if you mouth it, as many of our players do, I had as lief the town-crier spoke my lines. Nor do not saw the air too much with your hand, thus, but use all gently ; for in the very torrent tempest, and (as I may say) whirlwind of your passion, you must acquire and beget a temperance that may give it smoothness. O it offends me to the soul to hear a robustious periwig-pated fellow tear a passion to tatters, to very rags, to split the ears of the groundlings, who, for the most part, are capable of nothing but inexplicable dumb shows and noise ; I would have such a fellow whipt for o'erdoing Termagant ; it out-herods Herod : Pray you, avoid it.

"*First Player*. I warrant your honor.

"*Ham.* Be not too tame neither, but let your own discretion be your tutor: suit the action to the word, the word to the action, with this special observance, that you o'erstep not the modesty of nature ; for anything so overdone is from the purpose of playing, whose end, both at the first and now, was, and is, to hold, as 'twere, the mirror up to nature; to show virtue her own feature, scorn her own image, and the very age and body of the time his form and pressure. Now this overdone, or come tardy off, though it make the unskilful laugh, can-not but make the judicious grieve ; the censure of which one must, in your allowance, o'erweigh a whole theater of others. O there be players that I have seen play—and heard others praise and that high-ly—not to speak it profanely, that neither having the accent of Chris-tians nor the gait of Christian, Pagan, nor man, have so strutted and bellowed, that I have thought some of nature's journeymen had made men and not made them well, they imitated humanity so abominably.

"*First Player.* I hope we have reformed that indifferently with us.

"*Ham.* O reform it altogether. And let those that play your clowns, speak no more then is set down for them, for there be of them that will themselves laugh, to set on some quantity of barren spectators to laugh too, though in the mean time some necessary question of the play be then to be considered; that's villianous, and shows a most pitiful ambition in the fool that uses it. Go, make you ready.

. . . . . . . . . . . . . . .

"Aye, so, God be wi' you.—Now I am alone,
O what a rogue and peasant slave am I !
Is it not monstrous that this player here,
But in a fiction, in a dream of passion,
Could force his soul so to his own conceit,
That from her working all his visage wanned ;
Tears in his eyes, distraction in's aspect,
A broken voice, and his whole function suiting
With forms to his conceit ? And all for nothing !
For Hecuba !
What's Hecuba to him, or he to Hecuba
That he should weep for her ? What would he do
Had he the motive and the cue for passion
That I have ? He would drown the stage with tears,
And cleave the general ear with horrid speech ;
Make mad the guilty, and appal the free,
Confound the ignorant, and amaze indeed
The very faculties of eyes and ears.
Yet I,
A dull and muddy-mettled rascal, peak
Like John-a-dreams, unpregnant of my cause,
And can say nothing ; no, not for a king,
Upon whose property and most dear life
A vile defeat was made. . . . . . . . . . .
. . . . . . . . . Humph ! I have heard
That guilty creatures, sitting at a play,
Have, by the very cunning of the scene,
Been struck so to the soul, that presently
They have proclaimed their malefactions ;
For murder, though it have no tongue, will speak
With most miraculous organ. I'll have these players
Play something like the murder of my father

Before mine uncle.  I'll observe his looks;
I'll cut him to the quick; if he do blench
I know my course.  The spirit that I have seen
May be a devil; and the devil hath power
To assume a pleasing shape; yea, and perhaps
Out of my weakness and my melancholy,
(As he is very potent with such spirits,)
Abuses me to damn me: I'll have grounds
More relative than this.  The play's the thing
Wherein I'll catch the conscience of the king."

## C.—See page 38.

We cannot indorse the writer's view in this passage.  The reasons
assigned are invalid.  If it were true that "religious sentiment"
would not be universally received in a "mixed meeting," does that
show that such sentiments should not be used in such a place ?  We
might ask, What other persuasion would influence *all ?*  If we should
refuse to employ arguments or persuasions which would not have *universally* the desired effect, we should use none at all.  But he over-
looks the obvious fact, that man is *universally* a being of "religious
sentiment," with a profound inherent sense of right and wrong deep
seated in his moral nature.  However defective his standard of judgment may be, man everywhere is found with a strong admiration of
what he judges to be right, and detestation of what is wrong; the
operations of a universal conscience.  Hence, all men worship, however erroneously, and no depths of ignorance or degradation are so
great as to prevent it.  It may indeed be doubted whether any
other argument or persuasion is *so* universal in its adaptation and
success as a religious one.  This principle in man is as *strong* as
general, and as *safe* as it is strong.  The honest religious convictions
of men are the last they yield.  Even life itself will be sacrificed before these.  This is the primary and ultimate principle of our being,
to which earth and heaven make their final appeal, touching man's
highest interests, and we aver that all eloquence culminates around
this glowing truth.  When the orator has shorn himself of this mighty
impulse of the human heart, he has lost his leverage to move the
world.  What is it that imparts to the inspired penmen their superhuman eloquence, but their religious themes and their application to
man's spiritual nature.  Without *emotion* it is idle to talk of eloquence.
The *Christian* orator, in the fact that he is a Christian, is moved by a
*deeper*, *purer*, and *stronger* class of emotions than any other.  Hence it

has become notorious that pagan orators have fallen very far below when compared with the Christian. Whoever is constituted by nature or culture for high attainments in oratory, has a soul of the purest and most lofty conceptions and exquisite sensibilities; and such a soul kindles into a glowing eloquence on no subject as it does on moral truth and beauty, God's attributes and man's immortality.

## D.—See page 68.

What is here said of the House of Commons should be applied with a slight modification to the pulpit. Embellishment seems out of place in a Gospel sermon, except under strong excitement, and of the most thoroughly chastened and refined character. Dazzling, gorgeous, or flippant imagery attached to the solemn and weighty truths of God is an incongruity, obscuring those truths or diverting attention from them. Thoughtful people feel that their common sense is trifled with while the preacher seeks to amuse rather than instruct and save them, by which he shows he has no deep and abiding sense or truthful appreciation of what he utters.

Pulpit declamation produces a similar result. With many noble exceptions the training of modern scholars in our first institutions of learning tends directly to establish an empty, heartless, and declamatory style of speaking. Let almost any student for six or nine years repeat in public every two weeks the composition of others, composition which does not excite a single emotion of his own soul; let him also put on all the airs of some eloquent man, when he will appear like David in Saul's armor, and nothing but a miracle will prevent him from falling into this style of speaking.

*Habit* contracted during all these forming years will never be counteracted. A close observer will perceive that the most prominent feature in modern pulpit speaking is declamation, and it is not strange it produces no more effect. Cicero said: " We must never separate philosophy from eloquence."

We see no possible remedy for this lamentable state of pulpit oratory, except what our author here recommends, namely, that the basis of all delivery should be a conversational tone. What was true with the House of Commons is true with all informed and thoughtful hearers, either there, in the Senate, or in the house of the Lord. When public speaking varies from a conversational tone, under strong excitement of the speaker, producing a corresponding emotion of the hearers, they will move on together without repulsion. But when a speaker attempts to seize and carry by storm his auditors, while he is as cold and un-moved as they are, he commits a blunder by which he loses his power over all enlightened mind.    Such hearers feel at once that they are not reasoned with as rational beings, but that an attempt is made to sweep them away as by a whirlwind, they know not where.    Alas! for our modern eloquence, how much of it is of this kind?

----------◆----------

## E.—See page 76.

If what talent, learning, and piety there is in the pulpit were used to the greatest possible advantage, we believe the good accomplished thereby would be immensely increased.    There are several facts con-fronting us at once, as we come to pass judgment on the talents and success of clergymen.    *Success* not unfrequently bears no proportion to *ability*, but often seems to be the inverse ratio of it.    Men acknowledged to be powerful in thought and literary accomplishments, make but a small impression as speakers.    Why is this?    Their power is latent, "unde-veloped."    What has caused this?    It is not a lack of effort; for usually these men are laborious and faithful.    It is because the development has been *obstructed.*    Trace it back and it will be found to lie in their wrong *manner.*    If the style is monotonous, dull, and without emphasis; if the voice is harsh and unsuited to the utterances; if the logic is cold and unsympathizing; if the language and illustrations have not vivacity and pertinency, no matter what the strength, the populace will leave that speaker.    Were all hearers, scholars, and logical think-ers it would be otherwise.

But we see, again, some inferior man in all these respects, who draws after him the crowd, and is powerfully effective.    How is this? It is his *manner*, nothing more nor less.    Who believes that a Spurgeon bears any comparison in intellectual strength to a Butler, Paley, or Watson?    Yet it is no hyperbole to say that, as a speaker, he influences his thousands where they did their hundreds.    Every one knows there is something repulsive and deadening in a certain kind of speaking, while a different mode of utterance is attracting and moving.    Two things, however, trouble us greatly in contemplating this aspect of the subject; we can hardly discover *what it is* that constitutes this differ-ence, and to which of the two classes we ourselves belong.    Here we need very much the kind offices of some intelligent and thoroughly faithful friend, more faithful doubtless than we are with others, or we shall live and die in a perplexing ignorance of the causes of our ineffi-ciency, but greatly wondering that we are not better appreciated.

## F.—See page 78.

This is a terrible sarcasm. With a large class of English and American clergymen we are certain it is not true; but we are not sure but it applies to a minority, at least, in our own country. The fear of advancing an idea never before put forth; the fear of using an illustration never before used; the fear of making a gesture not named in the books, cripples the originality and naturalness of a minister. Hence the apparent constraint and stiff mechanical style so common in pulpit manner. Dullness and deadness among the hearers follow, while the clergy, like a becalmed sea, fall to a stupid level of a harmless mediocrity.

Because there are a few cardinal points of revealed truth which it is admitted should be often repeated and insisted upon, keeping them prominently before the public mind, many seem to suppose nothing else should be preached! This is called "loyalty to old Christianity," "abiding in the old paths." "Whatsoever is new in Christianity," it is said, "is false." This may be true of religion when spoken of as having been *exhaustively* studied, and the last truth and its application found out. But if everything in Christianity is false beyond what many clergymen *know* of it, there is very little in it either true or false. This is a fine subterfuge for forceless and unstudious men to hide behind: the orthodoxy of a few fundamental doctrines as an apology for non-progress in Biblical learning. The truth is, there is more in the book of God than has ever yet been taught or found out. Those ministers of Christ who study his word as closely and severely as they do their classics and philosophies, *are* able to bring forth things *both* new and old. Much of the sterility of pulpit themes and mannerisms grows out of a too close confinement to a few theological points, to the general exclusion of those subjects lying in the rich and comparatively unexhausted fields of Christian morality, or the application of Christian principles to practical life. This neglect has proved exceedingly detrimental to the Christian Church, not only as it affects the interest and vivacity of pulpit style, but also the intelligent and exemplary character of Christian life.

## G.—See page 96.

A public speaker who has a ready command of pleasantry, united with good sense, has a great element of power. It will impart variety and vivacity to his style, creating attention and interest with his hearers. This is as true of the minister of Christ as of any other speaker.

Yet we consider it one of the most dangerous talents ever introduced into the pulpit. Very few can use it at all without destroying the *gravity* with which sacred subjects should be treated. When used improperly it distracts attention, dissipates the mind of the hearers, lowers the dignity and influence of the speaker, throwing an air of levity over the subject and all its surroundings. All this is terribly destructive of the great end of preaching. Fewer still can use pleasantry or wit in the pulpit with perfect refinement of taste, without which it is most sadly out of place. Indeed, no class of public speakers requires so little wit, or can use it so seldom without detriment, as the minister of the Gospel. *His* chief object is to enlighten the mind and move the affections; while wit, so far from contributing to this object, has the opposite tendency, to destroy affection. Wit may serve to break the force of an opponent's unjust assault, or relieve one from a momentary embarrassment in debate—never required in pulpit discourse; but it can never reach and move the moral forces of our being. Hence its effect in the pulpit is usually worse than useless—it is *damaging*.

No sight is more melancholy than to see the sacred and sublime realities of God, the soul, and eternity, treated in a style bordering even upon the frivolous. Low witticisms, vulgar jokes, and coarse anecdotes may perhaps serve some purpose of third-rate lawyers and buffoons, but they ill become the embassador of Christ. The sprightly and flippant young clergyman is in great danger here. The senseless grin and unmeaning titter of an audience often mislead him into the opinion that his strength lies in wit and repartee; and thus incited he is led on blindly, till his habits are remedilessly fixed, which not unfrequently ruin his usefulness forever.

———◇———

## H.—See page 104.

Here lies the grand secret of all eloquence—*nature, nature in earnest.* Nature tortured is the common spoiler of good speaking. The trilling of the r, prolonging of certain vowel sounds, emphasizing certain words, not according to their importance, but according to their smooth and rolling sound, studying gesticulation according to rules only, thus putting an end to all eloquence. Extemporaneous speakers, especially, have not unfrequently a habit of holding on to, and drawing out many words when the next word does not readily occur, throwing in many connectives not necessary, simply as a sort of bridge over these chasms in language. A late author, Bautain, says: "You must not grope for your words while speaking, under penalty of braying like a donkey, which is the death of a discourse." The same disastrous results follow an effort to imitate some favorite speaker. Then the thoughts must be on that speaker, and the *heart* can be nowhere else. Mimic eloquence, if we could conceive such a thing, would be like a *mimic* volcano! Genuine eloquence cannot be counterfeited. It has its seat in the heart. Pure and benevolent intentions, with earnestness and artlessness, always result in eloquence, provided there are no impediments in the way of its utterance. Such impediments exist sometimes in the pathway of an eloquent nature. These are the cases where long and tedious training and practice are required, aside from a knowledge of the science, in order to success. A speaker with a feeling and enthusiastic heart, and soul of fire, may have a short breath, a stammering tongue, an indistinct enunciation, or a harsh voice. Then a critical drill is his only hope. While another speaker, with none of these impediments in his way, might be utterly ruined by that same process, as it might displace his naturally good qualities.

Many young speakers, with the best natural abilities for oratory, without any of these great hinderances, have entered upon the most elaborate and mechanical training, tampering with nature, spoiling its artless simplicity, and leaving upon it so many marks of the chisel, that in the end they have become less attractive and efficient than at first. Let nature alone, unless you or your friends can detect fault in her; but if so, remove them, however long the time it requires and whatever the cost.

Speakers are slow and unskillful in detecting their own faults; friends are slow, equally slow in pointing out these faults *to* the faulty parties, unless invited and *urged* to do so. Two men of the same abilities, acquirements, and tastes, will each detect in the *other* ten faults as a speaker to one in himself. He is a wise man who continually invites the closest criticism of his most intelligent and faithful friends. Nothing could possibly so much improve the pulpit oratory of this day as a resort to this means if well applied.

## I.—See page 107.

On the preparation and delivery of an extemporaneous sermon, we are allowed by the generous publisher, *Charles Scribner*, 124 Grand-street, New York, to make the following brief extracts from a late publication of his: "ART OF EXTEMPORE SPEAKING. HINTS FOR THE

Pulpit, the Senate, and the Bar;" a work which we most cordially recommend to all our readers.

"In every discourse, if it have life, there is a parent idea or fertile germ, and all the parts of the discourse are like the principal organs and the members of an animated body. The propositions, expressions, and words resemble those secondary organs which connect the principal, as the nerves, muscles, vessels, and tissues attaching them to one another, and rendering them copartners in life and death. Then amid this animate and organic mass there is the spirit of life, which is in the blood, and is everywhere diffused with the blood from the heart, life's center, to the epidermis. So in eloquence, there is the spirit of the words, the soul of the orator, inspired by the subject, his intelligence illumined with mental light, which circulates through the whole body of the discourse, and pours therein brightness, heat, and life. A discourse without a parent idea is a stream without a fountain, a plant without a root, a body without a soul; empty phrases, sounds which beat the air, or a tinkling cymbal. . . . . . .

"He who wishes to speak in public must, above all, see clearly on what he has to speak, and rightly conceive what he has to say. The precise determination of the subject, and the idea of the discourse, these are the two first stages of the preparation.

"It is not so easy as it seems to know upon what one is to speak; many orators, at least, seem to be ignorant of it, or to forget it in the course of their address; for it is sometimes their case to speak of all things except those which would best relate to the occasion. This exact determination of the subject is still more needful in extemporization; for there many more chances of discusiveness exist. The address not being sustained by the memory or notes, the mind is more exposed to the influences of the moment; and nothing is required but the failure or inexactitude of the word, the suggestion of a new thought, a little inattention, to lure it from the subject, and throw it into some crossroad which takes it far away. Add the necessity of continuing when once a speech is begun, because to stop is embarrassing, to withdraw a disgrace. Therefore, in order to lead and sustain the progress of a discourse, one must clearly know whence one starts, and whither one goes, and never lose sight of either the point of departure or the destination. But to effect this the road must be measured beforehand, and the principal distance marks must have been placed. There is a risk also of losing one's way, and then, either one arrives at no end, even after much fatigue, productive of interminable discourses leading to nothing; or if one at last reaches the destination, it is after an infinity of turns and circuits, which have wearied the hearer as well as the speaker, without profit or pleasure for anybody. . . . . . . . . . . A question well stated is half solved.

"It is necessary that the orator before speaking should be collected; he should be wholly absorbed in his ideas, and proof against the interruptions and impressions which surround him. The slightest distraction to which he yields may break the chain of his thoughts, mar his plan, and even sponge out of his mind the very remembrance of his subject itself. This appears incredible, and I would not believe it myself had I not experienced it.

"All who extemporize have had the misfortune some time or other, to fall into digressions, prolixities, and appendages, which cause the main object to be lost to view, and wear out or render languid the attention of the audience. In the warmth of exposition a man is not always master of his own words, and when new thoughts arise, they may lead a long way from the subject, to which there is sometimes a difficulty in returning. If he does not hold with a firm hand the thread of his thoughts he will never come to speak in an endurable manner; and though by his fine passages he may surprise, amuse, and dazzle the hearer, he will not suggest one idea to his mind, nor instill a single feeling into his ear, because there will be neither order nor unity, and therefore no life in his discourse.

"Most orators spoil their speeches by lengthiness, and prolixity is the principal disadvantage of extemporaneous speaking. In it, more than in any other, one wants time to be brief, and there is a perpetual risk of being carried away by the movement of the thoughts or the expressions.

"It sometimes happens, unfortunately, that you are barely into your subject when you should end; and then, with a confused feeling of all that you have omitted, and a sense of what you might still say, you are anxious to recover lost ground in some degree, and you begin some new development when you ought to be concluding. This tardy and unseasonable, yet crude aftergrowth has the very worst effect upon the audience, which, already fatigued, becomes impatient and listens no longer. The speaker loses his words and his trouble, and everything which he adds by way of elucidating or corroborating what he has said, spoils what has gone before, destroying the impression of it. He repeats himself unconsciously, and those who still listen follow him with uneasiness, as men watch from shore a bark which seeks to make port and cannot. It is a less evil to turn short round and finish abruptly than thus to tack incessantly without advancing; for the greatest of a speaker's misfortunes is that he should bore.

" They who have not learned first to write, generally speak badly and with difficulty, unless indeed they have that fatal facility, a thousand times worse than hesitation or than silence, which drowns thought in floods of words or in a torrent of copiousness, sweeping away good earth and leaving behind sand and stones alone. Heaven keep us from those interminable talkers, such as are often to be found in Southern countries, who deluge you relatively to anything and to nothing with a shower of dissertation, and a down-pouring of their eloquence! During nine tenths of the time there is not one rational thought in the whole of this twaddle, carrying along in its course every kind of rubbish and platitude. The class of speakers who produce a speech so easily, and who are ready at the shortest moment to extemporize a speech, a dissertation, or a homily, know not how to compose a tolerable sentence; and I repeat, that, with such exceptions as defy all rule, he who has not learned how to write, will never know how to speak.

" Nor must he rely on the notes which he may carry in his hand to help him in the exposition and save him from breaking down. Doubtless they may have their utility, especially in business-speaking, as at the bar, at the council board, or in a deliberative assembly. They are the material part, the baggage of the orator, of which he should disencumber himself to the utmost of his power. They are the most utterly worthless when they seem the most necessary. In the most fervid moments of extemporaneous speaking, when light teems, and the sacred fire burns, when the mind is hurried along upon the tide of thought, everything should proceed from within. Then nothing so thoroughly freezes the oratorical flow as to consult these wretched notes."

# SACRED ELOQUENCE: THE BRITISH PULPIT.*

ABOUT fifteen years ago our readers were presented with a critique on "French Sermons," concluding with an intimation that at some future period the subject would be resumed, with a special reference to the British pulpit.† In that article surprise was expressed that there should be so small a proportion of sermons destined to live; that out of the *million* and upward preached annually throughout the empire there should be so very few that are remembered three whole days after they are delivered; fewer still that are committed to the press; scarcely one that is not in a few years absolutely forgotten. "If any one," it was added, "were for the first time informed what preaching was; if, for example, one of the ancient critics had been told that the time would come when vast multitudes of persons should assemble regularly to be addressed, in the midst of their devotions, upon the most sacred truths of a religion sublime beyond all the speculations of philosophers, yet in all its most important points simple and of the easiest apprehen-

* *Edinburgh Review*, October, 1840.—*Sermons to a Country Congregation.* By AUGUSTUS WILLIAM HARE, late Fellow of New College, and Rector of Alton Barnes. 2 vols., 8vo.; London, 1839.

† No. LXXXIX, pp. 147, 148.

sion; that with those truths were to be mingled discussions of the whole circle of human duties, according to a system of morality singularly pure and attractive; that the more dignified and the more interesting parts of national affairs were not to be excluded from the discourse; that, in short, the most elevating, the most touching, and the most interesting of all topics were to be the subject-matter of the address, directed to persons sufficiently versed in them, and assembled only from the desire they felt to hear them handled, surely the conclusion would at once have been drawn that such occasions must train up a race of the most consummate orators, and that the effusions to which they gave birth must needs cast all other rhetorical compositions into the shade. . . . How then comes it to pass that instances are so rare of eminent eloquence in the pulpit?"

Though we are willing to believe that some improvement in this branch of eloquence is gradually taking place, we are still of opinion that the above question is as pertinent as ever. It seems proper, therefore, to investigate the causes of so singular a phenomenon, and to urge upon those who are intrusted with so powerful an instrument of instruction as the pulpit, the duty of endeavoring to turn it to better account.

To this important subject we propose to devote the present essay, premising that it is not at all our intention to discuss any doctrinal questions, or to examine how much of truth or error there may be in any given system of religious belief; we consider only the general conditions on which all religious instruction (presupposing it to be sound) should be conveyed, and especially the *style* and the *manner* peculiarly appropriated to this department of public speaking.

Without departing from the above resolution we may, however, be allowed to make one obvious remark, even in relation to what ought to be the *substance* of that eloquence of which we propose more particularly to consider only the form. It is this: that, whatever diversities of opinion and of doctrine it may present, it is of course implied that there are limits to these diversities. We cannot expect that any system will produce its proper effects, however eloquent and forcible the form in which it is professedly exhibited, unless its essential peculiarities be preserved. A Mollah must not preach the doctrines of a Brahmin if he wishes to see what are the genuine results of Islamism, nor a Pundit interpret his sacred books by the Koran of the prophet. In the same manner, if the Christian preacher (as was too often the case in times that are past) be nothing more than what Bishop Horsley calls "an ape of Epictetus," a bad personation of Seneca tricked out in a gown and cassock, or a doctor of metaphysics, who, by some strange blunder, has mistaken the church for the lecture-room, we cannot rationally expect that Christianity should produce its genuine results. What are the precise limits within which the essentials of Christian doctrine may be exhibited in their integrity it is not for us to determine; to do so would be to venture within that province which we have formally renounced. But that the essence of the doctrines and precepts of this peculiar system may be fully exhibited, notwithstanding considerable diversity of opinions on subordinate points, no man of candor will deny. The names of eminent men of very different parties will instantly suggest themselves to the memory of the reader, to whom, we are convinced, not one individual of the Christian community would deny the title of "preachers of righteousness."

But supposing the requisite purity of doctrine secured—of which we must leave men to form their own opinion—the mode in which that doctrine is exhibited and enforced is only second in importance. And the proof is found in this, that, if we appeal to an individual of *any* denomination, he will tell you that he knows preachers whom he cannot but account equally worthy and excellent, and equally in possession of the truth, (that is, who think exactly with himself, for that is the infallible standard by which each man measures the aberrations of his neighbor,) who yet shall produce the most opposite effects on him. The one shall send him to sleep in spite of himself, and the other shall not permit him to sleep even if he would. Yet the substance of their communications, he himself being the judge, is in each case precisely the same.

We have long been convinced that the inefficiency that so generally distinguishes pulpit discourses is in a great degree owing to the two following causes: First, that preachers do not sufficiently cultivate, as part of their professional education, a systematic acquaintance with the principles upon which all effective eloquence must be founded, with the limitations under which their topics must be chosen, and the mode in which they must be exhibited in order to secure popular impression; and, secondly, that they do not, after they have assumed their sacred functions, give sufficient time or labor to the preparation of their discourses.

Many and splendid exceptions to these statements no doubt there are. We only fear that some for whom the consolation of this saving clause was not intended will, nevertheless, complacently take the benefit of it. We shall offer some observations on both the causes of failure above specified at the close of the present article.

The appropriateness of any composition, whether written or spoken, is easily deduced from its object. If that object be to instruct, convince, or persuade, or all these at the same time, we naturally expect that it should be throughout of a direct and earnest character, indicating a mind absorbed in the avowed object, and solicitous only about what may subserve it. We expect that this singleness of purpose should be seen in the topics discussed, in the arguments selected to enforce them, in the modes of illustration, and even in the peculiarities of style and expression. We expect that nothing shall be introduced merely for the purpose of inspiring an interest, either in the thoughts or in the language, apart from their pertinency to the object; or of exciting an emotion of delight for its own sake, as in poetry, although it is quite true that the most vivid pleasure will necessarily result from perceiving an exact adaptation of the means to the end. We cannot readily pardon mere beauties or elegances, striking thoughts or graceful imagery, if they are marked by this irrelevancy, since they serve only to impede the vehement current of argument or feeling. In a word, we expect nothing but what, under the circumstances of the speaker, is prompted by *nature;* nature, not as opposed to a deliberate effort to adapt the means to the ends, and to do what is to be done as well as possible, for this, though in one sense art, is also the truest nature; but nature, as opposed to whatever is inconsistent with the idea that the man is under the dominion of genuine feeling, and bent upon taking the directest path to the accomplishment of his object. True eloquence is not like some painted window, which both transmits the light of day variegated and tinged with a thousand hues, and diverts the attention from its proper use to the pomp and splendor of the artist's doing; it is a perfectly transparent medium, transmitting light, without suggesting a thought about the medium itself. Adaptation to the one single object is everything.

These maxims have been universally recognized in deliberative and forensic eloquence. Those who have most severely exemplified them have ever been regarded as the truest models; while those who have partially violated them, though still considered in a qualified sense very eloquent, have failed to obtain the highest place. Nor, it may be safely said, would the irrelevant discussions, the florid declamation, the imaginative finery, the tawdry ornament which too often disgrace the pulpit, which too often are heard in it, not only without astonishment, but with admiration, be tolerated for a moment in the senate or at the bar.

Much of this is no doubt to be attributed to the deplorable fact that the great themes of religion are viewed (not by preachers alone, but by all mankind) with emotions so sadly disproportioned to their intrinsic importance. Hence the difficulty of finding the man who is as thoroughly interested in the subjects of religion as thousands are in discussions relating to the timber or sugar duties, to a grant of public money, or a vote of supply. Even a trial at the Old Bailey for stealing a couple of pocket handkerchiefs too often stirs deeper emotion, both in speakers and hearers, than the most momentous realities connected with the future and unseen world.

This, however, is only a partial solution of the difficulty; since the maxims we have above adverted to are often and grievously violated by multitudes of preachers, the consistency of whose lives, and whose diligent discharge of the ordinary duties of their office, bespeak them to be under the dominion of religious principle. Their failings, therefore, as public speakers, can be fairly accounted for only by their having adopted an erroneous idea of what the most effective style of speaking is; or, which is more frequent, from their never having attained any distinct idea of it at all.

We have long felt convinced that the eloquence of the pulpit, in its general character, has never been assimilated so far as it might have been, and ought to have been, to that which has produced the greatest effect elsewhere; and which is shown to be of the right kind both by the success which has attended it, and by the analysis of the qualities by which it has been distinguished. If we were compelled to give a brief definition of the principal characteristics of this truest style of eloquence, we should say it was "practical reasoning, animated by strong emotion;" or if we might be indulged in what is rather a description than a definition of it, we should say that it consisted in reasoning on topics calculated to inspire a common interest, expressed in the language of ordinary life, and in that brief, rapid, familiar style which natural emotion ever assumes. The former half of

this description would condemn no small portion of
the compositions called "Sermons," and the latter
half a still larger portion.

We would not be misunderstood. It is far, very
far, from our intention to speak in terms of the slightest
depreciation of the immense treasures of learning, of
acute disquisition, of profound speculation, of powerful controversy, which the literature of the English
pulpit contains. In these points it cannot be surpassed. In vigor and originality of thought, in argumentative power, in extensive and varied erudition, it
as far transcends all other literature of the same kind
as it is deficient in the qualities which are fitted to
produce popular impression. We merely assert that
the greater part of "Sermons" are not at all entitled
to the name, if by it be meant discourses *specially
adapted* to the object of instructing, convincing, or
persuading the common mind.

We are well aware that the very nature of pulpit
eloquence forbids anything more than a partial
assimilation to that of the senate or the bar; that
certain modifications will be instantly suggested by
the topics with which it deals and the objects which
it has in view. It must often be to a far greater extent simply didactic than eloquence of any other
kind; though the practical purpose to which all
matter of this sort is to be immediately applied, will
still secure an earnestness and animation in the style
in very observable contrast with the even tone and
measured periods of literary disquisition. It never
can appeal to those tumultuous passions, nor rouse
those vehement feelings which may be gladly abandoned to the arena of politics; while those sublime
realities, connected with the future and the invisible,

which form its great and inspiring themes, must necessarily demand more minute and ample description, in order vividly to impress the imagination, than would be readily tolerated either in deliberative or forensic eloquence. Still this is only saying that, as a peculiar *species* of eloquence, it has something peculiar; as a species of the *genus* it ought still to possess the generic qualities. The degree in which it can exhibit and embody those qualities is another question; and though it may be a point of some difficulty to ascertain how far this object may be attained, it is not difficult to show either that it might have been attained more completely than it has been, or that in many instances it has been neglected altogether.

We have said, for example, that the principal characteristic of all effective eloquence consists in reasoning on topics calculated to inspire a common interest in the mass of a common audience. Who can take even the most hasty inspection of our pulpit literature without perceiving how generally this obvious attribute has been neglected, especially till within a comparatively recent period? What can be more hopeless than the attempt to engage the attention, or interest the feelings of a common audience in metaphysical subtleties? And yet abstruse speculations on the "origin of evil," on "moral necessity," on the "self-determining power," on the "ultimate principles of ethics," on the "immortality of the soul," as proved from its indiscerptibility and we know not what, on the "eternal fitness of things," on the "moral sense," with other still more recondite speculations on themes which it is almost impious and perfectly useless to touch, were of common oc-

currence in our older pulpit literature; and they are
not infrequent, though not pursued to the same extent, even now.   For our own parts we believe that
the discussion of such subjects is about as profitable
in a popular assembly as would be that of the well-
known questions, as to whether angels can pass from
one point of space to another without passing through
the intermediate points, and whether they can visually
discern objects in the dark.   Dr. Donne has proposed
a series of questions for over-refined speculators in
which he keenly satirizes all such superfluous subt-
tilty.   It is only to be lamented that he did not more
effectually learn his own lesson in the composition
of his own sermons, in some of which he has touched
upon subjects more fit for Thomas Aquinas than the
Christian preacher.   We would not do even Thomas
Aquinas injustice, however; we verily believe that
the great schoolman would have stood aghast at the
idea of dragging such questions out of the obscurity
of the schools into common daylight, and making
them the themes of popular declamation.

We gladly admit that the modern pulpit is fast
outgrowing these extravagances; that such discussions are both less frequent, and pursued to a much
more limited extent, than they used to be.   Yet it is
no uncommon thing to find the young preacher, fresh
from his metaphysics or his philosophy, touching
upon them just to a sufficient extent to exhaust and
dissipate the attention of his audience before he
comes to more important and more welcome matter;
or indulging in allusions, and employing phraseology
with reference to them, wholly unintelligible to the
mass.   Others, and they form a much larger class,
are fond of subjects which are only one degree less

useful, and which, though they ought not to be excluded from the pulpit, need to be very rarely entered
upon. We allude to the discussions connected with
"Natural Theology," and the first "Principles of
Morals." Such preachers are continually proving
that there is a God, to those who readily admit there
is a divine revelation; that the marks of design in
the universe prove that there is an intelligent cause,
to those who never had a single doubt upon the subject; that death is not an eternal sleep, to those who
find no difficulty in admitting that there is a heaven
and a hell; that man is a moral agent, to those who
cannot even conceive that he can be otherwise; and
that those first principles of ethics are certainly true,
which even savages themselves would be ashamed to
disavow. We say not that such topics should be excluded from the pulpit, but only that they should
form a very inferior element in its ordinary prelec-
tions. The atheist and deist, though rarely found
in Christian congregations, should not be entirely
neglected; and those who are neither the one nor the
other should certainly be in possession of arguments
which may serve to confute both, and to give an intelligent reason "of the hope that is in them." But
it may safely be taken for granted, in ordinary cases,
that the great bulk of those who attend any Christian
place of worship already believe all these things; in
a word, admit the truth of that revelation, the exposition and enforcement of which are the preacher's
proper object. What should we say to a member of
Parliament who should treat the House of Commons
(characteristically impatient of whatever does not
bear on practical objects) to formal disquisitions on
points on which all the members are agreed: on the

first principles of law and government, for example; or on any of those abstract questions which were discussed properly enough by Filmer and Locke. Allusions to such matters, so far as they bear on the matter in hand, and brief references to general principles which embrace the particular instances under discussion, are all that would be tolerated.

Even where the topics are not such as are fairly open to censure, a large class of preachers, especially among the young, grievously err by investing them with the technicalities of science and philosophy; either because they foolishly suppose they thereby give their compositions a more philosophical air, or because they disdain the homely and the vulgar. We remember hearing of a worthy man of this class, who, having occasion to tell his audience the simple truth, that there was not one Gospel for the rich and another for the poor, informed them that, "if they would not be saved on 'general principles' they could not be saved at all!" With such men it is not sufficient to say, that such and such a thing must be, but there is always a "moral or physical necessity" for it. The will is too old-fashioned a thing to be mentioned, and everything is done by "volition;" duty is expanded into "moral obligation," men not only *ought* to do this, that, or the other, it is always by "some principle of their moral nature;" they not only *like* to do so and so, but they are "impelled by some natural propensity;" men not only *think* and *do*, but they are never represented as thinking and doing without some parade of their "intellectual processes and active powers." Such discourses are full of "moral beauty," and "necessary relations," and "philosophical demonstrations," and "laws of na-

ture," and "*a priori* and *a posteriori* arguments."
If some simple fact of physical science is referred to
in the way of argument or illustration, it cannot be
presented in common language, but must be exhibited in the pomp of the most approved scientific
technicalities. If there be a common and scientific
name for the same object, ten to one that the latter
is adopted. Heat straightway becomes "caloric,"
lightning, the "electric fluid;" instead of plants and
animals, we are surrounded by "organized substan-
ces;" life is nothing half so good as the "vital principle;" "phenomena" of all kinds are very plenti-
ful; these phenomena are "developed," and "combined," and "analyzed," and in short, done everything with, except being made intelligible. Not only
is such language as this obscurely understood, or not
understood at all, but even if perfectly understood,
must necessarily be far less effective than those simple terms of common life which for the most part
may be substituted for them. The sermons of Augustus William Hare, referred to at the commencement
of this essay, may serve to show how the abstract
terms of philosophy may be advantageously translated into simple and racy English.*

* The following extract from Dr. Campbell's "Lectures on Pulpit
Eloquence" is worth notice: "There is indeed a sort of literary diction, which sometimes the inexperienced are ready to fall into insensibly, from their having been much more accustomed to the school and
to the closet, to the works of some particular schemer in philosophy,
than to the scenes of real life and conversation. This fault, though
akin to the former, is not so bad; as it may be without affectation,
and when there is no special design of catching applause. It is, indeed, most commonly the consequence of an immoderate attachment
to some one or other of the various systems of ethics or theology
that have in modern times been published, and obtained a vogue
among their respective partisans. Thus the zealous disciple of Shaftes-

Equally at variance with common sense are the topics which *some few* preachers, much addicted to Biblical criticism, but strangely ignorant of its practical uses, and the limits within which alone it can be properly applied, sometimes think proper to introduce into sermons. Their talk is much of " collations of manuscripts," of " various readings," of the " Vulgate," of " Coptic and Syriac versions," of " interpolations," of the " original languages," of " Hebrew points," etc., etc., etc. They totally forget, if they ever knew, that all these things are the mere instruments with which they work; and that the *results*, expressed in simple language, and without any ostentatious technicalities, are all with which the people have to do. If such a man were building a house, he would doubtless suffer the scaffolding to stand about it as a notable embellishment; or if he were employed to lay down a carpet, he would leave the hammer and nails upon the floor as memorials of his labor and ingenuity.

The selection of inappropriate topics is the more bury, Akenside, and Hutcheson is no sooner licensed to preach the Gospel, than with the best intentions in the world, he harangues the people from the pulpit on the moral sense and universal benevolence; he sets them to inquire whether there be a perfect conformity in their affections to the supreme symmetry established in the universe; he is full of the sublime and beautiful in things, the moral objects of right and wrong, and the proportional affection of a rational creature toward them. He speaks much of the inward music of the mind, the harmony and the dissonance of the passions; and seems, by his way of talking, to imagine, that if a man have this same moral sense, which he considers as the mental ear, in due perfection, he may tune his soul with as much ease as a musician tunes his musical instrument. The disciple of Dr. Clarke, on the contrary, talks to us in somewhat of a soberer strain and less pompous phrase, but not a jot more edifying, about unalterable reason and the eternal fitness of things, about the conformity of our actions to their immutable relations and essential differences."

inexcusable, when we consider the large provision of subjects of enduring and universal interest which is made in the very book which the preacher professes to interpret. He may freely expatiate over the ample circle of its doctrines and precepts, in all their applications to the endless diversities of life, and the endless peculiarities of individual character; he may find an equally legitimate province in the interpretation of difficult passages, or the reconciliation of apparent discrepancies; in the illustration of manners, customs, and antiquities; and in the elucidation of those ever-varied and deeply interesting narratives in which, for the profoundest reasons, the doctrines of Scripture are everywhere imbedded, as if for the very purpose both of securing the requisite variety in pulpit discourses, and preventing the truths of religion from assuming the form of naked abstractions. Well would it be if in this respect, as well as in others, the preacher would make the Bible the object of his sedulous imitation. It is everywhere a practical book; it contains no over-curious speculations, no superfluous subtleties. On the contrary, as often remarked, there is a singular silence maintained in that volume on all that tends merely to gratify our curiosity. The very mysteries it discloses it discloses only so far as is necessary for some practical purpose; while it everywhere views man just as in common life man views himself and his fellows, recognizing at once, without discussion, all those facts connected with our intellectual and moral constitution, the true theory of which has occasioned such endless differences and inquiries in the schools.

If the topics selected by the preacher have often been very little calculated to inspire interest in the

13

mass of a common audience, it is equally true that, where they are liable to no such objection, the mode of treating them has as often been anything but popular. The argumentation is often too subtle or too comprehensive; or a too solicitously logical form is given to its expression. Unity of subject, indeed, there ought to be, and must be; that is, where the discourse is a "sermon," and not an "exposition." But it is one thing to exhibit that one subject by rapidly and powerfully touching those points which the common mind can seize and appreciate, and quite another to exhibit it after the manner of Euclid or Dr. Clarke. Unity of subject is a characteristic of Demosthenes; but continuous or subtle ratiocination never is. He *reasons*, indeed, perpetually, for reasoning, as already said, is the staple of all effective eloquence; but never was a truer criticism than that of Lord Brougham—"that his reasonings are not of the nature of continuous demonstration, and by no means resemble a chain of mathematical or metaphysical arguments." The following observations are well worthy the attention of every speaker: " If by this [the assertion that Demosthenes is chiefly character- ized by reasoning] is only meant that he never wanders from the subject, that each remark tells upon the matter in hand, that all his illustrations are brought to bear upon the point, and that he is never found making any step in any direction which does not advance his main object, and lead toward the conclusion to which he is striving to bring his hearers, the observation is perfectly just; for this is a distinguishing feature in the character of his elo- quence. It is not, indeed, his grand excellence, be- cause everything depends upon the manner in which he pursues this course, the course itself being one quite as open to the humblest mediocrity as to the highest genius. But if it is meant to be said that those Attic orators, and especially their great chief, made speeches in which long chains of elaborated reasoning are to be found, nothing can be less like the truth. *A variety of topics are handled in succession, all calculated to strike the audience.*"

We admit, however, that it is impossible to lay down any universal rule on this point. Different men will treat their subjects with more or less of logical severity, according to the structure of their own understandings; and, what is more, will form to themselves audiences who will appreciate their methods. A general caution against the extremes adverted to is all that can be given. But in order more effectually to guard against the faults in question, we are inclined to believe that it would be well if the ancient system of "Homilies," or expositions of considerable passages, were more frequently resorted to. If well executed, especially when the subjects are historical, we are disposed to think they would both be more fruitful of instruction, and secure, by variety of topics, a stronger hold upon the attention of a common audience. We are aware, indeed, that to present such subjects judiciously, to make the transitions easy and natural, and to secure something like unity of plan, notwithstanding the great variety of the materials, would require quite as much labor as the construction of a sermon on some single topic, probably more. And for this very reason we do not think it would be at all fair to judge of the effects of such expositions by what commonly pass under that name, in which a large portion of text is often

taken in order to *save* trouble; the preacher erroneously supposing that, where he has so much to talk
about he cannot fail to have enough to say, and that
he may therefore dispense with a diligent preparation. He forgets that, if the field be very wide, there
may be the greater danger, unless he take due care
of losing himself in it. We have heard of a preacher
of this stamp, who alleged, as a reason for resorting
to the expository method, that when he was "perse-
cuted in one text he could flee unto another."
Chrysostom, in his very best moods, admirably ex-
emplifies the homiletic style here contended for.*

* Whitefield's sermons very often consist of little more than a
familiar and lively exposition of a parable, or some short portion of
narrative; and to this we have no doubt they owed no slight degree
of their popularity. The sermons of Whitefield have come down to
us in a very imperfect form. They are, for the most part, mere notes
of what he said. It has often been remarked that his sermons are
strangely destitute of vigorous or original thought. Though it is certain they have greatly suffered from the mutilated form in which they
have reached us, we must confess it does not appear to us that the
sermons are very deficient in those qualities of thought or expression
which we have represented as so essential to popular eloquence. It
is true they often want method and arrangement, are disfigured by
repetitions, extravagances, and frequent and gross violations of taste.
These are to be attributed partly to the cause above specified, that is,
the imperfect manner in which his sermons have been preserved,
partly to the character of his own mind, and partly to the age. If,
indeed, any one look for profound speculation, or continuous and
subtle reasoning in these sermons, he will be disappointed; but so far
from wondering on that account that they could have produced such
an effect, he will feel, if he know anything of the philosophy of popular
eloquence, that they could not have produced such an effect if they
had been characterized by these qualities. It is certain they could not
have been destitute of the principal qualities. whether of thought or of
style, which constitute popular eloquence; and we think that even
now, amid great deformities, those qualities may be not obscurely
traced in them. Preaching of which the fastidious Hume said, that

As we have said that we wish preachers would let the Scriptures determine for them to what classes of subjects they should limit themselves, so we wish that they would imitate the same book in their general mode of treating the topics it supplies. There, assuredly, as Lord Brougham says of Demosthenes, the reasonings are not "chains of continuous ratiocination." The book is constructed with far too profound a knowledge of human nature for *that*. To use the expressive language already quoted, "a variety of topics are handled in succession, all calculated to strike the common mind." This is the very characteristic of the discourses of our Lord; and in this, as well as in all other respects, they are worthy of the profound study of the Christian preacher. A few philosophers would, no doubt, prefer a very different method, and have often very unphilosophically complained of Scripture because its method is not their method. But we are not speaking of what philosophers would best like, but what is most calculated to impress the common mind.

We shall now proceed to offer a few observations on those properties of style which peculiarly belong to the most effective eloquence. It was remarked that it is characterized by that brief, rapid, familiar, and natural manner which a mind in earnest ever assumes. It is best illustrated by the style of a man engaged in conversation on some serious subject— intent, for example, on convincing his neighbor of some important truth, or persuading him to some

it was "worth going twenty miles to hear it," which interested the infidel Bolingbroke, and warmed even the cool and cautious Franklin for once into enthusiasm, must have possessed great merit, independently of the charms of voice, gesture, and manner.

course of conduct. The public speaker will often manifest, it is true, greater dignity or vehemence, (the natural result of speaking on a more important theme, and to a larger audience,) but there will be the same general characteristics still; the same colloquial, but never vulgar diction; the same homely illustrations; the same brevity of expression; in a word, all those peculiarities which mark a man absorbed in his subject, and simply anxious to give the most forcible expression to his thoughts and feelings. It is not very easy to give an analysis of this peculiar style by an enumeration of its qualities; but it is instantly recognized wherever it is found, whether addressed to the eye or to the ear.*

The chief characteristics of this peculiar style are abhorrence of the ornate and the glittering, of the pompous and the florid; jealousy of epithets, a highly idiomatic and homely diction, a love of brevity and condensation, a freedom from stateliness and formality; rapid changes of construction, frequent recurrence to the interrogative—not to mention numberless other indications of vivacity and animation, marked in speech by the most rapid and varied changes of voice and gesture. Of all its characteristics, the most striking and the most universal is the moderate use of the imagination. Now as lively emotion always stimulates the imagination, it may at first sight appear paradoxical that this should be a characteristic at all. But a little reflection will explain this; for every one must recollect that if a speaker is

---

* No writer on rhetoric (if we except Aristotle) has been so uniformly alive to the peculiarities of this style, or has so happily illustrated them, as Dr. Whately. It must also be admitted that his own writings furnish many admirable exemplifications of his own maxims. It is well when precept is enforced by example.

in earnest he never employs his imagination as the
poet does, merely to delight us, nor indeed to delight
us at all, except as appropriate imagery, though used
for another object, necessarily imparts pleasure. For
this reason illustrations are selected always with reference to their force rather than their beauty, and
are very generally marked more by their homely
propriety than by their grace and elegance. For the
same reason, wherever it is possible, they are thrown
into the brief form of a metaphor; and here Aristotle,
with his usual sagacity, observes that the metaphor
is the only trope in which the orator may freely
indulge. Everything marks the man intent upon
serious business, whose sole anxiety is to convey his
meaning with as much precision and energy as possible to the minds of his auditors. But with the poet,
whose very object is to delight us, or even with the
prose-writer, in those species of prose which have the
same object, the case is widely different. He may
employ two or more images, if they are but appropriate and elegant, where the orator would employ
but one, and that perhaps the simplest and homeliest;
he may throw in an epithet merely to suggest some
picturesque circumstance, or to give greater minuteness and vivacity to description; he may sometimes
indulge in a more flowing and graceful expression
than the orator would venture upon; that is, whenever harmony will better answer his object than
energy. What does it matter to him who is walking
for walking's sake how long he lingers amid the
beautiful, or how often he pauses to drink in at leisure
the melody and the fragrance of nature? But the
man who is pressing on to his journey's end cannot
afford time for such luxurious loitering. The utmost

he can do is to snatch here and there a homely
floweret from the dusty hedge-row, and eagerly pursue his way.  So delicate is the perception attained
by a highly cultivated taste, of the proprieties of all
grave and earnest composition, that it not only feels
at enmity with the meretricious or viciously ornate,
but immediately perceives that the greatest beauties
of certain species of prose composition would become
little better than downright bombast if transplanted
into any composition the object of which was serious.
We may illustrate this by referring to a passage of
acknowledged beauty, the description, in the "Anti-
quary," of the sunset preceding the storm there so
grandly delineated: "The sun was now resting his
huge disc upon the edge of the level ocean, and gilded
the accumulation of towering clouds through which
he had traveled the livelong day, and which now
assembled on all sides, like misfortunes and disasters
around a sinking empire and falling monarch.  Still,
however, his dying splendor gave a somber magnificence to the massive congregation of vapors, forming
out of their unsubstantial gloom the show of pyramids
and towers, some touched with gold, some with pur-
ple, some with a hue of deep and dark red.  The
distant sea, stretched beneath this varied and gorgeous
canopy, lay almost portentously still, reflecting back
the dazzling and level beams of the descending luminary and the splendid coloring of the clouds amid
which he was setting."  No one in reading this passage can help admiring its graphic beauty.  The
numerous epithets, considering the purpose for which
they are employed—that of detaining the mind upon
every picturesque circumstance and giving vividness
and fidelity to the whole picture—appear no more

frequent than they ought to be. But suppose some naval historian, who has occasion to narrate the movements of two hostile fleets, (separated on the eve of battle by a storm,) should suddenly pause to introduce a similar description; would not the effect be so ridiculous that no one could read to the end of the passage without bursting into laughter?

It is against such a style that the young preacher, especially if he has or thinks he has a brilliant imagination, is called to be jealously on his guard; and the more so as the very themes on which he is often called to speak really require a certain fullness of description to bring them with sufficient fidelity and vividness before the mind of the hearer. But let him beware how he throws in epithets and employs images merely because he thinks them beautiful or picturesque. As regards real impression, there is no style which has so little practical effect, even when there is real genius in it. In general that style is characterized by anything but genius. There are some examples of it, however, to which this remark would not apply; it certainly would not to some of the sermons of Jeremy Taylor. That this style is often extravagantly admired is quite true; nay, even the downright florid is not without its admirers; but it is not the less ineffective for all that. This very admiration, as it is too often the subtle motive which has beguiled the speaker into such a vicious mode of treating his subject, so it at once affords a solution of the seeming paradox, for it shows that the minds of the auditors are fixed rather upon the man than upon the subject, less upon the truths inculcated than upon the genius which has embellished them. The speaker has been ambitious to attract the eye to himself and his doings, and it must be admitted that he too often succeeds; but it is at the expense of what is his *avowed*, and ought to be his *real* object. If we cannot endure this style in the public speaker, even where there is intrinsic beauty in it, simply because we do not think it natural that a man in earnest should indulge in all this wanton dalliance with imagination, how much more repulsive is that far more frequent style which is but a mockery of it, in which there is a constant *effort* to be fine; where there is not only excess of ornament, but all of a bad kind! The former style may be natural to the *man*, as in the case of Jeremy Taylor, however unnatural in relation to the subject and the occasion; the latter is alike unnatural in relation to both.

As the severe style for which we contend is best illustrated by examples, we shall mention two or three of those who have strikingly exemplified it. And as we are speaking simply of style, the authors to whom we shall refer are selected without relation to the systems of doctrine which they preached, and without implying either approbation or censure in that point of view. If the whole of those who have illustrated the principles here expounded were given, the catalogue would not be very long. It is true that this style is more frequently cultivated than it was; and if it were not invidious to refer to living preachers, we might mention not a few, both in the Establishment and out of it, who have attained it in a very high degree; some few in whom it is found nearly in perfection. But if we search the printed literature of the pulpit, it is not one sermon in a thousand that possesses any traces of it. The style is often that of stately or elegant disquisition, often of loose and florid declamation, but rarely indeed do we recognize the qualities of what Aristotle has happily and aptly called the "agonistical" or "wrestling" style; that style by which a speaker *earnestly strives* to make a *present* audience see and feel what he wishes them to see and feel. A large portion of our sermons differ not at all in style from that of a theological treatise or a philosophical essay; and they may be read by the individual in the closet without the slightest suspicion, were it not for the assurance on the title-page, that they were discourses delivered to a public audience. We would fain believe that the printed sermons of many of our preachers have in this respect done injustice to their ordinary discourses, and that they have been greatly altered previous to publication. In one case, and that a striking one, we know that this belief is well founded. We allude to perhaps the greatest of modern English preachers, the late Robert Hall. The few discourses which he so elaborately prepared for the press are full of exquisite thoughts, expressed in most exquisite language; but the style is almost everywhere that of disquisition, and in no sensible degree different from what he has adopted in his "Apology for the Freedom of the Press," or his work on "Terms of Communion." Now it is well known that his ordinary discourses were distinguished by a much higher degree of those qualities of style for which we have been so earnestly contending; and there can be little difficulty in affirming that, *in this one point of view,* many of the sermons which were imperfectly taken down in shorthand from his own lips, are superior to the most polished of those compositions which he slowly elaborated for the press.

But though it is difficult to point out many specimens of the style in question, such specimens are to
be found.  Of all the English preachers, probably
those who have been most strongly marked by the
peculiarities of the true genius for public speaking, are
Latimer, South, and Baxter;  and, notwithstanding
some defects, and those not inconsiderable, they are
also probably the preachers in whom specimens of
the style we are speaking of will be found the most
frequent and perfect.

The first of these certainly possessed talents for the
most effective eloquence in a high degree.  Indeed,
it may be said of many of the preachers of the Reformation, that, though their uncouthness, quaintness,
ridiculous or trivial allusions, wearisome tautologies
and digressions, incessant violations of taste and dis-
regard of method, render it difficult to read them,
they are in many important points very superior to
the more erudite and profound preachers of the next
century.  The subjects they selected were such as
more generally interested the common mind.  These
subjects are briefly touched and rapidly varied.
Though the structure of the sentence is often most
uncouth, (as might be expected from the state of the
language,) the diction is more idiomatic and purely
English;  while the general manner is decidedly more
that of downright earnestness, more direct and pungent.  This effect is in a great measure to be attributed to the circumstances in which they were placed.
In that great controversy to which they consecrated
their lives, they appealed to the *people*, and were
naturally led both to adapt their subjects to the popular mind, and to express themselves in the popular language.  The preachers of the next century

were men who lived in seclusion, far from common
life, buried among books, and incessantly reading
and often writing in a foreign tongue. To all this it
is owing that their subjects and their style are too
often as little adapted to produce popular impression
as those of Thomas Aquinas himself.

Of all the English preachers, South seems to us to
furnish, in point of *style*, the truest specimens of the
most effective species of pulpit eloquence. We are
speaking, it must be remembered, simply of his style;
we offer no opinion on the degree of truth or error
in the system of doctrines he embraced, and for his
unchristian bitterness and often unseemly wit would
be the last to offer any apology. But his robust intellect, his shrewd common sense, his vehement feelings, and a fancy always more distinguished by force
than by elegance, admirably qualified him for a
powerful public speaker. His style is accordingly
marked by all the characteristics which might naturally be expected from the possession of such qualities. It is everywhere direct, condensed, pungent.
His sermons are well worthy of frequent and diligent
perusal by every young preacher. He has himself
taught, both by precept and example, the chief peculiarities of that style for which we are pleading in
a discourse on Luke xxi, 15: "For I will give you a
mouth and wisdom, which all your adversaries shall
not be able to gainsay or resist." In one passage of
this sermon he takes occasion to expose the folly of
that florid declamation to which his manly intellect
and taste were so little likely to extend indulgence. In
doing this he introduces some brief specimens of the
style which he condemns. Though he mentions no
names, and though we might be unable to refer the

expressions to any particular author, any one might be sure, from the expressions themselves, that he intended his admonitions for the special benefit of his illustrious cotemporary, Jeremy Taylor. More bold than courteous, he has been at no pains to *invent* expressions for his purpose, but has actually selected them out of Taylor's own writings. There is certainly some malice in the passage; but it is itself so impressive an example of the style he is recommending, that we cannot refrain from extracting it: "'I speak the words of soberness,' said St. Paul, and I preach the Gospel not with the 'enticing words of man's wisdom.' This was the way of the apostle's discoursing of things sacred. Nothing here 'of the fringes of the north star;' nothing 'of nature's becoming unnatural;' nothing of the 'down of angels' wings, or the beautiful locks of cherubim;' no starched similitudes introduced with a 'Thus have I seen a cloud rolling in its airy mansion,' and the like. No; these were sublimities above the rise of the apostolic spirit. For the apostles, poor mortals, were content to take lower steps, and to tell the world in plain terms, that he who believed should be saved, and that he who believed not should be damned. And this was the dialect which pierced the conscience, and made the hearers cry out, Men and brethren, what shall we do? It tickled not the ear, but sunk into the heart; and when men came from such sermons they never commended the preacher for his taking voice or gesture; for the fineness of such a simile, or the quaintness of such a sentence; but they spoke like men conquered with the overpowering force and evidence of the most concerning truths, much in the words of the two disciples going to Emmaus: *Did not our hearts burn within us while he opened to us the Scriptures?*

"In a word, the apostles' preaching was therefore mighty and successful, because plain, natural, and familiar, and by no means above the capacity of their hearers; nothing being more preposterous than for those who were professedly aiming at men's hearts to miss the mark by shooting over their heads."*

We are tempted to give another short extract from this great preacher; we might select some which would still better illustrate our present subject, but they would be too long. The following is from his sermon entitled "Good Inclinations no Excuse for Bad Actions:" "The third instance, in which men use to plead the will instead of the deed, shall be on duties of cost and expense. Let a business of expensive charity be proposed; and then, as I showed before that in matters of labor the lazy person could find no hands wherewith to work, so neither in this case can the religious miser find any hand wherewith to give. It is wonderful to consider how a command or call to be liberal, either upon a civil or religious account, all of a sudden impoverishes the rich, breaks the merchant, shuts up every private man's exchequer, and makes those men in a minute have nothing at all to give, who, at the very same instant, want nothing to spend. So that instead of relieving the poor, such a command strangely increases their number, and transforms rich men into beggars presently. For, let the danger of their prince and country knock at their purses, and call upon them to contribute against a public enemy or calamity, then immediately they have nothing, and their

* South's "Sermons," vol. iv, pp. 152, 153.

riches (as Solomon expresses it) never fail to make themselves wings and to fly away."*

Of the preachers of the seventeenth century, Baxter possessed as largely as any those endowments which are essential to the best kind of popular eloquence. He presents the same combination of vigorous intellect and vehement feeling which distinguished South; but he conjoined with these a devotion far more pure and ethereal, and a benevolence most ardent and sincere. It is a pity that the slovenly manner in which he threw off his works, and which was too commonly the fault of the age in which he lived, has deformed so large a portion of them by repetitions and redundances. Continuous excellence is not to be looked for, indeed, in any of the writers of that period. There are single passages of great power occurring here and there, but imbedded in a mass of deformities—gems of marvelous value and splendor incrusted in their native earth. Numerous as Baxter's defects in point of style are, he often presents us with passages which are genuine examples of the most effective pulpit eloquence, and, if our space would permit, we should be glad to insert some of them. Baxter was almost equally distinguished by those talents which go to form a great public speaker, (hence his constant desire to make a direct and practical use of all his knowledge,) and by that excursiveness and subtilty of intellect which impels to a thorough investigation of every subject, however worthless. It is not a little ludicrous sometimes to see these two propensities of his intellect struggling for the mastery. At one time he forms a magnanimous resolution to forego speculations which are

* South's "Sermons," vol. i, pp. 278, 279.

curiously useless, and the next is found deep in the discussion of them. Thus, in his "Dying Thoughts," after telling us of the futility of the greater part of those questions which relate to the *modes* of existence in a future world, he proceeds very deliberately to expend about threescore pages in the examination of some of them!

Even in Jeremy Taylor, the exuberance of whose imagination too often betrayed him into puerilities and extravagances which are utterly inconsistent with true eloquence, and whose cumbrous erudition perpetually suggested allusions and phraseology equally inconsistent with it, passages which in a considerable degree illustrate the style in question are not seldom to be found. Take the following from his sermon entitled, "Christ's Advent to Judgment:" "And because very many sins are sins of society and confederation, it is a hard and a weighty consideration what shall become of any one of us who have tempted our brother or sister to sin and death; for though God hath spared our life, and they are dead, and their debt-books are sealed up till the day of account, yet the mischief of our sin has gone before us, and it is like a murder, but more execrable; the soul is dead in trespasses and sins, and sealed up to an eternal sorrow; and thou shalt see at doomsday what damnable uncharitableness thou hast done. That soul that cries to those rocks to cover her, if it had not been for thy perpetual temptations, might have followed the Lamb in a white robe; and that poor man that is clothed with shame and flames of fire, would have shined in glory, but that thou didst force him to be partner of thy baseness. And who shall pay for this loss? a soul is lost by thy means;

14

thou hast defeated the holy purposes of the Lord's bitter passion by thy impurities; and what shall happen to thee by whom thy brother dies eternally?"

Of recent writers there is none with whom we are acquainted who, in point of diction, so well deserves to be a model as the late Augustus William Hare, to whom reference has been already made. We by no means assert that (as was the case with Latimer, South, or Baxter) the general structure of his intellect was that which plainly predestines a man to be a great public speaker. Of many of the qualifications of ,one' he was certainly possessed; and it is equally certain that his early death, and the humble sphere to which his talents were restricted, render it impossible to say what he might have become. He possessed in an eminent degree the art of making difficult things plain; of setting obvious truths in novel lights; of illustrating them by familiar images; and of expressing them in a style habitually animated, and now and then singularly vivacious. His sermons to a " Country Congregation" will probably disappoint, by their very simplicity, the highly cultivated and intelligent, for whom, indeed, they were never intended; although we cannot conceal our opinion that the extreme simplicity of the language would often deceive even such readers as to the value and importance of the thoughts it expresses. But for an illiterate audience, an audience of rustics, they appear to us, in point of *diction*, perfect models of what discourses ought to be.

Their author was a man of powerful intellect, and of the most varied accomplishments, and affords a striking example of the success with which high endowments may be made subservient to a very humble object whenever a man is honestly bent upon so employing them. His great knowledge, instead of being employed for ostentation's sake, only taught him more precisely what was to be done, and hów he ought to set about it. To the most extensive acquaintance with ancient and modern literature, he added no inconsiderable knowledge of Anglo-Saxon, and consequently possessed (what no public speaker should be without) an acquaintance with the capabilities and resources of his mother tongue, with the vocabulary and idioms of the *people*. When he left Cambridge to undertake the charge of a congregation in a remote rural district, he resolved so to express himself that all should understand him; and his eminent success shows what may be done by one who forms a definite notion of the style he ought to adopt, and deliberately bends his best energies to attain it. The above-mentioned sermons to a "Country Congregation," we consider a greater triumph of his genius than all the splendid acquisitions he had made; and if Dr. Johnson's sentiment be true, that a "voluntary descent from the dignity of science is perhaps the hardest lesson that humility can teach," the triumph of his humility was still greater than that of his genius.

We are well aware of the many difficulties which beset the man who honestly resolves to speak only in the style we have recommended; difficulties sometimes arising from the intellectual pursuits to which he has been necessarily addicted; sometimes from the peculiarity of his own mental character. Nursed in the lap of learning, and familiar with the language of science and literature; necessitated in the very course of those preparatory studies which form an essential part of his professional education, to read much in foreign tongues, and to prosecute profound or abstruse inquiries, he will be apt, insensibly, to select subjects, or adopt a style utterly inconsistent with pulpit eloquence. He may still more frequently be betrayed into such conduct by affectation and vanity. The very peculiarities of his own mental constitution may expose him more fatally to the danger, and require continual efforts to counteract them. If he be a philosopher he will be tempted to indulge too much in abstruse speculation, or to treat those subjects on which he may rightfully expatiate in a *philosophic manner*—in language too abstract and remote from common life. If he have a brilliant imagination he will often be tempted to employ it inopportunely or to excess, and will find it hard to restrain it within the moderate limits in which alone it can be useful. In order to counteract the accidental evils arising from the necessary prosecution of various branches of study, which, in relation to public speaking, may injuriously affect the habits of thought or of expression, it is proper that every one who is destined for such engagements should cultivate acquaintance with the most idiomatic writers, understand the genius and resources of his own language, the modes of thought and expression prevalent among the common people, and, above all, be diligent in the perusal of the best models of that severe and manly eloquence of which we have said so much. The success of Mr. Hare may serve to show how much may be done by honesty and diligence. Nor can it fail to encourage the young preacher to know that if he gets but a clear idea of the task which he has to perform, and honestly resolves to perform it, there is not one of those things which we have mentioned as possible impediments that may not be made to facilitate his object. All that is requisite is a determination, that, as he has a practical object in view, everything shall be strictly subordinated to it. Philosophy, for example, may be made useful ; but it must be principally by teaching him to understand the mechanism and movements of that mind on which he is to operate. The audience must not perceive or suspect that the speaker is following the suggestions of any such invisible guide ; or, if it be employed directly at all, it still must be unsuspected by the common people to be philosophy : it must be employed merely to insure greater accuracy and comprehensiveness in the views propounded ; and to determine the circumspect limits within which every subject must be treated ; that is, so far, and so far only, as it may be made conducive to a practical end. In a word, it must be philosophy without the forms of it ; philosophy in its working dress ; philosophy that has learned one of its hardest lessons, that it is often the truest philosophy not to appear such. In like manner, the speaker may have a knowledge of logic ; but it must be seen only in the greater perspicuity of his statements, and the greater closeness of his reasoning. He must never trouble the people with the mysteries of mood and figure, or bewilder them with a single unintelligible technicality. He may possess a knowledge of rhetoric ; but he is not to confound his audience with the distinctions of trope and metaphor, with the uses of synecdoches or metonymies, with those principles of the human mind which give them energy, or the rules by which, at the very time he is speaking, he is regulating his own taste in the employment of them. Here is a

" hard lesson! who can hear it?"  To be employing
profound and extensive knowledge without suffering
those you address to know any thing of the matter!
To be contented to produce results which seem cheap
and common, without once lifting the curtain to bewilder and dazzle the multitude with a sight of the
imposing and complicated machinery which is re-
volving behind it!

It is happily unnecessary to caution the modern
preacher against many of the abuses which pervade
our older pulpit literature, especially that of the
seventeenth century; a period, notwithstanding, in
which many of our most eminent preachers flourished.
We allude more particularly to the abuse of *learning*.
Most of the sermons of that age are full of quotations,
absolutely unintelligible to the common people.
Numberless passages of Jeremy Taylor, in particular,
are little better than a curious tessellation of English, Greek, and Latin.  The people, however strange
the fact may appear, came at last not merely to like
these displays, but to be sometimes discontented if
they did not hear a great deal which they could not
understand!  It is recorded of the profoundly learned
Pococke, that when he successfully studied to divest
his pulpit style of the traces of erudition, and, with
a magnanimity and good sense very unusual in that
age, made it a point to say nothing but what the people could understand, his congregation absolutely
despised his simplicity, and said that " Master Pococke, though a very good man, *was no Latiner.*"
And South tells us, "that the grossest, the most
ignorant and illiterate country people, were of all
men the fondest of high-flown metaphors and allego-
ries, *attended and set off with scraps of Greek and*

*Latin,* though not able even to read so much of the latter as might save their necks upon occasion."

Equally unnecessary is it to caution the preacher against those complicated divisions and subdivisions into which our forefathers thought proper to chop up their discourses, to the entire frustration of the very object they had in view, and the utter discomfiture of the most retentive memory. In one discourse of Bishop Hall's, we have counted no less than eighty heads, principal and subordinate; in one of Baxter's, not less than one hundred and twenty, besides a formidable array of "improvements." But the most amusing examples of this abuse are those recorded in Robinson's notes to Claude's Essay " On the Composition of a Sermon :" " But allowing the necessity of a *natural* and easy division, it does by no means follow that these are to multiply into whole armies. A hundred years ago most sermons had thirty, forty, fifty, or sixty particulars. There is a sermon of Mr. Lye's on 1 Cor. vi, 17, *the terms of which,* says he, *I shall endeavor, by God's assistance, clearly to explain.* This he does in thirty particulars, *for the fixing of it on a right basis,* and then adds fifty-six more to *explain* the subject, in all eighty-six. And what makes it the more astonishing is his introduction to all these, which is this: Having thus *beaten up and leveled* our way to the text, I shall not stand *to shred the words into any unnecessary* parts, but shall *extract* out of them such *an observation* as I conceive *strikes a full eighth* to the mind of the Spirit of God.

" If Mr. Lye is too prolific, what shall we say to Mr. Drake, whose sermon has (if I reckon rightly) above a hundred and seventy parts, besides queries and solutions; and yet the good man says he *passed sundry useful points, pitching only on that which comprehended the marrow and substance."*

Equally superfluous would it be to caution the modern preacher against the quaintnesses, the quirks and quibbles, the fantastic imagery, the alliterations, and other curious devices of composition in which many of our older writers so much delighted. In truth, the tendency is all the other way. In the laudable effort to avoid the *vulgar*, there is not un-frequently a danger of sinking down into tame pro-priety. Our old writers, in their free and reckless resort to every mode of stimulating attention, were often, it is true, betrayed into gross violations of taste; but the very same audacity of genius also often pro-duced great felicities, both of imagery and diction. The too frequent characteristic of modern discourses is what the Germans would denominate "Wasserig-keit," "waterishness:" there is little to *strike* either the one way or the other; all is blameless common-place, accurate insipidity.

We now proceed, conformably with the intention mentioned at the commencement of this essay, to offer a few remarks on what we conceive to be the two chief causes of the mediocrity of the generality of sermons. One of them in our opinion is, that too little time is given to the preparation of public dis-courses. Far be it from us to involve in indiscrimi-nate censure the thousands of preachers whom we have never heard, or to pronounce absolutely on the indolence or the industry even of those to whom we have listened. We only think that the failing in question is not a very partial one, from the internal evidence supplied by the sermons of no inconsiderable

number of the different preachers whom we have
heard. We are also willing to admit, that the duties
of the pulpit are not the only duties which claim the
attention of the Christian minister; and that his other
engagements, in an age like this, are neither few nor
small. But we must also contend, that as his principal office is that of public instructor, the duties of
that office must ever be his chief business; and that,
to whatever extent he may undertake other engagements, he should sacredly reserve sufficient time for
the due discharge of his proper functions. The construction of a discourse which shall be adapted in
matter, arrangement, and style, to produce a strong
impression upon a popular audience, seems a task
which requires much more time and labor than, as
we conceive, are generally bestowed upon it. But
we are convinced that this task, difficult as it is,
might be performed much better than it generally is.
We are well aware, of course, that there must always
be an immense interval between the productions of a
man of genius and those of a man who has no genius
at all, between those of a fertile intellect and those
of a barren one; but there are few men possessed of
that measure of vigor and elasticity of mind, without
which they have no business out of the rank of
handicraftsmen, who could not, with diligence, compose a discourse which might be generally useful and
interesting, at least much more so than discourses
are often found to be. Prolonged study and meditation are never without their reward. Either some
new materials are collected, or they strike by a new
arrangement, or some new truth is elicited, or some
old truth is exhibited under a new aspect, or illustrated in a manner which gives it an importance never

felt before, and extends its influence from the under-standing to the imagination, and thence to the affec-tions.    Such sources of interest as these are sure to reveal themselves, sooner or later, to the mind that honestly and diligently sets itself to seek them with the conviction that they are to be had, and that they must be obtained.*

* How much force is imparted to the most familiar and obvious truths in the following passages, merely by the novel mode of exhibit-ing them?

" 'Come unto me, all ye that are weary and heavy laden, and I will give you rest.'  If an inhabitant of some distant part of the uni-verse, some angel who had never visited the earth, had been told that there was a world in which such an invitation had been neglected and despised, they would surely say: The inhabitants of that world must be a very happy people; there can be few among them that 'labor and are heavy laden.'  No doubt they must be strangers to poverty, sorrow, and misfortune; the pestilence cannot come nigh their dwell-ing, neither does death ever knock at their doors, and of course they must be unconnected with sin, and all the miseries that are its ever-lasting attendants."— *Wolfe's Remains.*

"Though the arguments which the Christian hath for his faith may not be the strongest, yet a tree but weakly rooted often brings forth good fruit; and if it doth, will never be hewn down and cast into the fire."—*Secker's Sermons*, vol. i, p. 20.

The following is a passage from Hare's sermon on the text, "And forgive us our sins; for we also forgive every one who is indebted to us:"

"Conceive a revengeful, unforgiving man repeating this prayer, which you all, I hope, repeat daily.  Conceive a man with a heart full of wrath against his neighbor, with a memory which treasures up the little wrongs, and insults, and provocations he fancies himself to have received from that neighbor.  Conceive such a man praying to God Most High to forgive him his trespasses as he forgives the man who has trespassed against him.  What, in the mouth of such a man, do these words mean?  They mean—but, that you may more fully under-stand their meaning, I will turn them into a prayer, which we will call the prayer of the unforgiving man: 'O God, I have sinned against thee many times from my youth up until now.  I have often been for-getful of thy goodness; I have not daily thanked thee for thy mercies;

Without intending to implicate Christian ministers generally in the charge now made, it will not be denied that the internal evidence of many a discourse justifies us in saying that it is widely applicable. In the first place, it can hardly be affirmed that those give time enough to their sermons who give none at all; who, if they are ever eloquent, are eloquent at other people's expense; who are contented to be wholesale plagiarists, and to shine Sunday after Sunday in borrowed finery,

> "And cheat the eyes
> Of gallery critics with a thousand arts."

We well know all the arguments by which this combination of vanity and indolence usually supports itself.

I have neglected thy service; I have broken thy laws; I have done many things utterly wrong against thee. All this I know, and besides this, doubtless, I have committed many secret sins which, in my blindness, I have failed to notice. Such is my guiltiness, O Lord, in thy sight. Deal with me, I beseech thee, even as I deal with my neighbor. He has not offended me one tenth, one hundredth part as much as I have offended thee; but he has offended me very grievously, and I cannot forgive him. Deal with me, I beseech thee, O Lord, as I deal with him. He has been very ungrateful to me, though not a tenth, not a hundredth part as ungrateful as I have been to thee; yet I cannot overlook such base and shameful ingratitude. Deal with me, I beseech thee, O Lord, as I deal with him. I remember and treasure up every little trifle which shows how ill he has behaved to me. Deal with me, I beseech thee, O Lord, as I deal with him. I am determined to take the very first opportunity of doing him an ill turn. Deal with me, I beseech thee, O Lord, as I deal with him.' Can anything be more shocking and horrible than such a prayer? Is not the very sound of it enough to make one's blood run cold? Yet this is just the prayer which the unforgiving man offers up every time he repeats the Lord's prayer; for he prays to God to forgive him in the same manner in which he forgives his neighbor. But he does not forgive his neighbor, so he prays to God not to forgive him. God grant that his prayer may not be heard, for he is praying a curse on his own head!"—*Hare's Sermons*, vol. ii, pp. 207–299.

The principal is, that a man of little talent can buy or borrow a much better sermon than he can make. We freely acknowledge it, and should not make so great an objection to the practice if the preacher would avow the fact. This we think common honesty requires; but if it be felt, as every one must feel, that such an avowal would put the speaker to shame, or, if *he* were past that, would make his audience ashamed for him, it is a tacit admission of the impropriety of the practice.

But we think the argument altogether fallacious. Supposing the preacher not to be destitute of that measure of talent without which he has no business to assume the office of a public instructor at all, we deny *in toto* that a borrowed discourse, whatever its merit, can be so impressive as one, even though intrinsically inferior, which has been made his own by conscientious study. The latter is the fruit of diligent effort; prolonged meditation will insure familiarity with the subject, and both together insure, what nothing else can, adequate *emotion*. It will, accordingly, be delivered with an earnestness and glow of natural feeling of which the reading of a borrowed discourse is altogether destitute. The treasures of theological literature, whatever is valuable in other men's thoughts, are freely open to the preacher; but he should ever seek to make them his own by new combinations, arrangement, and expression. The matter he borrows should be made his by chemical affinities with his own thoughts, not by mere mechanical appropriation.

As to those discourses which are commonly called extemporaneous, we mean extemporaneous with regard to the *expression*, for the bulk of the thoughts ought never to be extemporaneous, it is our firm belief that no inconsiderable portion to which the Christian communities of this country are treated are hastily huddled up on the evening preceding their delivery. But we believe that not a few are quite as extemporaneous in relation to the *thought*, as they are in relation to the expression. When this is the case, the fact usually proclaims itself with sufficient clearness; the painful process by which the mind is endeavoring to manufacture the material as the discourse proceeds is abundantly visible both in face and manner. The frequent hesitation, the curiously bewildered look, the endless repetitions of commonplace, the wire-drawing of obvious truths, all unequivocally proclaim the speaker's unenviable confusion and embarrassment, his utter bankruptcy of intellect. The wonder is, that any man who has felt the misery of such an exhibition, or subjected his congregation to the pain of witnessing it, should ever again allow himself to be found in so painful a situation.

Even of discourses where the thoughts are not properly extemporaneous, (and if the subject has been duly pondered, the matter properly distributed, and the principal illustrations selected, we cannot but think this the most effective, as it is certainly the most natural mode of preaching,) very few, comparatively speaking, are prepared with the requisite degree of deliberation and care. Owing to the hasty manner in which they are *got up*, the subjects are rarely sufficiently digested; the several parts of the discourse do not present themselves to the mind with sufficient distinctness; and, what is as bad, the great task of selection is not adequately performed after the materials have been got together. Knowing that he must have a sufficient mass of matter of some kind or other, conscious that there is not much time to collect it, and grievously fearing lest he should not have enough, the preacher takes everything that offers, relevant or irrelevant, simply because it cannot be dispensed with. The process too often adopted in the manufacture of these extemporaneous discourses we take to be this. A text is selected; critics and commentators hastily consulted; and as it is felt that everything must be used, all that is collected *about* the text, whether relevant or not, whether calculated to instruct and edify, or quite unlikely to do either the one or the other, goes into the notes, simply because it cannot be spared. It is owing to this that we have sometimes heard preachers occupy a quarter of an hour, or twenty minutes, (exhausting the patience and dissipating the attention of their flocks,) in disposing of some whimsical, far-fetched, and palpably untrue interpretation of the text, benevolently assuring them, at the same time, that such interpretations are utterly worthless, never dreamt of except by the solitary author who originated them, and perfectly inconsistent with common sense!

There are not a few fallacies by which some preachers impose upon themselves the belief that less preparation is necessary than is really indispensable. They think that the topics on which they have to insist are so familiar and obvious that it is easy to discourse about them to any extent. It is clear that this argument *ought* to tell just the other way; it is precisely because the topics on which the Christian minister has to expatiate are so familiar and obvious that the more diligence is requisite to set them in new lights; to devise new modes of illustration, and to secure the requisite variety by changing the form where we cannot change the substance. In this way only can exhausted attention be stimulated and renewed; but in this way it can. As the instances recently adduced will show, even the most obvious and threadbare truths may be made striking and forcible by a new setting.

Sometimes men will tell us that they prefer a *natural* and *artless* eloquence, and that very diligent preparation is inconsistent with such qualities. We veribly believe that this fallacy, though it lurks under an almost transparent ambiguity, is of most prejudicial consequence. Nature and art, so far from being always opposed, are often the very same thing. Thus, to adduce a familiar example, and closely related to the present subject, it is *natural* for a man who feels that he has not given adequate expression to a thought, though he may have used the first words suggested, to attempt it again and again. He, each time, approximates nearer to the mark, and at length desists, satisfied either that he has done what he wishes, or that he cannot perfectly do it, as the case may be. A writer, with this end, is continually transposing clauses, reconstructing sentences, striking out one word and putting in another. All this may be said to be *art*, or the deliberate application of means to ends; but is it art inconsistent with nature? It is just such art as this that we ask of the preacher, and no other; simply that he shall take diligent heed to do what he has to do as well as he can. Let him depend upon it that no such *art* as this will ever make him appear the less natural.

A similar fallacy lurks under the unmeaning

praises which are often bestowed upon a *simple* style of address. We love a true simplicity as much as any of its eulogists can do; but we should probably differ about the meaning of the word. While some men talk as if to speak naturally were to speak like a natural, others talk as if to speak with simplicity meant to speak like a simpleton. True simplicity does not consist in what is trite, bald, or commonplace. So far as regards the thought it means, not what is already obvious to every body, but what, though not obvious, is immediately recognized, as soon as propounded, to be true and striking. As it regards the expression it means, that thoughts worth hearing are expressed in language that every one can understand. In the first point of view it is opposed to what is abstruse; in the second to what is obscure. It is not what some men take it to mean, threadbare, commonplace, expressed in insipid language. It can be owing only to a fallacy of this kind that we so often hear discourses, consisting of little else than meager truisms, expanded and diluted till every mortal ear aches that listens. We have heard preachers commence with the tritest of truths, "all men are mortal," and proceed to illustrate it with as much prolixity as though they were announcing it as a new proposition to a company of immortals in some distant planet, skeptical as to the reality of a fact so portentous, and so unauthenticated by their own experience.

True simplicity is the last and most excellent grace which can belong to a speaker, and is certainly not to be attained without much effort. Those who have attentively read the present article will not suspect us of demanding more deliberate preparation on the

part of the preacher, that he may offer what is pro
found, recondite, or abstruse; but that he may say only
what he ought to say, and that what he does say may
be better said. When the topics are such only as
ought to be insisted on, and the language such as is
readily understood, the preacher may depend upon
it that no pains he may take will be lost; that his
audience, however homely, will be sure to appreciate
them, and that the better a discourse is the better
they will like it.

We have stated as the other great cause of the
failure of preachers, that they are not sufficiently
instructed in the *principles* of pulpit eloquence. We
are far from contending that a systematic exposition
of the laws in conformity with which all effective
discourses to the people must be constructed, should
be made a part of *general* education, or that it ought
to be imparted even to him who is destined to be a
public speaker, till his general training, and that a
very ample one, is far advanced. But that such
knowledge shall be acquired by every one designed
for such an office, and that all universities and col-
leges should furnish the means of communicating it,
we have no manner of doubt. It is sometimes said,
indeed, that all systematic instruction of this sort
tends to spoil nature, prevent simplicity, and encourage vanity; in short, that it is sure to produce one or
other of the forms of spurious or artificial eloquence.
We ask: Does the objector mean any such system
as approves of such things, or one that condemns
them? If the former, we know of no such system;
if the latter, then he must defend the paradox that
such systems have, somehow or other, a tendency to
produce the very faults which they expose and

15

denounce, and to prevent the attainment of those
very excellences which they describe as the only ones
worth seeking! Now is it possible for any sane
mind to conceive that the ridicule which Campbell
and Whately, for example, pour upon such faults, can
foster in any youth a perverse passion for them? or
that the severity, simplicity, earnest, businesslike
style which these writers everywhere enjoin as essential to all effective eloquence should provoke any
man to the imitation of the opposite vices?   The
supposition is an absurdity.  So far as such writers
produce any effect at all, it must be to prevent the
follies which they so unsparingly condemn.  Those
who attribute vicious eloquence to sound criticism
have been guilty merely of the common blunder of
assigning effects to wrong causes; only it must be
confessed that in the present case they show singular
ingenuity in referring them to the only causes which
could not by possibility produce them.  The simple
truth is that the bent of the young mind is so strong
toward various forms of this spurious eloquence that
it resists the most powerful counteraction; and time
and experience alone will avail, and not always even
these, to give precepts their due weight and their
just practical influence.  To charge such effects upon
such causes is about as wise as it would be to say of
some spot which had been but partially cultivated,
and from which the weeds which nature had so
prodigally sown had not been completely eradicated,
"This comes of gardening and artificial culture!"

Youthful vanity and inexperience alone sufficiently
account for the greater part of the deviations from
propriety, simplicity, and common sense now adverted
to.  Those who laud nature in opposition to art are

too apt to forget that this very vanity forms a part
of it. It is natural for a youth, whether with or
without cultivation, to fall into these errors; and
all experience loudly proclaims that on such a
point nature alone is no safe guide. Who that has
arrived at maturity in intellect, taste, and feeling,
does not recollect how hard it was in early life to put
the extinguisher upon a flaunting metaphor or dazzling expression, to reject tinsel, however worthless,
if it did but glitter, and epithets, however superfluous, if they but sounded grand? How hard it was
to forget one's self and to become sincerely intent
upon the best, simplest, strongest, briefest mode of
communicating what we deemed important truth to
the minds of others! Surely then it is not a little
ridiculous, when so obvious a solution offers itself, to
charge the faults of young speakers upon the very
precepts which condemn them. It is sufficient to
vindicate the utility of such precepts if they tend only
in some measure to correct the errors they cannot
entirely suppress, and to abridge the duration of
follies which it is impossible wholly to prevent.

But it is further said that, somehow or other, *any*
such system of instruction does injury, by laying
upon the intellect a sort of constraint, and substituting
a stiff, mechanical movement for the flexibility and
freedom of nature.

The reply is, that if the system of instruction be
too minute, or if the pupil be told to employ it
mechanically, it may easily be conceived that such
effects will follow, but not otherwise. We plead for
no system of minute technical rules; still less for the
formal application of any system whatever. But to
imbue the mind with great general principles, leaving

them to operate imperceptibly upon the formation of habit, and to suggest, without distinct consciousness of their presence, the lesson which each occasion demands, is a very different thing, and is all we contend for. One would think, to hear some men talk, that it was proposed to instruct a youth to adjust beforehand the number of sentences of which each paragraph should consist, and the *lengths* into which the sentences should be cut; to determine how many should be perfect periods and how many should not; what average allowance of antitheses, interrogatives, and notes of admiration shall be given to each page; where he shall stick on a metonymy or a metaphor, and how many niches he shall reserve for gilded ornaments. Who is pleading for any such nonsense as this? All that is contended for is that no public speaker should be destitute of a clear perception of those principles of man's nature on which conviction and persuasion depend, and of those proprieties of style which ought to characterize all discourses which are designed to effect these objects. General as all this knowledge must be, we cannot help thinking that it would be most advantageous. One great good it would undoubtedly in many cases effect: it would prevent men from *setting out wrong*, or at least abridge the amount or duration of their errors. In other words, prevent the formation of vicious habits, or tend to correct them when formed. Nothing is more common than for a speaker to set out with false notions as to the style which effective public speaking requires, to suppose it something very remote from what is simple and natural. Still more are led into similar errors by their vanity. The young especially are apt to despise the true style for what are its chief excellences, its simplicity and severity. Let them once be taught its great superiority to every other, and they will at least be protected from involuntary errors, and be less likely to yield to the seductions of vanity. Such a knowledge would also (perhaps the most important benefit of all) involve a knowledge of the best models, and secure timely appreciation of them.

But it is frequently urged that, after all, the practical value of all the great lessons of criticism must be learned from experience, and that mere instruction can do little. Be it so. Is this any reason why that little should be withheld? Besides, is it nothing to put a youth in the right way? to abridge the lessons of experience? to facilitate the formation of good habits, and to prevent the growth of bad ones? to diminish the probabilities of failure, and to increase those of success? Is there any reason why we should suffer the young speaker to grope out his way by the use of the lead-line alone, when we could give him the aid of a chart and compass; or to find his way to truth at last by a series of painful blunders, when any part of the trouble or the shame might be spared him? Can any one doubt that a great speaker may be able to give a novice in the art many profitable hints, which would save him both much time and many errors, and make the lessons of experience not only a great deal shorter, but vastly less troublesome? If this be so, we cannot see how it should be affirmed that instructions founded on an accurate analysis of eloquence, and compiled and digested by critics like Campbell and Whately, will altogether fail of producing similar benefits.

Lastly, it is urged that such instructions are of very

little benefit, because, do what we will, we cannot *make* great speakers; that nature has the exclusive patent for the manufacture; that, like the true poet, the true orator is " born, not made," facts which we fully admit, but deny to be relevant. The argument contains a twofold fallacy. First, it is not true that even those to whom nature has imparted this heaven-born genius can do themselves justice without assiduous cultivation, or afford to dispense with early instruction. Certain it is, that none of them have ever thought it wise to venture upon such a display of independence. Secondly, if it were ever so true that such men could do without instruction, the cases are so few that they would in no wise affect the general question. The highest oratorical genius is of the very rarest occurrence; it is as rare as the epic or dramatic, if not more so, there being but two or three tolerably perfect specimens to be found in the whole cabinet of history. The great question is, how to improve to the utmost the talents of those who must be public speakers, but who yet have no pretensions to the inspiration of genius; on whom, in truth, no one ever suspects that the mantle either of Demosthenes or of Cicero has descended. Nor should it ever be forgotten, (for it powerfully confirms the correctness of the views now insisted upon,) that, though the constitution of mind which is necessary for the highest eloquence is very seldom to be met with, there is no faculty whatever which admits of such indefinite growth and development, or in which perseverance and diligence will do so much, as that of public speaking.

THE END.

# Harmony of Divine Dispensations.

Harmony of the Divine Dispensations. Being a Series of Discourses on Select Portions of Holy Scripture, designed to show the Spirituality, Efficacy, and Harmony of the Divine Revelations made to Mankind from the Beginning. With Notes, Critical, Historical, and Explanatory. By GEORGE SMITH, F. A. S., Member of the Royal Asiatic Society, of the Royal Society of Literature, Fellow of the Genealogical and Historical Society, etc., etc.

8vo., pp. 319. Sheep ............................................... $1 50
————— Half calf.................................... 2 00

This is a new work, being reprinted from the London edition to correspond with the "Patriarchal Age," "Hebrew People," and "Gentile Nations," by the same distinguished author. It will be sold in connection with the others, or separately. It is a profound work, and will have a large sale.

# Lady Huntingdon Portrayed.

Including Brief Sketches of some of her Friends and Co-laborers. By the Author of " The Missionary Teacher," " Sketches of Mission Life," etc.

Large 16mo., pp. 319. Muslin ............................ $0 75
————————————— Morocco ............................ 1 75

# Hibbard on the Psalms.

The Psalms Chronologically Arranged, with Historical Introductions, and a General Introduction to the whole Book. By F. G. HIBBARD.

8vo., pp. 589. Muslin.................................... $2 00
————————— Half Morocco................................ 2 50
————————— Morocco .................................... 5 00

This book occupies an important place in Biblical interpretation, and is a valuable contribution to Biblical literature.

# The Object of Life:

A Narrative Illustrating the Insufficiency of the World, and the Sufficiency of Christ. With four Illustrations.

Large 16mo., pp. 357. Price.................... $0 75
————————————— Morocco.................... 1 75

# The Living Way;

Or, Suggestions and Counsels concerning some of the Privileges and Duties of the Christian Life. By Rev. JOHN ATKINSON.

16mo., pp. 139. Price..... ....................... $0 40

# Compendium of Methodism.

A Compendium of Methodism: embracing the History and Pres
ent Condition of its various Branches in all Countries; with a
Defense of its Doctrinal, Governmental, and Prudential Pecu
liarities. By Rev. James Porter, D.D. Revised edition.

12mo., pp. 501. Price.................................... $1 00

This work has received universal favor. The facts that our bishops have put
it in the course of study for local preachers, and that it has been translated into
the German and Scandinavian languages, commend it to the confidence of all
Methodists. Its peculiar advantages are, 1. That it gives a connected history of
Methodism from the beginning in all countries, and in all its denominations.
2. That it shows our doctrinal agreements and disagreements with other sects.
3. That it exhibits the different systems of church government in the world, and
the relative merits of each. 4. That it explains and defends all our prudential
means of grace and other peculiarities as no other book does. It is a WHOLE
LIBRARY in one volume, and is a *labor*-saving as well as a *money*-saving production. Its importance to preachers and others is indicated by the following
testimonials:

It is, in fact, a digest of Methodism. The arrangement and execution of the
several parts are admirable. The style is a model of perspicuity, ease, and vigor;
and in point of condensation, the volume is literally crowded with important
matter. We have hardly seen as great compactness without confusion, or an
equal number of pages from which so few could be eliminated without detriment.
But what is far more important than the mode of composition is the spirit which
pervades the work. The author writes with that candid discrimination so essential to the proper discussion of the topics which he handles.—*Ed. of North. Adv.*

This work is a valuable acquisition to our Church literature. It embodies
much important information, arranged in a natural and convenient form, and
affords a good general outline of Methodism. It is a work of much merit. I do
cheerfully commend it, as a whole, to the favorable consideration of our friends
and the public generally.—T. Morris, *Bishop of M. E. Church.*

I like the book much. It will do good. Our people and friends ought to read
and study it thoroughly. It furnishes a satisfactory answer to the petty objections urged against the Methodists by a set of ecclesiastical croakers with which
we are everywhere beset. One gentleman, whom I let have a copy, after reading
it carefully, remarked, "It is the book needed; I would not take *twenty dollars*
for my copy if I could not obtain another."—Rev. Justin Spaulding.

I have just finished the reading of this book, and I wish to express my decided
approbation of it. *It should be a family book,* a Sunday-school book, and I would
add especially, *a text-book for all candidates for the ministry.*—J. T. Peck, D.D.

The work throughout is *not* a criticism on Methodist usages, but a statement
and defense of them. As such, we trust it will meet with the wide circulation it
deserves, both in and out of the Church.—*Methodist Quarterly Review.*

We have examined the book, and most cordially recommend our friends, one
and all, to procure it immediately. No Methodist can study it without profit,
and gratitude to the great Head of the Church for the wisdom imparted to those
who have been the instruments employed in constructing the rules and regula-
tions under which the operations of this most successful branch of the Church
are conducted.—*Editor of the Christian Guardian, Toronto.*

It is precisely the volume needed to instruct our people in the peculiarities of
our system. The *special* character of Methodism is here developed in such a
manner as to show that it is specially excellent, and worthy of *special* zeal and
*special* sacrifices. It is very systematically arranged, and therefore convenient
for reference on any given point. To the Methodist, especially the "official"
Methodist, this book is fitted to be a complete manual; and to all others who
would understand what Methodism precisely is, as a whole, or in any specific
respect, we commend Dr. Porter's work as an ACKNOWLEDGED AUTHORITY.—
A. Stevens, LL.D.

# Ministering Children.

A Story showing how even a Child may be as a Ministering Angel of Love to the Poor and Sorrowful.

Large 16mo., pp. 542. Price ............................. $0 90
————————————— Illustrated edition, gilt edges.... 1 25
————————————— Morocco, gilt..................... 2 00

This is one of the most moving narrations in the whole list of our publications. Its sale in England has reached FORTY THOUSAND copies. The illustrated edition contains more than a dozen superb cuts on plate paper.

# Life in the Itinerancy;

In its Relation to the Circuit and Station, and to the Minister's Home and Family.

12mo , pp. 335. Price ...................................... $1 00

# Life in the Laity;

Or, the History of a Station. By Rev. L. D. DAVIS, Author of " Life in the Itinerancy."

16mo., pp. 200. Price................................... $0 50

# Chart of Life.

By Rev. JAMES PORTER, D.D.

12mo., pp. 259. Price................................... $0 60

The design of this book is to indicate the dangers and securities connected with the voyage of life, all which are accurately and admirably described.

# Heroines of Methodism;

Or, Pen and Ink Sketches of the Mothers and Daughters of the Church. By Rev. GEORGE COLES.

12mo., pp. 336. Price................................... $0 90

# Heroes of Methodism.

Containing Sketches of Eminent Methodist Ministers, and Characteristic Anecdotes of their Personal History. By Rev. J. B. WAKELEY. With Portraits of Bishops Asbury, Coke, and M'Kendree.

12mo., pp. 470. Price................................... $1 00
————————— Morocco ................................... 2 00

Life-like and interesting sketches of early Methodist preachers, their toils, hardships, and achievements, interspersed with anecdotes lively and entertaining.

# Reasons for becoming a Methodist.

By Rev. I. SMITH, for some Years a Member of the Close-Communion Calvinist Baptist Church. Including a brief Account of the Author's Religious Experience up to the Time of his becoming a Methodist.

18mo. pp. 160. Price.................................... $0 30

This work was written by Rev. I. Smith, now a member of the New England Conference. It was printed in Boston a few years ago, and seventeen thousand copies have been sold. Knowing the work from its first issue, and believing it to be calculated to do great good, we have recently bought the plates, and shall soon bring out the nineteenth edition, with some improvements. Brother Smith was formerly a Calvinistic Close-Communion Baptist, but being placed in circumstances obliging him to consider the principles he professed to believe, he was led to renounce them. He subsequently joined the Methodists, and became a preacher. This book develops the reasons which influenced his action in the premises, and they are well stated. Preachers who are molested by Baptist influences, will find this work just the thing to circulate. We have put it upon our list to extend its usefulness, more than to make money out of it.

# The Pioneers of the West;

## Or, Life in the Woods. By W. P. STRICKLAND.

12mo., pp. 403. Price.................................... $1 00

This decidedly popular book, which sketches to the life the Pioneer Explorers, Settlers, Preachers, Hunters, Lawyers, Doctors, School Teachers, and Institutions of the West, is meeting with an extensive sale.

# The True Woman;

Or, Life and Happiness at Home and Abroad. By JESSE T. PECK, D.D., Author of "The Central Idea of Christianity."

| 12mo., pp. 400. | Price | $1 00 |
|---|---|---|
| | Gilt edges | 1 25 |
| | Gilt edges, beveled | 1 50 |
| | Morocco | 2 00 |

In this volume the author has illustrated his ideal of female character by a series of didactic precepts and familiar examples. His standard is not taken from the prevailing customs and opinions of society, but from the highest teachings of Christian ethics. In his remarks on the intellectual cultivation of woman, he condemns novel-reading in decided terms, regarding it as a "crime, murderous to the heart, the intellect, and the body;" while he as warmly recommends the perusal of literary periodicals, and insists on having access to at least one daily or weekly newspaper. The work is written with great earnestness and feeling, with an occasional exuberance of expression.—*N. Y. Tribune.*

# Stevens's History of Methodism.

The History of the Religious Movement of the Eighteenth Century, called Methodism, considered in its Different Denominational Forms, and its Relations to British and American Protestantism. By ABEL STEVENS, LL. D. Vols. I & II. From the Origin of Methodism to the Death of Wesley.

Large 12mo. Price per vol. ............................... $1 00

A charming work—full of thrilling facts, combined and stated in the most interesting manner. The work has been read and highly indorsed by the most distinguished authors. One says, "It is wonderfully readable;" and another, "I have been interested beyond measure." It will be a standard for all Methodists for all time to come, and will be read by thousands of Christians of other denominations.

It contains a new steel engraving of Rev. JOHN WESLEY, the best ever seen in this country.

The volumes which are to follow will be put up in the same style, so that those who get the whole will have uniform sets, though they buy but one volume at a time.

# Hymns and Tunes.

Hymns for the Use of the Methodist Episcopal Church. With Tunes for Congregational Worship.

8vo., pp. 368. Roan, (20 per cent. discount to the trade.)... $1 25
————— Morocco, marbled edges...................... 1 50
————————— extra gilt ........................ 2 00

This work embraces all the hymns in our standard Hymn Book, and no more. It contains also more than three hundred of the most popular old and new tunes in print, and is offered at a very low price for a book of its cost, in the hope that it may be generally adopted.

# Autobiography of Peter Cartwright.

## Edited by W. P. STRICKLAND.

12mo., pp. 525. Muslin...................................... $1 00

This is one of the most interesting autobiographies of the age. The sale of this remarkable book has averaged two thousand copies per month since its appearance. Thirty-two thousand have been printed, and still the orders come. It is useless to add anything by way of commendation. The people *will* have it, and we are prepared to supply the continued demand.

# What must I do to be Saved?

## By JESSE T. PECK, D.D.

18mo., pp. 192. Price............ ......................... $0 35

A new revival book, written by request, designed to awaken the sinner, guide the penitent to Christ, and establish the young convert.

# NEW BOOKS,

## PUBLISHED BY CARLTON AND PORTER,

### 200 Mulberry-street, New-York.

FOR SALE ALSO BY J. P. MAGEE, 5 CORNHILL, BOSTON, AND
H. H. OTIS, SENECA-STREET, BUFFALO.

## GIFT AND LIBRARY BOOKS. Square Form.

### *EVERY-DAY BOOK FOR BOYS AND GIRLS.*
### Harry Budd.

*In various styles of binding, at prices from 50 cents upward.*

This is decidedly the *best book* of its class *we have ever read.* The Orphan's story has nothing of the marvelous in it, yet it is so conducted as to impress—indelibly impress—the most instructive lessons of religion—true evangelical piety in its most delightful form—on the heart and conscience; so to direct the life and secure the great end of our being; so to worship and serve God, as to obtain his favor here and eternal life at his hand in the world which is to come -*Dr. Bond, Editor Christian Advocate and Journal.*

### Pictorial Catechism.

Pictorial Catechism, muslin, 55 cents; gilt, 70 cents.

### Pictorial Gatherings.

Pictorial Gatherings, muslin, 50 cents; gilt, 65 cents.

### Child's Sabbath-Day Book.

Child's Sabbath-Day Book, paper covers, 20 cents; muslin, 25 cents.

### Little Frank Harley.

Little Frank Harley, paper covers, 20 cents.

### The Great Journey.

The Great Journey, muslin, 35 cents.

### Here and There.

Here and There, paper covers, 15 cents.

### Childhood; or, Little Alice.

Childhood; or, Little Alice, 37 cents.

### A String of Pearls.

A String of Pearls. Embracing a Scripture Verse and Pious Reflections for Every Day in the Year, 30 cents.

### Henry's Birthday.

Henry's Birthday; or, Beginning to be a Missionary, 35 cents.

# NEW BOOKS,

## PUBLISHED BY CARLTON AND PORTER,

### 200 Mulberry-street, New-York.

FOR SALE ALSO BY J. P. MAGEE, 5 CORNHILL, BOSTON, AND
H. H. OTIS, SENECA-STREET, BUFFALO.

## A Model for Men of Business.

A Model for Men of Business: or, the Christian Layman contemplated among his Secular Occupations. Revised and Modified from the Lectures of Rev. HUGH STOWELL, M. A., Incumbent of Christ's Church, Salford. With an Introduction, by Rev. D. CURRY. 16mo., pp. 322. Price, 35 cents.

An excellent little volume, indicating its character in its title-page, and forcibly presenting the morality of the Gospel to the acceptance of men of business. There is so much in every day life to call our thoughts away from God—so much to blunt our sensibilities to the moral principles which should govern and direct every Christian man in all his intercourse with the world, that a book like this cannot but be a most profitable companion for all who desire to be at last accepted in Christ Jesus. We welcome its appearance. For sale at the Methodist book-stores generally.—*Meth. Protestant.*

This is a work much wanted to carry the sanctity of the Sabbath into the business of the week—to make religion, with business men, an ever-present and all-pervading principle. It is well written, and highly edifying. Let it be widely circulated.—*Pittsburgh Christian Advocate.*

## The Life and Times of Bishop Hedding.

Life and Times of Rev. Elijah Hedding, D. D., late Senior Bishop of the Methodist Episcopal Church. By Rev. D. W. CLARK, D. D. With an Introduction, by Rev. Bishop E. S. JANES. Pp. 686. Price, large 12mo., $1 50; 8vo., $2 00.

## The Temporal Power of the Pope.

The Temporal Power of the Pope: containing the Speech of the Hon. Joseph R. Chandler, delivered in the House of Representatives of the United States, January 11, 1855. With Nine Letters, stating the prevailing Roman Catholic Theory in the Language of Papal Writers. By JOHN M'CLINTOCK, D. D. 12mo., pp. 154. Price, 45 cents.

Last winter Hon. Joseph R. Chandler, a Catholic, and Representative in Congress from Pennsylvania, being hard pressed by anti-Romanist influences, made a speech, in which he denied the political supremacy of the pope. In doing this, he showed himself possessed of the cunning of a Jesuit, or the weakness of a neophyte. Dr. M'Clintock, in a series of nine letters, has thoroughly exposed the weakness and sophistry of Mr. Chandler's speech. It is a volume for intelligent readers—none others will relish the learning and the nice discrimination which pervade the work.—*Northern Christian Advocate, Auburn, N. Y.*

A series of letters to the Hon. J. R. Chandler, stating the prevailing Roman Catholic theory in the language of papal writers, forms the substance of this volume. They were prepared in reference to the speech of Mr. Chandler, delivered at the last session of Congress, and from the position and character of the writer, as well as from his mode of treating the subject, are eminently deserving of public attention.—*N. Y. Tribune.*

Carlton & Phillips, No. 200 Mulberry-street, New-York, have just issued a neat duodecimo volume of one hundred and fifty-four pages, with the foregoing title. It needs not that we say the work is a most timely and masterly production.—*Western Christian Advocate.*

# NEW BOOKS,

## PUBLISHED BY CARLTON AND PORTER,

### 200 Mulberry-street, New-York.

FOR SALE ALSO BY J. P. MAGEE, 5 CORNHILL, BOSTON, AND
H. H. OTIS, SENECA-STREET, BUFFALO.

## Bishop Baker on the Discipline.

A Guide-Book in the Administration of the Discipline of the Methodist
Episcopal Church. By OSMON C. BAKER, D. D. 12mo., pp. 253. Price,
60 cents.

We are glad this long-expected and much-desired book has at length made its appearance. Since the first announcement that such a book was forthcoming, our
ministry have looked for it with no little degree of impatience as a sure aid to
their right and beneficial administration of Discipline. The title of this work, and
the source from whence it was furnished, warranted such expectation. After a
careful perusal of the volume, we have no hesitancy in asserting that the most san-
guine of those expectants will more than realize all they hoped for. We have here
striking proof of that careful, patient investigation which precedes all the decisions
and productions of Bishop Baker. Our author has evidently made our "excellent book of Discipline" a subject of long and earnest study. For many years
he has been making note of the decisions given in annual and General Confer-
ences by his able predecessors in office, on all difficult questions pertaining to our
denominational administration. This result of his labors is an invaluable boon
to our ministry. No Methodist minister can well afford to be without it. The
possession of this volume will save our *junior* preachers a great amount of study,
much perplexity, and many troublesome errors. The clearness, conciseness, and
evident correctness of this production are marvels of mental investigation, acumen,
and discernment.—*Zion's Herald.*

## The Young Man Advised.

The Young Man Advised: Illustrations and Confirmations of some of
the Chief Historical Facts of the Bible. By E. O. HAVEN, D. D. 12mo.,
pp. 329. Price, 75 cents.

Let no one suppose that we have here a book of commonplace counsels to the
young. The writer has seized upon some of the chief historical facts of the Bible,
from which he has drawn illustrations, which he commends to the study and instruction of his readers, and thus in a new and most striking form has conveyed
great practical truths which can hardly fail to make a deep impression upon the
youthful mind. He displays no slight degree of research in his own studies, and
the whole is clothed with such historical beauty as will charm while his words
will instruct the student.—*New-York Observer*.

This book differs from all others we have ever seen addressed to this class of
readers. It plods not o'er the old beaten track of the numerous volumes bearing
similar titles. Its design is to fortify the young against the assaults of infidelity,
never perhaps more generally, more craftily, or more insidiously made than now.
In prosecuting this design it presents the greatest leading facts of the Bible, con-
firming them by the most conclusive evidence, historical and philosophical,
proving beyond all controversy the superhuman, the divine origin of the Word
of God. This volume has none of that cold, stiff, dry argument which has characterized similar productions, repelling the young from their perusal. Dr.
Haven's method of defending the "book of books" has a novelty about it which
must hold the attention of every young man who commences the perusal of
his work. His style and diction are of such a character as invest a powerfully
argumentative treatise with all the charms of a "well-told tale." If this book
does not sell extensively, and do immense good, the author is not at fault. We
commend it to parents who would save their sons from moral wreck. Let pas
'ors join issue with parents in scattering this potent antagonist to the infidelity
of the times ZETA.—*Zion's Herald.*